OTHER BOOKS BY EDWARD McCLELLAND

Midnight in Vehicle City: General Motors, Flint, and the Strike That Created the Middle Class, 2021.

Folktales and Legends of the Middle West, 2018.

How to Speak Midwestern, 2016.

Nothin' But Blue Skies: The Heyday, Hard Times, and Hopes of America's Industrial Heartland, 2013.

Young Mr. Obama: Chicago and the Making of a Black President, 2010.

The Third Coast: Sailors, Strippers, Fishermen, Folksingers, Long-Haired Ojibway Painters, and God-Save-the-Queen Monarchists of the Great Lakes, 2008.

Horseplayers: Life at the Track, 2005.

WORKING LIVES SERIES

BOTTOM DOG PRESS

RUNNING FOR HOME
A NOVEL

EDWARD MCCLELLAND

WORKING LIVES SERIES
BOTTOM DOG PRESS
HURON, OHIO 44839

ISBN: 978-1-947504-26-4
Bottom Dog Press, Inc.
PO Box 425, Huron, OH 44839
Lsmithdog@aol.com
http://smithdocs.net

CREDITS:
General Editor: Larry Smith
Layout and Cover Design: Susanna Sharp-Schwacke
Cover Image: Rich Moll of Rich Moll Photography
Author Photo: Sarah Elizabeth Larson

For my children: Lark, Birch, and Rose.

ONE

The Empire Motors body plant, across the street from my high school, was girded with a corrugated skin the same shade of green as the Statue of Liberty. Like the Statue of Liberty, it seemed a permanent symbol of my hometown, as well as a gateway to opportunity. My father worked there, as had his father, my Gramps, for forty-two years. When I started Wenniway Central as a freshman, the plant was still turning out two hundred thousand bodies a year, which were trucked over to the big assembly plant on the river and plopped on top of chassis. That wasn't an efficient way to build cars, I guess. By the time I graduated, the plant was gone, demolished, replaced by a fenced-in field that looked like a combination of Hiroshima and the Badlands.

What I remember most about the plant was the smell—the sweetish, chemical tang of atomized paint, drifting across the street. I smelled it most, inhaled it most, when I was running on the track, inside the football stadium behind the school. My high school athletic idols were not the husky baseballers and footballers who excelled at the sports for which I was too small, but marathoners as slight as myself: Bill Rodgers, Frank Shorter, Alberto Salazar. I wanted to win a state championship, just as they had, and then I wanted to run in the Olympics, just as they had. I knew that running was the one sport in which I could accomplish that, even from a little town like Wenniway. We had roads, and we had trails, and that was all I was going to need.

And, of course, we had the track, six lanes of asphalt, painted with peeling white stripes and lane numbers. I'll start my story there, during the fall cross-country season of my junior year. Every Friday—the day after a meet—we ran a workout Coach Funkhouser called Indian Running. It went like this: ten guys ran in a file, and the trailing runner sprinted to the front of the pack. When he took the lead, the guy in last place started sprinting. And so on for three miles, a ladder constantly re-forming itself. Coach called it Indian Running because it was how Indians helped each other endure long runs through the forests.

"They were all working together to get to their destination as fast as they could without losing anyone," he said, when he introduced the drill during our first week of practice. "Teamwork. Running is not an individual sport. You're a team, even if you don't throw a ball to each other, like those guys in football and basketball. Your job is to make your teammates faster."

Coach always put me in the outside lane, with the other varsity runners. The slowest guys, the freshmen, were in lane 1, and middle-of-the pack guys in lane 4—mostly sprinters and hurdlers who just ran cross country to stay in shape for track, which was where Wenniway Central really kicked ass. We were one of those rare integrated schools, with black guys who could win the sprints, and white guys and Mexicans for the long distances. Most schools only had one or the other, but we scored points all across the board. The year before, we had finished third at the state meet. James Harris, who was stretching over in lane 4, was runner up in the 110-meter hurdles.

I lined up behind Joaquin Duarte, the only guy on the team who could outrun me. I had never beaten Joaquin, at any distance. The day before, we had finished one-two at the meet against Wenniway South. Once Joaquin knew he'd won the race, he slowed down a little bit in the last mile to fool me into thinking I could catch him. As soon as I got close enough to hear his footsteps, he sprinted off, and beat me by ten seconds.

"You almost got me, buddy," he told me on the bus back to school, even though we both knew I hadn't almost gotten him, that he was just a cocky bastard messing with my head. "You made me work for that one."

Joaquin was full of himself, but as Varsity One—the runner who lines up in the pole position at meets—and defending conference champ, I guessed he had the right to be. He was a senior and I was a junior, so next year, I'd be Varsity One. When that happened, I'd try to be less of a dick to Varsity Two.

Coach blew his whistle. Joaquin led us at a pace that only Joaquin could keep up for three miles. After half a lap, Coach screamed, "Duarte, slow it down! No racing in practice. You only run hard when you're running to the front."

On the backstretch, we ran toward the plant. After a lap, when the rubbery feeling in my legs settled, and I began inhaling deeply to absorb all the oxygen I was going to need for three miles, I became especially aware of the industrial aroma in my nostrils. As I said, my dad worked in that plant, as a tool-and-die maker. The first day we ran on the track, during my freshman year, I went home and complained about the smell.

"You know what that smell is?" Dad lectured me. "That's the smell of money. That smell puts food on the table and Nikes on your feet. When you don't smell that paint anymore, that's when you should start worrying about it."

That was the last time I mentioned the smell of paint to my dad, although some said it was why our band teacher, Mr. Gray, developed a hole in his heart and spent a semester on sick leave. The band room windows opened toward the plant. We only ran on the track once a week, at least during cross-country season, so I supposed the smell of money wasn't going to kill me.

Coach blew his whistle again, a signal to the trailing runner to make his move. One by one, I was shuffled back in the pack, always staring at Joaquin's Mexican flag shorts. He ran with a hunched stride, hands slung below his waist, but he always looked like he was jogging, as though his joints had been greased. His muscular thighs tapered to ankles as narrow as a racehorse's. He was an animal, built to endure high speeds.

Ever since the start of cross-country season, I had run five miles every morning before school, and still I couldn't beat Joaquin. I told him he could be state champ if he ran twice a day. He shrugged and said, "I just want to run with the team, buddy." My chest was burlier than Joaquin's, my legs thicker, my stride ganglier and more urgent, or so it appeared when I watched myself in plate glass windows. That meant I had to work harder just to come in second. No sport rewards hard work over talent more than running. I'm sure a lot of little guys who took up running because they couldn't cut it in real sports like baseball or football tell themselves the same thing. Every time Joaquin settled into the lead, I sprinted past the pack at a speed I imagined was faster than what he—my rival, my nemesis, my teammate, the repository of all my envy—had just run. It probably wasn't, but I needed to convince myself that I was grit, and he was grace—the recipient of a God-given talent for which he never had to work—and that someday, grit would overcome. So it went for a dozen laps, each revolution around the track another turn of the vise constricting my chest. Finally, Coach blew the whistle. We shortened our strides to a jog, then a walk. The vise loosened. My chest felt like a hollow frame, filled with relief and release.

"Good run, guys!" Coach shouted. The brim of a black Saucony baseball cap was pushed down to his brow to conceal his baldness. Entangled over the logo of his Wenniway Central Warriors sweatshirt were a whistle, stopwatch, and faculty ID lanyard. "Wenniway all the way! Go home and get some rest this weekend, and I'll see you Monday after school."

I would go home. I wouldn't rest. At seven the next morning, I'd be up to run ten miles. I ran every day except Sunday, when my mom made me go to church. She had switched our family to the eight a.m. service this year, specifically to make me take the day off.

"God made the Sabbath even for runners," she told me. "If you run every day, you'll hurt yourself and you'll be too tired for races."

Before I went home, though, I had to meet my dad. Dad worked first shift, so he got off at two-thirty. Friday was the one afternoon a week Mom let him do whatever he wanted. "My sacred time," he called it. Dad spent his sacred time at Pete's Place, the bar across the street from the main gate of Empire Body, where he drank Stroh's beer and presided over the Gary Ward Memorial Friday Afternoon Euchre League. It wasn't really a league, just a card game with whichever guys from the shop lingered at Pete's past shift change.

"You're not dead," I pointed out when he told me the name.

"But I will be someday," he said, "and I don't want them to have to change what we call it."

I put on a sweatshirt and jeans in the locker room, walked across the railroad tracks separating the school from the shop, past the floral emblem growing on the front lawn of Empire Body, the chrysanthemums' colors fading in these first days of autumn. The flowers formed the shape of a horse-drawn carriage, which the company had manufactured until the automobile came along. "Wenniway Put the World on Wheels" was our civic slogan. Wheel City was our nickname. We built a million cars a year. The Empire Body logo was pasted on the inside of every driver's side door, next to the tire pressure chart. "Empire's got something for everyone from the janitor to the boss," my dad bragged. The Wenniway, a cheap little, two-door named for our town. The Durant, for the middle-class fellas who couldn't afford fancy but wanted a car that wouldn't break down after twenty-five thousand miles. And the Marquette, the luxury sedan the rich folks drove, its name a synonym for quality. They all started in this plant, where the American flag and the Empire Motors standard flew from poles on either side of the main gate, snapping crisply against a pale September sky.

I walked past Nakfoor's Party Store, the Arab grocery where the guys on the line nipped across the street on their lunch breaks for a pint of Jameson's or Canadian Club to take the edge off the last half of a shift. My dad drank when he was on the line but quit once he was promoted to skilled trades: "Tool and die ain't as monotonous, and if you fuck up, there's no one to fix your mess. When I was a kid on the line, I could act like life was one big party. When you're in the trades, you've got responsibilities."

Pete's Place: a brick façade with a few frosted glass blocks that let in the light, but didn't let out anything that happened inside. Embedded in the wooden door was a smoked, diamond-shaped window that performed the same function. Pete got so much business from the shop that he didn't need, or want, any other customers. I ignored the "Must Be 21 to Enter" sign and walked into the weekly First Shift Payday Party. The cigarette smoke was as thick as morning fog. Bob Seger's "Still the Same" boomed out of the jukebox, but its volume couldn't compete with the cacophony of a hundred temporarily liberated, temporarily enriched shoprats barking their orders across the bar—"Pete! Pete! Pete! Need a pitcher o' Stroh's for the table in the corner"— and dirty jokes that might be funny if told loudly enough. "This Halloween, I'm gonna tie a potato around my waist and go as a dictator. My wife's gonna get a lemon and go as a sourpuss." My dad was sitting at the bar, his Auto Workers Alliance Local 151 windbreaker bunched on the stool beside him. As soon as I gathered it up—exposing a vinyl seat patched with duct tape—Pete got in my face.

"I thought I say no Central students," he shouted at me from behind the bar, and from behind his still-black mustache. At the same time, he sneaked a glance at my dad. I saw him smirk. "I have some students come in here once and loosen all the lids on the sugar shakers. People try to put sugar in their coffee, pssht." He dropped his outspread palms toward the surface of the bar, whose gloss had been everywhere chinked by keys, lighters and penknives. "They got all sugar, no coffee. That's why I put that '21 to Enter' sign out there. Plus, you don't drink no beer."

"Pete," my dad implored, pretending that he needed to defend my presence, because he knew Pete enjoyed any argument, real or not, "that happened ten years ago. I told Kevin to meet me here. I *promise* I'll drink enough beer for the two of us. I'll have another Stroh's. Get Kevin a pop. What do you want?"

"Vernors," I said.

"Vernors!" Dad repeated.

Pete poured me a Vernors, but he didn't look happy about it. He never looked happy. I don't think he'd ever gotten over the fact that he ended up in Wenniway, instead of Frontenac, the big city in our state, with a million people and all the pro sports teams, all the auto company headquarters, the big newspapers, the big TV stations, the big concerts, a Greektown full of Greek restaurants. He'd had his choice. Thirty-five years before, when Pete was a refugee from the

Greek Civil War, the resettlement agency told him he was going to our state and asked where he wanted to live. Pete had heard they made cars here, so he told the immigration officer he wanted to go to the city that made the biggest, fanciest car. That would be the Marquette, in Wenniway, the immigration officer said. "Send me to Wenniway," Pete demanded, figuring it must be the biggest, fanciest city, with all the action, and all the glamorous girls. So here he was in little Wenniway, pop. 99,000, where we don't even have a minor league hockey team, where Gordon Lightfoot played a concert last year, or maybe two years ago. (My parents went, for that Edmund Fitzgerald song; I only listened to baseball and hockey on the radio, so it didn't bother me that not too many musicians stopped here.) But as long as Empire Body was across the street from Pete's Place, he would always earn a living off thirsty shoprats shoving dollar bills across his bar and continue to buy the burgundy Marquettes he parked in the street out front.

"You want anything to eat?" my dad asked.

At Pete's, you had three choices: hamburgers, cheeseburgers and grilled cheese. Always with fries.

"Cheeseburger," I said.

"How'd the meet go yesterday?"

"We won. I finished second."

"You beat that Mexican kid?"

"Nah. He acted like he was slowing down in the last mile, but he pulled away. I think he was just messing with me."

(I think Dad called him "that Mexican kid" because he couldn't pronounce Joaquin. A lot of old guys couldn't. Once, at an award ceremony after a race, the meet director announced the winner as "Jacqueline Duarte." Joaquin was lucky he was the fastest guy on the team. Otherwise, we would have called him Jacqueline for the rest of the season. Coach did, once, when Joaquin dogged it on a quarter-mile interval.)

"You need to teach that kid a lesson," Dad said. "Keep getting up at five-thirty and you will. Hard work always beats talent. That's why the Japs are kicking our asses now. They never invented a thing, but they'll work sixteen hours a day to make it better than the people who did."

Pete set a Stroh's, a Vernors and an ashtray on the bar. Dad picked up the beer and pushed away the ashtray. He hadn't smoked in three years, not since my grandmother was diagnosed with the lung cancer that killed her. Not even on his sacred Fridays, when my mother couldn't complain about it.

"I'm sorry I couldn't make it to your meet yesterday. I had to work overtime. You don't turn down time and a half. We may have more expenses coming up."

"What's so expensive?"

Dad had paid for our house in cash, five years after he started working in the shop. He paid for all our cars in cash, with the employee discount. Every time a credit card offer appeared in our mailbox, he cut it up. "The more you owe, the more you're owned," he liked to say.

"Your sister's pregnant, and they're not making any money. She just started working for that dentist and Dan is *still* getting that degree. I think he's working in a copy shop. I don't know why they're havin' a kid now."

"You and Mom were only twenty when you had Deb."

"I was already full time at Empire then." He exhaled, as he would have when he was still smoking—a reflex he had retained despite giving up cigarettes. "But nothing can stop young love. Young, dumb and full of...you know what, just like every other twenty-one-year-old in history."

As I finished my cheeseburger, Dad asked if I wanted to stick around for the Gary Ward Memorial Euchre League. He had never asked me before, but the previous Sunday, me and my mom had beaten him and Deb three games in a row. Now, apparently, he believed me to be a card-playing savant.

"You have a photographic memory," he said. "You remembered every card that was played. You should be getting A's in algebra. If you develop that talent, you can go to Vegas and count cards. Then you won't need to get a job."

There was a football game that Friday night: Central vs. South. Same as the cross-country meet the day before, but much better attended. Which is to say, attended. No fans stood in the woods to cheer the cross-country team. No cheerleaders waved pom poms at the finishing chute. Before I left the house to walk back to the stadium, I buttoned myself into my letterman's jacket. It wasn't just because the evening was chilly; it was because I wanted everyone to see that I was an athlete too—all five feet, seven inches, one hundred and thirty-two pounds of me—even if I didn't play football. The spring before, I'd been the only sophomore to break five minutes in the mile. I was also the only sophomore to earn a varsity letter.in track. I pinned a tiny pair of gold-plated winged shoes to the letter, to identify my sport (as if, looking at me, anyone could have any doubt).

Outside the gate, I met Dave and Tim, two of my cross-country teammates. We each paid our dollar and climbed to the top row of the wooden bleachers, where we could look down on the track encompassing the gridiron, the track where Coach had sent us off on our Indian Run a few hours before. (We were only allowed to use the track on Friday afternoons because the football team didn't practice then, it being game day.) Not only were the home bleachers full, but across the street, autoworkers watchinedthe game from the darkened balconies of Empire Body, smoking cigarettes and staring down on the floodlit field, where, probably, some of them had once butted heads.

As the home team sprinted out from under the bleachers, and the pep band blared our fight song, "Wenniway, All the Way," I honestly wished I were down there on the field, instead of up in the stands, hunched inside a jacket that billowed around my chest, because they didn't make them small enough for jocks my size. Any runner who tells you that running was his first-choice sport is a liar. When I was eight years old, I was a football fanatic. I had an electric football set, with plastic players I painted in the blue-and-silver colors of my favorite team, the Frontenac Foxes. The Foxes played every Thanksgiving Day, and the TV screen always turned fuzzy when Dad fired up his electric knife to carve the turkey. I slept under a bedspread with the logos of every NFL team. I flipped and traded football cards with my classmates, demanding ten offensive linemen for Terry Bradshaw or Larry Csonka.

On the afternoons I couldn't get my friends to the park for a game of touch, I pitched a Nerf football against the garage door, practicing my spiral. When I saw a newspaper ad for Pop Warner League, I asked my dad to take me to the tryouts. He did, even though I was one of the shortest boys in my class. The pads drooped off my shoulders. The helmet slipped over my eyes. The jersey sagged to my thighs. The coach started me at offensive guard, probably to teach me right away that I didn't belong on a football field. On the first snap, I got knocked on my back by a pass rusher who sacked the quarterback. Then the coach tried me at running back, where you don't have to be big, only quick. I wasn't quick enough. I sidestepped through a gap between two linemen, then collided with a linebacker who seemed to have materialized through a wormhole in the pack. I never saw him before he hit me. The blow lifted me off my feet so violently that my oversized helmet flew off my head and spun around in the grass like a dying top. I put the helmet back on, snapping the button of my chinstrap into its station while telling myself that even Larry Csonka had to shake off hard tackles. I had no more need of football equipment, though. I was relegated to the sidelines until the end of practice, when the coach announced, "Those of you who made first cuts will be getting a phone call."

I never got a phone call. After that, I lost interest in football. I shucked off invitations to play touch. Instead of spending Sunday afternoons watching the Foxes—Wenniway was just far enough from Frontenac so we could see the games on TV, even if they weren't sold out—I sat up in my room, piecing together and painting model sports cars. Only Empire brands of course, especially the Corsair, with its long, sloping hood, shaped like a steel tongue. I was too young to understand what that design represented, but I'd seen young, single, permed, mustachioed autoworkers driving them down my street with Montrose or Led Zeppelin pounding out of the open windows, and I wanted my own miniature version.

My mother must have noticed I'd lost interest in sports. Even though my father had been no athlete—he was only an inch taller than I was—she understood that boys work out their pecking orders on playing fields. "Good at sports" equals popular. The summer after my football washout was an Olympic year. Mom sat me down in front of the television and insisted I watch three sports with her: wrestling, gymnastics, and track and field.

"The thing about the Olympics is there's a sport for every body type," she explained. "All the sports they show on TV the rest of the time are for the big fellas. You have to be six feet tall to play football or basketball. No one in our family has ever been that tall! I'm five foot-two, and your dad's five-eight. I think that's why I liked him. A big guy would have been too much for me. But look at some of those guys. They're not much bigger than you or me and they're going to win gold medals."

This was true. But wrestling involved two muscular guys hugging each other. Gymnasts wore tight-fitting shirts and ran around in bare feet. Also, no high school has a boys' gymnastics team. On the last day of the Games, we watched the final event, the marathon. I was disappointed that the American runner couldn't keep up, but when the leading runner emerged from the stadium tunnel onto the track, every spectator stood and cheered. An entire stadium—eighty thousand people!—screaming for a sweaty little guy in shorts and a tank top. It was almost as loud as a football game.

"Is that something you'd like to try?" my mother asked.

It was. That week, she took me to a little running shoe store in a strip mall. The Athlete's Foot was wedged between a health food co-op and a hi-fi boutique. Taped to its walls were posters of running champions: Bill Rodgers, winner of the Boston Marathon; Frank Shorter, the American who had finished second in the marathon I had just watched (and who had won the Olympic Marathon four years previously); Jim Ryun, who ran a four-minute mile in high school. I had never heard any of those names, but in the years to come I would idolize them far more than Terry Bradshaw or Larry Csonka. I chose a white pair of Tigers with red and blue stripes, because it was the Bicentennial year.

"So you need a singlet? A pair of split shorts?" asked the clerk, a skinny guy whose moustache seemed too broad for his bony face. He nodded at my Evil Knievel iron-on t-shirt. "Nylon wicks away the sweat better than cotton."

"He can wear his gym clothes," Mom said. "It never gets that hot around here. We don't need wicking."

On the drive home, she asked me, "You run in gym, don't you?"

"We run *around*," I said. "In tennis shoes. The only time we have races is on Field Day. They have a marathon on Field Day."

The "marathon" was one lap around the school's playground, no longer than half a mile. But as I trained for it, I imagined myself as Frank Shorter, in his red USA singlet. I began with a run around the block, treading cubes of concrete whose solidity radiated through the thin gum soles of my new shoes.

The morning after my first run, my legs were so stiff I walked like a bowlegged cowboy. But I ran again that evening. An Olympic medal began with a boy's stumble. Soon I could circle the block twice without stopping. In our neighborhood of tall, narrow, closely spaced houses, and sheltering elms whose roots cracked and heaved the sidewalks, a jogger was a novelty. After a few runs, the old folks on the porches raised their copies of the *Wenniway Star* to salute my efforts. After a few more runs, they called out "Get those knees up," and "Can you do the mile in four?"

After a week, I could run a mile, or so I calculated by holding my thumb and forefinger apart on the scale of a map of Wenniway and laying this digital measurement along my course. I saw a magazine ad in which a couple boasted about running five miles, while tugging at the waistbands of their loosening sweatpants. Five miles seemed like an unimaginable, unconquerable journey, but I had run twice as far as the distance of the Field Day Marathon. I was ready for my first race.

On Field Day, I wore my red, white and blue Tigers to school. All through math and English, I rehearsed my strategy: start slowly, then pass every winded classmate who ran flat out. It almost worked, too. Our principal, Mr. Crenshaw (the only adult male in the school, other than the janitors), lined up the fourth, fifth and sixth grade boys' division. "All right, gentlemen," he announced. "One lap around the playground. Race ends back here on the tennis court. Mr. Peck and Mr. Sweet"—the janitors—"will be holding a tape for the winner to break."

I started in the middle of the pack. By the second corner of the playground, I began passing kids who were huffing heavily, their eyes darting this way and that, searching for relief, their arms and shoulders heaving to compensate for exhaustion. I passed everyone except Joaquin Duarte. Our rivalry began that Field Day. Or, at least, my rivalry with Joaquin began that Field Day. He still thought of me as his little buddy, his sidekick, Godzooky to his Godzilla, if you watched that Saturday morning cartoon. I took home a red second-place ribbon, my first award for an athletic achievement; it was still pinned to the bulletin board in my bedroom, even as its color had faded to pink and its toothed bottom edge had frayed.

So that's the story of how and why I became a runner, instead of a football player. When I went to a football game, I didn't pay attention to what the players were doing. Because my enthusiasm for the sport never really recovered from that Pop Warner tryout. I just went to show off my letterman's jacket.

At halftime, though, something finally drew my attention to the field. The score was tied, six to six, because high school kickers can't even convert extra points. The band blatted "Proud Mary" and wheezed through "Centerfold," a big hit the year before, and then...every eye in the stadium was suddenly following the progress of a Silly Putty-colored figure racing along the visitor's sideline at a five-minute mile pace, wearing only a green ski mask, a green jockstrap, and a green W painted on each untanned ass cheek. At least he was representing the home team. Even the band stopped playing and watched him race for the end zone. Our principal, portly Dr. Bexley, broke downfield after the streaker, holding down the fedora that covered his gray head, while the straps and buckles of his trench coat flapped and jingled. I thought of that song, "The Streak," when the hillbilly drawls, "Here he comes right out of the cheap seats. Didn't have nothin' on but his PFs."

"Holy shit!" Tim shouted. "It's Carter."

"How do you know?" Dave retorted. "Do you recognize his ass from the showers?"

"No. That's Carter's stride. And those are his red Nikes."

A runner's stride is as distinctive as his face. Straight torso, arms high and tight, high-kicking heels. That was Carter, one of our varsity seven. He made it to the end zone ahead of the principal, the assistant principal, and assorted other narcs chasing after him, then scaled the Cyclone fence and dove into the back seat of an automobile that departed without igniting its headlights. Dave and Tim were bumping forearms in celebration, but I knew what was going to happen if the narcs found out Carter was inside that jockstrap: that was going to be his last run in Warriors green, and we were going to miss his points in the meet against East Wenniway. I also knew that no one in this stadium was going to be talking football on Monday. That was the first time I saw Carter's ass, but it wouldn't be the last: both times he exposed it in public, he kind of messed up my life. The second time way more than the first, actually; but that's another story.

Two

That Sunday morning, after church, we stopped by Gramps' house, to pick him up for Sunday dinner. He was dressed and waiting for us in a sweater, tie, and slacks. He climbed silently into the shotgun seat my mother had vacated for him. Gramps had never been much on church. He wasn't an atheist, but only because he didn't think of God as someone he ought to have an opinion about. The one time I asked him why he didn't come to church with us, he said, "God's got his business, and I've got my business; I don't interfere with his, and I don't ask him to interfere in mine." Gramps was in church when Mom and Dad were married, and when Deb and I were baptized, and he attended every Christmas Eve, but that was it for Gramps and religion.

Ever since Gram's death, these Sunday dinners were about the only time Gramps left the house at all. On the drive home afterwards, Dad would take Gramps to the supermarket and watch him buy twenty-one frozen dinners and a case of beer—all the provisions he needed to survive until the following Sunday. Inside the house, he sat in his recliner and watched television. Game shows. *Card Sharks.* Judge Wapner. Reruns. *The Andy Griffith Show.* Johnny Carson. Right up until the national anthem and test pattern, after which he fell asleep in his chair.

"He's been living alone for two years, and it's making him weird," Dad had told us at supper, earlier that week. "It's not natural to live alone. This Sunday, we're gonna drag him out for dinner, and I'm gonna tell him he's moving into

Deb's old room. He needs to be with his family. None of this 'independent living' bullshit where they store old people in a room until it's time to store 'em in a coffin. Wards don't do that. We look out for each other, cradle to grave."

My dad had been preparing all his life for this particular Sunday dinner: it would be the moment he took over from Gramps as patriarch of the Ward family. Dad hired in at Empire Body when he was eighteen, just three months out of high school. ("I got all my dicking around done in one summer" he told me. "It wasn't like later, with the hippies. And then I was broke, so it was time to get a job.") He married Mom when he was twenty. ("If you find a girl you think wants to sleep with you, don't let her go. You might not find another one.") When he was twenty-five, he bought our house. When he was thirty, he was promoted to tool-and-die maker. And now, at forty-three, he was ready to spend the rest of his life saying grace at the head of the Sunday dinner table and making the rest of us feel guilty for borrowing money from him. As far as Dad was concerned, that was the best thing money could buy.

Gramps didn't say anything when he got into the car, so I didn't say anything, either. I knew today was the day Dad was going to talk to Gramps about moving in with us, and I knew it was going to be uncomfortable; it was uncomfortable in the car, and Dad hadn't even brought up the subject yet.

Gramps was just as morose during dinner, morbidly chewing his ham and scalloped potatoes. Fortunately, Deb and Dan were there, so Mom filled the silence with baby talk. (Deb looked about ten months pregnant; I was amazed me that someone five feet tall could carry a fully formed human being inside her.) Finally, during dessert, Dad made his move. Mom had baked an apple pie, because it was Gramps' favorite, and served it with butter pecan ice cream, also his favorite.

"I made this with apples we picked at the orchard last week," Mom said. "Kevin picked most of them. He climbed up the ladder for the apples way up in the branches. They're Macintoshes. The best baking apples."

Gramps nodded, then sliced off a forkful of pie and ice cream. As his lips closed over that first bite, Dad spoke up.

"Dad," he said, "I was just thinking about how great it would be if we could have dinner like this every day."

(He wasn't "just thinking." All the day before, I had heard him rehearsing the "family together" speech with Mom. "I want him to think *we* need him, not that he needs us," he'd said.)

As Gramps silently chewed his pie and ice cream, Dad forged on. I could tell by Dad's halting, high-pitched voice that the skin beneath his dress shirt and v-neck sweater was prickling.

"Jo Anne and I have been talking about how nice it would be if you came here to live with us, especially now that Deb's room is empty. You always taught us that family should stay close. That's why me and Dick and Karen are all still here in town. We just don't want you to live alone. No one should live alone."

"You could come live with me," Gramps said stonily. "I've got a bigger house than this; I've got *three* empty bedrooms now."

Dad receded into the back of his chair. He was unwilling to press the argument, at least for now. The fact was, Gramps was a more prominent and powerful man than my dad would ever be. Gramps had participated in the Great Wildcat Strike all the way back in the thirties, which had led to the founding of the Auto Workers Alliance, the union that represented everyone working at Empire and all the other auto plants in the U.S.A. The strike began during Gramps' night shift at Empire Body. Gramps and two hundred other guys stopped working until the line shut down, then escorted the guards out the front door and told them, "This plant is ours until we sign a union contract." When the police showed up with tear gas, Gramps helped bar the main gate, then pelted the cops with door hinges until they hightailed it back across the railroad tracks, shooting at the plant to cover their retreat. Gramps didn't get shot, but the guy beside him took a flesh wound to the leg. Gramps has never let Dad forget that he put his life on the line so Dad could have job security and health insurance, and a new car every two years and the precious "thirty and out"—the opportunity to retire with full benefits after three decades in the shop. Gramps worked forty-two years, retiring as an engine inspector in the assembly plant on the river. For the last ten, he was vice president of the local. Whenever union elections were coming up, I heard his campaign ads on the radio between innings of baseball games—"Vote for the Unity ticket, president Dennis Cordile and vice president Sam Ward"—and I'd run downstairs to announce "I just heard Gramps' name on the radio." Dad just turned red. He had no interest in union politics himself, but it bothered him that every time he met someone new at the plant, they'd ask, "Are you Sam Ward's son?" Both were short men with cleft chins, so there was no denying the relationship.

Gramps decided that was still how it was going to be in this family. Gary Ward was still going to be Sam Ward's son. Sam Ward wasn't going to be Gary Ward's father, living under his roof. After dessert, Dad drove Gramps home to his empty house and his television.

By noon on Monday, everyone at Wenniway Central knew that the Football Streaker and his co-conspirators had been identified and would all face the consequences of his near nudity. The streaker himself was Jason Carter, the cross-country team's Varsity Three, as his teammates had recognized. It turned out the other guys involved were also on the cross-country team. Right after Carter climbed the fence, one of the assistant principals (a fancy title for a narc) spotted Phil Tracewski power walking toward the stadium exit with a bundle of clothes stuffed inside his letterman's jacket. Carter's clothes. The narc blocked Tracewski's path, dragged him by the arm into the locker room, and ordered him to identify the streaker or face expulsion. He did, and the getaway driver too: Darren Hinsdorf. Three varsity runners. Almost half our top seven.

That afternoon, when we circled up to stretch before practice, all three were absent. Coach explained why. "You may notice that three of your teammates are not here today," Coach bellowed. He was exasperated, and exasperation raised his voice at least a dozen decibels. "I don't need to tell you who they are, or why they're not here, because A, you know your teammates, and B, if you were in the hallways of this high school and have a pair of functioning ears, you heard all about what happened on Friday night. If you were at the football game, and have a pair of functioning eyes, you saw what happened. Now, I don't know if that guy was jealous of the attention the football team gets and wanted to get some of that attention for the cross-country team. I don't know if he thought a short and a singlet is too cumbersome an outfit and wanted to go for a run in something more casual..."

Nobody was laughing yet, but a few guys were pressing their grins together to trap the laughter inside their mouths. Including me.

"Whatever the motivation, streaking is not permitted at football games! We don't have a sign outside the stadium saying, 'No Shirt, No Pants, No Service,' because we assume you all have sense enough to wear both. But apparently not everyone does. The streaker is going to be expelled from school. We have zero tolerance for streaking at Wenniway Central, in case any of you think you can run faster with no clothes on."

Coach's Sergeant Friday grimace broke into a half grin.

"Also, no matter how fast you run, you can't outrun your own identity. You're still gonna be you. You might be a faster you, but it's still you. I was at the game, and the streaker was running pretty fast. He should have. I coached him."

That we laughed at. But Carter had been Varsity Three, right behind me. His expulsion would cost the team points.

"The streaker's accomplices will be suspended. All three of them are off this team. All those guys were varsity runners, so I'm going to need three of you JV guys to step into their spots and score this team some points. I'll be watching you in practice this week to see who's got the balls to do that. All right. Jumping jacks."

We jogged out to our home course, a riverfront park two miles from school, where we ran thousand-meter repeats through the woods. On the jog back to school, I came up with a plan for Thursday's meet against East Wenniway: I was going to win the race, to make up for the points that Carter's and Tracewski's and Hinsdorf's absence would cost us. Cross-country scoring works like this: there are seven runners on a team, but only the top five finishers count toward the team's score. However, the sixth and seventh guys can push the other team down in the finishing order. The best possible score is 15 to 50; your guys finish one through five, theirs finish eight through fourteen. East Wenniway had one of the fastest runners in the conference, a guy named Steve Schaden. If I could beat him, I'd get us the 1. Of course, getting the 1 would require beating Joaquin, too. I devised a strategy: instead of chasing Joaquin, I would run with him from the gun to the finish line. I had watched enough track races and marathons on TV to see that the winner was never a guy who comes from behind. He was always the last survivor of the lead pack. Jim Ryun had tried to come from behind against Kip Keino at the 1968 Olympics, but he couldn't catch the frontrunner. Whenever Bill Rodgers ran the Boston Marathon or the New York City Marathon, he went out hard, and dropped his rivals one by one, until he was alone in front. That would be Kevin Ward, at Thursday's cross-country meet.

It would have been easy to call Steve Schaden a queer, or a freak, if he weren't so fast. His look came straight from an English New Wave band on MTV. Like a lot of runners, he was gaunt, with cheekbones that asserted themselves at the points where miles and miles of effort had pared away all the flesh, but he completed the affect by styling his blond hair into a crest that swept from his left temple to just above his right eyebrow. A few strands of hair crept down the nape of his neck to form what we called a "rat tail," which he had dyed even blonder than his natural blonde, a platinum tint approaching chlorine green. In his left ear—the heterosexual lobe, it was claimed—he wore, on some race days, a gold hoop, on others, a black lightning bolt. For this race, he wore the lightning bolt, as an advertisement of his speed. I took it as a challenge. So did Joaquin.

"Their best runner is such a fag," he said, as we jogged our home course to warm up for the race. "I'm not gonna let some fag beat me."

I don't think Joaquin was commenting on Steve Schaden's sexual proclivities, but on the fact that he fell short of Joaquin's personal standard of machismo. Which was pretty high, since Joaquin was a varsity letterman, and a Mexican. Whatever. It gave me an opening to discover how fast I was going to run to win the race.

"We should both beat him," I said.

"We should both beat him" Joaquin agreed. "We have to win this meet. Their whole school is a fag school. We can't lose to a fag school."

I got what he was saying. A lot of doctors and office workers lived out in the suburb of East Wenniway, and their kids dressed kind of…androgynously. The guys wore earrings and parachute pants, and the girls wore cotton dresses with thermal underwear and high-top Chuck Taylors.

"How fast are you going to go out?" I asked.

"About five-ten," he said. "I don't know any fags who can hang with that."

I drew a sharp breath as I did the calculations in my head. A 5:10 mile, if sustained for five kilometers, projected to a final time of just over sixteen minutes. My personal record on our home course was 16:31. If I was going to win, I'd have to run with Joaquin.

As Varsity Two, I lined up behind the lime stripe next to Steve Schaden, our opponent's fastest runner. As the home team's Varsity One, Joaquin had the pole position. The starter raised a pistol above his head. Its cap cracked the crisp blue afternoon. We charged up a long grassy slope, made a hard right at a yellow flag (on a cross-country course a yellow flag means to turn right, a red flag means turn left, and a blue flag means run straight). Down a shaded straightaway past a file of evergreens, a tight hairpin at another blue flag, and up the short, steep slope we called the Mickey Mouse Hill, because it was a hill only by the standards of our flat hometown. Coach had taught to attack a hill with pitty-pat steps, get to the top as quickly as possible without expending effort by overstriding. In every other race on this course, Joaquin had beaten me to the top of the Mickey Mouse Hill by ten yards; this time, I was stepping on his shadow. When we reached the bottom of the grassy slope and entered the woods, Joaquin, Schaden and I were three abreast. The trail was only wide enough for two runners, though, so I sprinted ahead and took the lead. Behind me, I heard Joaquin shout "Motherfucker!" Glancing back, I saw Schaden stiff-arming my teammate to claim a narrow path between two trees.

The first mile ended just past a fallen log. We hurdled it, and there stood Coach, holding a stopwatch, calling out splits from among the underbrush.

"Five-oh-nine, Ward! What the hell are you doing running five-oh-nine? Slow...the...hell...down!"

I could not slow down. Joaquin was right behind me. I could hear his breathing so distinctly that I was aware of myself breathing even harder. Winning this race was going to hurt like a bitch. It was going to feel like being stabbed in the chest over and over again, and then being crushed to death by boulders. I told myself I could run one more mile at this pace. Get to mile two. That was as far ahead as I could think. As we reached the midpoint of the race—further than I had ever run so fast—I tried to detach my mind from the pain, from the feeling of my chest constricting as I desperately inhaled air to fuel my legs. I packed the essence of myself into a little pouch, allowing it to float above my head, where it could simply observe a body moving independently of any mental pleadings. Kevin Ward was not going to win this race—a body wearing his face and my uniform was going to win. I just had to get out of its way, disassociate myself from the pain. Even if my brain decided to stop running here and now, my legs would not obey.

According to my watch, we hit the two-mile mark in 10:23, still a lead pack of three. My new goal became the light at the end of the woods, two hundred yards away. Beyond was an open field, another climb of the Mickey Mouse Hill, and then a downhill run to the finish line. I could not imagine enduring this agony for the six more minutes it would take to cover that ground. This was like a torture test, like seeing how long I could hold my hand on a burning stove. I ran only for the seam of light between two pine trees. Once I reached it, Joaquin and Steve fanned out on either side of me and ran off to settle the race. I had never been a serious contender. Only a rabbit. A pacer. A guy whose ambitions didn't match his abilities.

If you don't hate running at some point on the last mile of a 5K, you didn't run the race hard enough. But as I watched my chance to win this race recede, in the persons of my lifelong archrival and a pretentious quiff from the suburbs, my feelings went beyond a mere betrayal of the sport to an earnest wish for the end of my existence. Maybe a lightning bolt or a meteor would deliver me from having to run the final thousand yards of this race. I was on the mile three death march, urging forward legs that seemed to accumulate weight with every shortening stride. As I reached the bottom of the Mickey Mouse Hill, I could hear members of the girls' team—which had raced before us—shouting my name.

"C'mon Ward! Go! Don't let 'em catch you! Turn it on! Eye of the Tiger!"

That's when I looked behind me to see two East Wenniway runners, in blue and white singlets, hauling ass out of the woods. I held them off until the top of the hill, but they sprinted past me on the downslope. My body was indeed independent of my brain—it refused to run as fast as commanded. I gave up, jogged into the finishing chute, fell on my back in the grass. Joaquin won the race, but we lost in the team scoring, 26-29, and I was the egotistical fool whose delusions of victory cost us the meet. If I had run my usual race, I would have finished third, and we would have won. Coach let me know about it, too. Not there on the course, or on the car ride back to school, or in the locker room. Coach would never embarrass a runner in front of the rest of the team. He asked me to stick around for a minute after everyone else had left, sat me down on a bench in front of the lockers, and lit into me.

"What were you thinking going out in five-ten?" he demanded.

I looked up at a sign above the doorway to the dank locker room. It read SACRIFICE BLOOD AND SWEAT FOR WENNIWAY CENTRAL, in hand-painted green letters. I wanted to tell Coach that's what I had been thinking; instead, I told him the truth.

"I was trying to win," I said. "I was trying to make up for the points we were gonna lose because of Carter and Tracewski and Hinsdorf."

"We don't *need* you to win," Coach said. "We've got a guy who can win. He wins every conference meet. We needed you to finish third; if you hadn't gone out so fast, you *would* have finished third and we would have won the meet. I keep trying to explain to you guys that cross country is a *team* sport. It's not about who's the fastest runner, but who's the fastest bunch of runners, and that was still us, even without those three guys."

I also wanted to tell Coach that we would have won the meet if the runner he refused to name hadn't streaked across the football field—the JV runners promoted to replace Carter and his confederates all finished in the bottom half of the field—but I knew better than to talk back to a teacher.

"I'm glad you're ambitious," Coach said, by way of apologizing for having to chew me out. "You train harder than anyone on this team. I'm glad you want to win races. You're going to win plenty of races. Next year, after Joaquin graduates, you're gonna be my go-to guy. So be patient. You've got all your fastest races ahead of you. I envy you that. I'm thirty-four years old. I'm never gonna run as fast as I did when I was in college. Every runner's got this little window"—Coach held his hands a few inches apart—"between maybe twenty-one and twenty-eight, when he can set his PRs. Then, after that, they never change. You're on one side of that and I'm on the other. For me, it's gone, but for you, it's coming. For now, though, don't go out in five-ten until I tell you you're ready."

Dad worked overtime again that day, as usual, so he missed my race, as usual. The next afternoon, when I saw him at Pete's, preparing to preside over the Gary Ward Memorial Euchre League, he asked me the same question he always asked after a race.

"D'ja beat that Mexican kid?"

THREE

The run from school to our home course always took us past Empire Body. Past the floral emblem, past the South Gate, where the bodies were loaded onto trucks, across the railroad tracks, and past Pete's Place. The day we found out the plant was closing we were jogging back from a 5 x 1000 workout in the woods. It was late October, so we were wearing our sweats, with the green emblem of Chief Wenniway in a feathered headdress. The smoke unfurling from the slim chimneys was outlined sharply against the chilly sky, like pale pennants of steam. As our pack approached the plant, we saw workers milling on the sidewalk. My first thought was to cross the street, to avoid having to run through the crowd, but then I saw my dad out there, sucking hard on a cigarette. I never saw my dad hanging around outside the plant, and I hadn't seen him smoke since Gram was diagnosed with cancer, so I stopped running, while the other guys went on ahead.

"What's going on?" I asked my dad. He was coatless, shivering in a flannel shirt. "How come everyone's standing around?"

"We're shuttin' down."

"What happened?" I figured the plant must have been evacuated due to a fire, or else the shift was sent home because the line broke down.

"A bunch of assholes in Frontenac decided we're obsolete is what happened," a voice beside my dad spat.

My dad raised his hand: "Jim, my son is here." Then he turned back to me.

"We were called into a meeting today, with the head of the Empire Body division. He told us this plant and the plant down by the river are gonna close next year. They don't think it's quote-unquote efficient to build bodies in one place and truck 'em somewhere else for final assembly. So instead they're gonna build one big plant..."

"In Tennessee!" my dad's angry co-worker shouted. "It's bullshit!"

"Jim!"

"Gary! How about getting angry for one red hot minute?"

"You're making me angry," my dad retorted. "Number one, you're cussing up a storm while my son's standing here. And number two, nothing you or I say is gonna change what the company said today or what the company's gonna do."

Dad put his arm around me and guided me to the curb.

"Go finish your run and meet me at home," he said. "I'm gonna head over there right now, so I can tell your mom before she sees it on the six o'clock news. There's a TV truck interviewing guys going in and out of Pete's. I hope they get 'em goin' in, 'cause as outspoken as they're gonna be then, they're gonna be a lot more outspoken coming out."

"We're done running," I told Dad. "I just have to go inside and change."

"All right, I'll pick you up outside the locker room. We'll tell her together."

By the time we got home, Mom already knew. Everyone in Wenniway knew, it seemed. Mom had gotten a phone call from Gramps, who had gotten a phone call from a union buddy who still worked in the plant.

"Your father sounded really angry," Mom told Dad. "He was calling Empire a bunch of backstabbers. It was the most I've heard him say since your mom died. I had to hang up the phone when he started swearing."

Dad grimaced.

"He doesn't even work there anymore," Dad said.

"He still takes it personally. Once a Wildcat Striker, always a Wildcat Striker."

Dad sat us all down on the rust, red and beige tartan couch that had been the central feature of our living room for my entire life. My mother's afghan, hand-knitted in a green and orange zigzag pattern, was draped over the back, to be pulled down on sick days, or TV watching nights when the close-to-zero cold seeped through the plastic sheeting insulating our windows.

"First of all," Dad told us, "it doesn't look like I'm going to lose my job. The new plant in Tennessee isn't going to require as many workers. They're streamlining the process. It makes sense. But I've got twenty-five years seniority, so I can transfer down there if I want. The question is, do I want to?"

As Mom listened, she kneaded the afghan in her hands, gathering bundles of yarn.

"It'd only have to be for five, six years, and then I can retire on full benefits," Dad said to Mom. "We wouldn't be as well off as if I stayed on for forty like Dad, but I can't see moving the whole family down South. I'm not gonna leave Dad up here all alone, and Deb's about to have a baby. You got your job at the hospital, and Kevin's in school, and we been going to Friendship Methodist for twenty years now. You can't just interrupt a life in the middle and start it all over again. The other alternative is I stay here and look for something else, but I don't know what else there's gonna be for a guy my age, especially in a town that's losing two auto plants. And quitting Empire before I get my thirty in would mean throwing away my lifetime health benefits."

"How are you gonna work in Tennessee while we're up here?" Mom asked.

"There'll be plenty of other guys going. We can room together, carpool up and down every week."

37

Dad walked to the bookshelf beside the TV set and pulled out a road atlas. The atlas had been published in 1976, but its cover was still glossy, its pages crisp. The Wards didn't travel to many places we didn't already know how to get to. My dad had never flown on a plane, and the only letters he ever wrote were to my Uncle Dick when Dick was in the Army. Dad didn't have to leave Wenniway to see or speak to anyone he knew. He'd thought he was set for life at Empire. He hadn't counted on having to move to Tennessee.

As Dad paged to the big map of the United States, I looked back and forth between my parents, sitting hip to hip on a couch whose springs had sagged to settle them close together. Since they were married, they had probably never spent a night apart. Any time they had gone out of town—mostly to Gramps' cottage Up North—they had gone together, with Deb and me. And now they would have to sleep apart five nights a week, forty-eight weeks a year.

Dad pressed his little finger atop the name of the small town where Empire was building its new plant. Just south of Nashville, halfway from Wenniway to the Gulf of Mexico. And Dad would have to make that drive twice a week.

"I've only been through Tennessee once," he said to Mom. "That time we visited my brother when he was stationed at Fort Rucker, before he shipped out to Germany."

When Dad talked about that trip down South, to Alabama, I realized something else; that, and our one-time hop across the border to Canada just to say we'd been to a foreign country, were the only times Dad had even left the state. His world—our whole family's world—was about to get a lot bigger, exploding across the map from this tight little kernel we've always inhabited here in Wenniway. When Dad hired on at Empire, he didn't sign up for a lifetime of travel. The shop was an antidote to adventure:

a guarantee that in exchange for spending eight hours a day (or more) in that huge smelly windowless room, he'd have enough money to marry my mom and take care of Deb and me, with a little left over for summer vacations. That was all he'd ever wanted in 1958, when everyone in America had driven a big Empire car. This was 1982, and even people in Wenniway were driving farty little Volkswagens and Japanese rice burners, as my dad called them. Empire had to cut costs.

I left my parents alone to plan this unexpected future, and went up to my room, where I laid down on my bed and picked up a book called *Great Runners of the 20th Century*. It wasn't easy to get me to read—I'd rather be outside moving around, like any athlete—but I had read every book about running in the school library, and once I'd finished those, I'd gotten into the public library's collection. Lately, I'd been hero-worshipping a guy named Gerry Lindgren, who had run back in the '60s, in Washington State, but still held every high school record. Just a scrawny guy with big glasses from the photo with his bio, but he ran the 5,000 in 13 minutes and 44 seconds, and the two-mile in eight forty. He did it by training two hundred miles a week. He ran ten miles in the morning, ten miles in the evening, and then he'd get up in the middle of the night and run *another* ten miles. That made him so fast that when he was still in high school, he beat the Soviet Union's best runners in a 10,000 meter race. In high school. Like me. Who couldn't even beat Joaquin Torres. Or Steve Schaden. Or those two other guys from East Wenniway. But I only ran ten miles a day. If I ran thirty miles a day, could I break Gerry Lindgren's high school records, I wondered.?. And then I wondered what would drive a guy to run that much. After high school, he ran in the Olympics at 18. I would be 18 during the next Olympics, in Los Angeles. And then he won eleven NCAA championships. Steve Prefontaine, the guy they just called

"Pre," was the running idol of the '60s and '70s, because he was blond and handsome and died in a car crash when he was twenty-four, but he lost to Lindgren in the NCAA cross-country championships. Lindgren wasn't the best athlete; he just ran the most. Maybe I couldn't run thirty miles a day, but I could run more than anyone else in Wenniway... maybe in the state.

The next morning, at six-thirty, I pulled on a pair of red nylon shorts and a t-shirt from the Pumpkin Fest 5K, the first timed race I ever ran, when I was fourteen. Out on the porch, the skin of my bare arms and legs clenched against the autumn chill. Every fall, I tried to run as far into the season as I could in a t-shirt and shorts, and every spring, I tried to bareleg it as soon as I could. (My personal records: November 11 and March 4.) I was only cold for the first mile, anyway. I was running five miles, to the zoo and back, a distance I had measured in my dad's car the day I got my learner's permit. My morning run was usually my time to think about nothing but running, but that was hard the morning after I found out Empire Body was closing, and my dad wasn't going to be home much for the next five years. I tried to push those thoughts away by imagining myself winning a gold medal in the 1500 meters at the Los Angeles Olympics. In my head, I heard the voice of Howard Cosell, the loud, nasally sportscaster in the gold blazer: "... the first Olympics the United States has competed in in eight years, since the Montreal Games of nineteen hundred and seventy-six...now, here is Team USA on home soil, in Los An-ge-les, looking for gold in the golden state of California...Steve Scott, considered the USA's greatest hope to defeat the British champions Steve Ovett and Sebastian Coe, defending their medals from four years ago in Moscow. But miraculously, a young man named Kevin Ward, who graduated from high school just two months ago, has qualified for the final. Echoes of Jim Ryun, another Midwestern schoolboy phenom who broke the world mile record while still a teenager. They're lining up. There's the gun. Coe and Ovett take the lead. They pass the first lap in a swift fifty-five seconds…the first half mile in one fifty-one. A suicidal pace. Here's the bell. And look who's moving up from the back of the pack. It's young Kevin Ward of the US of A."

At this point in Howard Cosell's commentary, I fixed my eyes on a mailbox I estimated to be a hundred yards distant, surging toward it at what I imagined was a four-minute pace. I was coursing not over a track under the floodlights of the L.A. Coliseum, with eighty thousand cheering me on, but over an uneven sidewalk—cracked by frost, heaved by roots—in the gray autumn dawn of Wenniway, with nobody watching. But I had to run a hundred yards as fast as Coe, Ovett and Scott before I could run a mile as fast as they did.

The crisp brown leaves scattered across the sidewalk crumbled under my soles. I headed for the river: there was a hole in the fence separating Riverside Park from the Empire Motors assembly plant railyards. Ducking through it, I had the riverbank to myself. To my left, boxcars awaiting automobiles. To my right, the ever-visible rainbow slick on the river's surface, the effluent of automaking. Past the dam with the stair-stepped fish ladder, where a lone angler in a quilted winter jacket dipped his line into the current. Then I was in the coal yards of the municipal power plant, where grimy mud blackened the nubs of my waffle-iron soles. I ran beneath the plant's six hundred foot smokestacks, the tallest anything in Wenniway, their almost-as-long shadows spread out across the coal and the dirt and the water by the rising sun. Past the guard house where the coal trucks checked in. I wasn't supposed to run on the power plant's property, but the guards had seen me in my Wenniway Central sweatshirt, and now they just waved. I emerged onto a street busy with first-shift autoworkers trying to make it to the plant for clock in. Bar. Bakery. Windowless clubhouse of a motorcycle gang, with a sign warning, IF YOU DON'T KNOW IF YOU'RE WELCOME—YOU'RE NOT! Crossing the street, I ran across a vast weedy lot where, a dozen years before, a truck factory had burned down, after sitting empty for a dozen years before that. I barely remembered the midnight dawn of the fire, but my father still insisted it was arson. ("The insurance was worth way more than that polluted land. Why do you think no one's ever built on it?") Then another mile along the planked Riverwalk, to the zoo. If I looked inside the gate, I could see a lion pacing behind the metal bars of his concrete cell. I didn't like looking at that lion, because everything with legs should have the freedom to run, the way I was running. I touched the brick wall that surrounded the zoo, turned around, and ran the course in reverse. As I turned onto my block, I resumed the Olympic race in my head, sprinting the last two hundred yards to our house.

"And here comes Ward!" Howard Cosell shouted. "Coe and Ovett struggling toward the finish. They look utterly depleted. Can they hang on? They cannot. Ward is passing them in the home stretch, looking like a thoroughbred racing broken-down milk horses. It's Ward! Kevin Ward, the first American to win this event since 1908. The gold medal that eluded Jim Ryun will hang around the neck of Kevin Ward!"

One of our neighbors hung an American flag from his porch. In my mind, it represented all the flags waving in the stands, and the flag I would drape over my shoulders as I took a victory lap around the Coliseum. Every runner had that voice running through his head, whether he wanted to admit it or not. It may not have been Howard Cosell's voice, but it was a voice telling him he was a champion. Why run if you didn't have that goal?

FOUR

My homeroom class was physics, taught by Mr. Erwin. He was the most famous teacher at Wenniway Central, because every year, he held the Stadium Egg Drop Contest. (Also, he always dressed in a button-up cardigan and a bow tie, one of each for every day of the week.) Contestants began with two items: a shoebox and an egg. The goal was to drop both off the top row of the bleachers without breaking the egg. One kid stuffed his egg into a loaf of bread. (It didn't break.) Another suspended his egg within a cradle of rubber bands. (It broke.) I stuffed my shoebox with gummy worms, Big League Chew and marshmallows, the softest substances I could find at the party store across the street from the stadium. Not only did my egg break, it fell out of the shoebox in mid-descent, splattering yolk all over the sidewalk milliseconds before its insulation arrived. Next year, I planned to slide my egg into the toe of an old running shoe. Those things cushioned my feet. Why not an egg?

After that morning's 7:55 bell, Mr. Erwin took attendance, but he didn't begin the day's class with a physics lesson. Instead, he sat on the edge of his desk and asked, "How many of you have parents who work at Empire?"

My hand went up. So did the hands of half my classmates.

"My job," Mr. Erwin said, slowly and quietly (he always spoke slowly and quietly, because he knew that made us lean in to listen), "is to prepare you to get jobs. And my job is about to become a lot more important. When I started teaching here, a young man didn't have to study to get a good job. He could walk straight from the graduation line to that assembly line across the street and start making more money than I was. I've been here long enough so that I taught some of your parents. I'm not going to point any fingers, but I had this one student, he was such a chucklehead. Never did his homework. I gave him a D just so he wouldn't repeat my class. About a year after he graduated, he came to visit me and pointed to his brand-new Corsair in the parking lot. This is when I was driving a ten-year-old station wagon. I think he was an electrician's assistant or something. He stood under a ladder and handed the electrician a lightbulb to screw in."

"That was probably my dad," a kid in the second row mumbled.

"Your dad studied harder than you ever did, Mr. McNair," Mr. Erwin said, breaking up the room with laughter. "You oughta go home and ask him to help you with your homework."

Fixing his smirk, settling his features again behind is horn-rimmed reading glasses, Mr. Erwin went on.

"You're all going to have to study hard and go to college," he said, "because by the time you graduate, that plant is going to be gone. And even if it were going to stay, now they've got robots to do all the idiot jobs they used to have you high school students for. No more assistant electricians handing lightbulbs to master electricians. The job market isn't going to be as easy for you as it was for your parents. OK, that's my effort to get you to pay attention this morning. Now we're going to talk about Newton's First Law of Motion."

My dad had never talked about my working in the shop, one way or the other. He hadn't given me an "I want you to follow in my footsteps" or an "I want something better for you, son" speech. I knew it wasn't as easy to hire in at Empire as when my dad graduated from Central. Back then, all a guy had to do was present himself at the personnel office and demonstrate a pulse. Now, whenever Empire hired, every employee was allowed one "recommendation." Of course, my dad would recommend me if I wanted. To hire in at Empire, you had to know someone, or be related to someone, and I was. I didn't want to work in the shop, though. I wanted to run, and win big races, and own a running shoe store, like Frank Shorter and Bill Rodgers. But until yesterday, I had known that the shop would be there to fall back on, if that didn't work out. You *could* be a factory worker and a champion runner. A guy from Iowa named Phil Coppess trained around working eight-hour shifts in a food processing plant and beat Frank Shorter in the Chicago Marathon. I had read about him in *Runner's World*, one of the two magazines I subscribed to, along with *Track and Field News*. Now, though, I wouldn't be able to do that in Wenniway.

That afternoon, as cross-country practice began, I saw another group on the sidewalk in front of the plant. These guys were all hoisting signs with the same screen-printed message: EMPIRE MOTORS STABS WORKERS IN THE BACK. They were older than the workers milling around outside the day before. Among the gray heads, I saw Gramps, wearing his Auto Workers Alliance Local 151 windbreaker, and an adjustable baseball cap bearing the union's logo. Every time a car slid by, he waggled his placard, hoping to elicit a honk. Car. Honk. Car. Honk. Car. Car. Car. Honk. There were a lot of union members in Wenniway: not just autoworkers, but pipefitters, electricians, nurses, even teachers—most everyone who peddled a skill for a paycheck. We were headed to the park for our workout, so I couldn't depart from the rubber stampede on the sidewalk to talk to Gramps. But after I got home from practice, I told Dad I'd seen him picketing. Dad just shook his head.

That Sunday, Gramps drove himself to our house. He looked tense and determined as he plodded up our driveway, his right arm waving at the air to balance an arthritic leg. He still wore his union windbreaker, even though it was Sunday, and cold. As soon as he walked in the door, before he even unfastened all the snaps, Gramps began haranguing Dad about Empire Motors.

"Well, you're finally seeing that they'll always screw you over," Gramps said, hanging his jacket in the closet. "Have you got any beer, by any chance?"

"We don't drink alcohol on Sundays, and you look like you want to start an argument, so no and no," Dad said.

They went into the living room, as far as possible from Mom and the kitchen. I sat down at the dining room table, so I could hear what they were saying.

"Kevin said he saw you out picketing," Dad began.

"That was me."

"I'm glad you're keeping busy, but I don't know what good it's going to do."

"You don't care that they're shutting your plant down, moving your job six hundred miles away?"

"Yeah, I care. Leaving Wenniway is the last thing I want to do."

"Maybe you should have been out there, then," Gramps said.

"I still have to work with that company. Which is what I was doing while you were out there with a sign."

"Your generation just had the easiest ride imaginable," Gramps said, sounding disgusted.

"I'm sure every father in the history of the world has said that to his children."

"I mean it. Someone else fought for everything you've got. We fought the war for your freedom. We fought the Wildcat Strike so you wouldn't have to go to work every day worried about getting fired so's the foreman could put his brother-in-law on the line."

"That was about fifty years ago."

"Maybe you should fight now, so Kevin can have what you've got."

"It's an obsolete plant."

Gramps shook his head. "Weak."

"Dad, every time you and the other union brass called a strike, I was out there with a sign. When we struck for thirty and out, I did picket duty every day. But after that, we had it all. We didn't need to go on strike for floating holidays, but we did. The Wildcat Strike needed to happen, but you just couldn't let it go. You beat the company once, and from then on, it was 'strike, strike, strike, let's beat 'em again.' Every time we get a transfer from Frontenac, they talk about how militant everyone here is. You know, Empire didn't have to build a new plant in Tennessee. There's plenty of farmland around here. Maybe they wanted to get away from that attitude."

"Now you sound just like that president you voted for."

"Dad, let's not talk politics on a Sunday."

"He fired them air traffic controllers when they went on strike, and he'll fire every union member if he could. Is that what you wanted?"

"I wanted someone to get tough with the Ayatollah and boom, as soon as he gets in, we get our hostages back," Dad said. "You're never gonna agree with any president on everything. FDR is dead, ya know."

"I just can't believe I'm sitting here listening to my ingrate son tell me the union cost him his job," Gramps retorted in a tense, quiet voice. "If it wasn't for the union, you might not even have a job. When you got caught giving another guy your badge so he could punch you out while you run over to Pete's, we saved your ass."

"I know, and I never did it again."

"And that's good, because if you'd done it again, we couldn't'a saved you and we wouldn't'a tried. What's Jo Anne cooking for dinner?"

"Meatloaf and mashed potatoes, with apple pie for dessert."

"Tell her I'm sure it's as good as it always is, but I'm not feeling well enough to stay and eat."

I heard footsteps on the living room carpet, then the closet door, then a jangle of hangers, then the front door open and shut. Not loudly. It sounded no differently than Dad leaving the house in the morning. I looked out the dining room window to see Gramps walking to his car. The Auto Workers' Alliance logo, a pair of interlocking A's encompassed by a gear, covered the back of his windbreaker. I went into the living room, pretending I'd heard nothing, and asked Dad why Gramps had left.

"I know you don't remember the Vietnam War," Dad explained, "but during Vietnam, you had a lot of old guys who'd fought in World War II and thought it was the greatest thing they'd ever done, and wouldn't it be great for the country if we could do it again. Well, we needed to fight World War II, but we didn't need to fight that other war. Your grandfather's the same way about the Wildcat Strike. It was the greatest thing he ever did, so why isn't every strike great? He's a little mad at me right now because I don't agree, so I want you to go over to his house after practice this week and check on him, OK?"

Mom set the table, sliced the meatloaf, and spooned out the potatoes without asking about Gramps. I think she'd heard everything I'd just heard and was glad not to have him at her table.

*   *   *

Jim Ryun was an even faster high school runner than Gerry Lindgren. He broke the four-minute mile *when he was a junior*, just like I was. (I had only just broken the five-minute mile: 4:53 last track season). Jim Ryun got into running like all the rest of us did. He got cut from the church baseball team and the junior high basketball team, so he figured there was nothing left to do but join all the other uncoordinated wimps on the cross-country team, which never cuts anyone. He got a letter jacket and started thinking maybe that would get him a girlfriend, too. Which I guess is what all guys are thinking about when they go out for sports. One of the best things about cross country was that the girls were right there. Girls didn't play football, but the girls cross-country team rode the bus back and forth to meets with us and joined us on our easy three mile runs the day before a race. You can tell where this is going, so I'll cut it short: her name was Sara. She wasn't the fastest girl on the team. She wasn't even on the varsity. Mostly, she just jogged through the races, then sprinted the last hundred yards. But as I said, nobody got cut in cross country. We had a two hundred pound guy on our team who joined to lose weight. It took him half an hour to run the 5K, which meant he *always* finished last, so after the rest of us were done, we stood out on the course and screamed, "Go, Dean!," "Pour it on, Dean!," and "If you're out here long enough, you'll win next week's race," until Dean busted up laughing. As Coach said, "You're not all gonna be champs, but this is a sport you can do the rest of your life. I'm still running and I'm thirty-four. You're not gonna see those lunkheads playing football when they're thirty-four."

Anyway, Sara. She was short, her legs were short, which was kind of cute, but maybe why she was not so fast. Everyone knew who she was because her mom was the hippie English teacher at Clarence Parks Junior High

School, a short (of course) woman with long, straight hair. Mrs. Coonley wore gold-framed octagonal eyeglasses, and hand-knitted shawls. Every year, she conducted a folk music unit, playing "Barbara Allen" and "Wayfaring Stranger" on her acoustic guitar. Mrs. Coonley had also organized the *Free to Be You and Me* pageant with Mrs. Braverman, the drama teacher. (They asked me to play William, the boy who wants a doll. I refused.) During every boys' race, Sara stood at the edge of the woods and shouted, "C'mon Ward!" when I emerged from the trees. (Cross-country teams didn't have cheerleaders, so we cheered for each other.) After the last meet of the season, Coach took both teams out for pizza. Sara sat down next to me.

"Good second place," she said, as though congratulating me for losing was a compliment. (It may have seemed like a compliment to her, because she had never finished in any place.) I was so obtuse, so wrapped up in my own competitive ego, that I didn't realize the conversation *was* the compliment. Sara, as I was to find out over and over again, knew exactly what was going to happen between us before I ever did.

"I just ran my race," I said, shrugging. "I went out too fast last time because I was trying to beat Joaquin."

"No one can beat Joaquin."

"I know. I totally crashed and burned that race. Coach told me not to do it again."

I thought Sara just wanted to talk about running, but when the pizzas were served, she and another girl started giggling about a sign by the window: NO SHIRT, NO SHOES, NO SERVICE. (This was not a fancy pizza parlor. As a history teacher who took on coaching duties for extra money, Coach was too broke for a place with tablecloths, or plates. The menu was spelled out on a white board in little plastic letters, some of which had fallen from their slots, so the toppings on offer included AN HOVIES and PIN APPLE. The tables were naked Formica, with the glitter worn away in the spots where diners had rested their elbows. A Galaga console had been fitted into the corner beside the bathrooms. It was exactly the kind of place that might attract half-naked skateboarders and BMX riders in the summer.)

"No shirt, no shoes, NO DICE!" Sara shouted, pointing at the sign. Her friend laughed. Sara saw that I didn't get it. (I would come to realize that she made the joke precisely because she thought I wouldn't get it. But at that moment, I did not yet understand that Sara's mind was always a step ahead of everyone else's. Such subtlety for one who ran so slowly.)

"You haven't seen *Fast Times at Ridgemont High*?" Sara asked me.

"Uh-uh," I said.

I had heard a lot of people talking about *Fast Times at Ridgemont High*, since it was a movie about high school, but it came out right at the start of cross-country season, and I couldn't go to the movies and still get up at six to run. (Later, I found out that Sara had known my running schedule, too. Sara knew a lot more about me than I knew about her.)

"Oh, my God, you're like the only person." Sara ribbed me with an elbow. "I've seen it twice, but I would totally go a third time. Just to get you up to speed, so to speak."

When I was tardy to respond, she said, "It's still playing at the Triplex." When I still didn't respond, she continued, "On Saturday."

I went home with Sara's address and phone number, written in looping 3s, 2s, and 0s on a napkin. Fifty hours later, I parked my father's car in front of her house, wearing my letterman's jacket, a flannel shirt, a pair of jeans, and, of course, running shoes. I wore running shoes everywhere, not just as a badge of identity (my athletic identity was inseparable from my personal identity), but because I was terrified that walking in anything that didn't support my feet would cause my knees to buckle and result in patellar tendinitis, or some other season-ending injury. I even wore running shoes to church. If God hadn't wanted me to wear them, he would not have made me the second-fastest runner on the Wenniway Central cross-country team.

I meant to walk up to the front door and ring the bell, as my father had counseled me when I'd told him why I wanted to borrow the car. ("Be a gentleman, and, uh, be safe," he said.) The moment I jerked the gearshift up to "P," though, the storm door flapped open. Sara bounded over the little concrete porch, down the steps—faster that I'd ever seen her run on a cross-country course—and was suddenly rapping on the passenger's side window. I leaned across the seat to pull up the lock.

"My dad"—Sara was short of breath, even after that brief sprint. Belting herself into the seat, she gathered a few deep drafts of wind to power the monologue about to ensue: "When I told him I was going out with a guy from the cross-country team, he wanted to know *all* about your times, *all* about your races. My dad got me into running. He started doing laps on the little track at the Y, and now he does four miles, four days a week. I started going with him when I got old enough. I told him you broke seventeen minutes and he was like, 'Whoa! I have got to get some tips from this guy.' He did the 5K for the hospital and I think it took him, like twenty-five minutes. That's what I run."

That speech was very Sara. We were not even three blocks away from her house, on our first date, and already she had sussed out that I was vain about my race times, and suggested a coaching session with her father, as a pretext to get me inside her house.

At the theater, I paid for the tickets. I was about to pay for the popcorn, too, when we had our first disagreement: she wanted butter, I didn't.

"Most people eat their popcorn with butter," she said.

Most people can't run five thousand meters over fallen logs and up hills in under seventeen minutes, but I didn't point that out. Instead I said, "I'm trying to keep my weight between one twenty-five and one twenty-seven. I might let myself go a little between Thanksgiving and New Year's. After states, if we get there, and before indoor track."

I bought a small buttered popcorn for Sara, and a plain one for myself.

"I'll bet you don't eat Milk Duds, either," she said.

I shrugged. I didn't eat candy, at least not during racing seasons.

"OK," she said. "I'll buy those myself."

"You think it's weird that I won't eat buttered popcorn?" I asked, as we sat in the twilit theater, before the curtains opened and the previews of coming attractions rolled. I ate my unseasoned kernels. Salt, I had read, caused high blood pressure.

"It doesn't surprise me."

"Why not?"

"It seems like who you are. Every time you race, you look so gaunt and intense."

I had often imagined that the physical qualities that made me so well-suited for distance running—shortness, leanness—made me less attractive to girls, in proportion as they aided my speed and endurance. When my mother had told me, as we watched the Olympics, that there's a sport for every body type, she hadn't promised there would be a girl for every body type as well.

"Are you gonna run indoor?" I asked. Indoor track was how we kept in shape over the winter, between cross country and real track.

"I don't like running indoors," Sara sniffed. "My dad used to take me to the Y. The track was twenty laps to the mile, and the air was all sweaty and stuffy. I'm gonna audition for pit orchestra in the school musical this winter. They're doing *Camelot*. I used to love listening to that record when I was little."

"So, you're not doing any more running?" I hoped she didn't think I was disappointed by her lack of interest in indoor track. Now that we were on a date, I wanted to see her at every track meet.

"I need to be more well-rounded. I want to go to the U, and they look for a lot of activities on your resume."

I thought of my future senior yearbook line: cross country, 1, 2, 3; indoor track 1,2,3; track 1,2,3.

"*You* don't have to be well-rounded," Sara said—she always knew what I was thinking, and if I wasn't thinking it, she knew how to make me think it. I hadn't been thinking of taking her to the movies, but now here I was, with only six dollars left of the twenty my dad had lent me for the date. "You have a talent. All you have to do is run, and they'll give you a scholarship. I have to be average at a lot of little things, so I can look well-rounded, like running and playing the flute, which is the instrument I play in band class, since you didn't ask."

The lights faded, sparing me from telling Sara I hadn't asked because I'd seen her carrying her flute case around school. Everyone knew Sara's flute case, because it was decorated with a VISUALIZE WHIRLED PEAS bumper sticker, which she had undoubtedly gotten from her mother, who had undoubtedly purchased it from the Wheel City Food Co-op, or from the classified section of *Mother Jones*, a magazine she liked to leave lying around her classroom.

Fast Times at Ridgemont High was a pretty funny movie, although kind of an awkward choice for a first date, since one of the scenes is about two characters going on an awkward first date. Sara ribbed me with her elbow again, during the scene when the surfer dude and his friends see the NO SHIRT, NO SHOES, NO SERVICE sign at the

restaurant and shout "No Shirt, No Shoes, No DICE!"
We did have guys like that at Wenniway Central. Not surf-
ers, because Wenniway is a thousand miles from an ocean.
But guys who smoked pot and did laid back, non-com-
petitive stuff like hiking or watching TV. Some were guys
I'd known since elementary school: we'd played with G.I.
Joes and Matchbox cars and ridden dirt bikes over would-
be Evel Knievel jumps improvised from plywood and
cinderblocks. But they'd gotten into weed and I'd gotten
into running, so we didn't even talk to each other in the
hallways anymore. We belonged to different cliques: they
were *burnouts*; I was a *jock*. Sara, on the other hand, didn't
seem to belong to any clique: most band kids didn't run,
and most runners didn't play flute in the school musical.
Sara did what Sara wanted to do. Honestly, after she ribbed
me with her elbow, I couldn't keep my mind on the movie.
I wanted to put my mouth on her mouth, my hands on
her five-foot-two-inch body, and all the little worlds it contained. She seemed a lot deeper than me. I was just deep
enough to run in a straight line for hours without getting
bored.

After the movie, as my dad's car idled in front of her
little house, I kissed her goodnight; she pushed open the
passenger door after the first faint, dry contact of our lips,
but then she leaned back inside to tell me, "Come over after practice on Monday to meet my dad. My mom's gonna
be cooking something really *healthy*. You'll like that."

"I have to go see my grandfather on Monday," I said.

"Well, then come over on Tuesday. Every night's the
same at Chez Coonley!"

FIVE

Gramps answered the doorbell in his Autoworkers Alliance baseball cap. He seemed to wear it everywhere now.

"Sorry, I'm on the phone," he told me, walking back to the kitchen to pick up a receiver lying atop a stack of union literature.

"Jerry, I'll have to call you back. My grandson's here, but yes, a rally at the courthouse on the 30th. I'll be there. Make those assholes at Empire give back the tax breaks they've been getting all these years. There's an election coming up, so the idiots under the dome will listen...Solidarity to you, too, buddy."

Gramps heaved himself into his stuffed La-Z-Boy, its nap worn smooth by many years of retirement. He swirled it away from the blank television set.

"Sit down." Gramps gestured at the couch, but I had come straight from cross-country practice, and was still wearing my sweats. I sat on the floor.

"You run over here?"

"Yeah."

"I spent forty years building cars, and my grandson goes everywhere on foot."

"We've got the conference meet this week, then regionals. I'm trying to qualify for state."

"You beat that Mexican kid yet?"

"Nah, I tried, but he burned me out and I faded so bad a bunch of guys from East Wenniway passed me. Coach told me to just finish second."

"Well, you gotta learn teamwork. That's how we got through the Wildcat Strike. The whole family pitched in. Your grandmother brought home-cooked meals, and we tied a rope to a basket and hoisted it through the window. The boys used to love her chocolate cake."

Gramps glanced at the black-and-white wedding portrait on the mantel. The only piece of art in his living room. His hair was dark and thick; Gram's was pinned beneath a veil that flowed over her shoulders. For a moment, neither of us spoke. Then he asked, "Did your dad send you over here?"

"Yeah."

"To apologize?"

"No." My father could do that for himself. "Just to see how you're doing."

"Well, tell him that for the first time since your grandmother died, I've got something better to do than watch the cop shows on TV. I've been around long enough to understand the plant closing is all about revenge. That's the plant where the Wildcat Strike started. Empire used to fire guys whenever they felt like it—no job security, no health insurance, no pension—so one day, a couple hundred of us shut down the line and said, 'This is our plant now.' And we didn't leave 'til we got a union, even when the cops came at us with tear gas and bullets."

Gramps walked over to the dining table, picked up a flyer, handed it to me. HOLD EMPIRE ACCOUNTABLE, it read. THE STATE GAVE EMPIRE MOTORS A TAX BREAK. NOW EMPIRE IS MOVING THE PLANT TO TENNESSEE. MAKE THEM GIVE IT BACK!

"This Thursday afternoon at the county courthouse." Gramps fixed me with an expectant look.

"We have the conference meet then," I said. I folded the flyer into a paper football and slid it into my calf-length cotton sock. "I'll give it to my dad, though."

*   *   *

57

Chez Coonley, as Sara called her family's house, was a bungalow with only three bedrooms: one for Sara, one for her parents, and one for Mrs. Coonley's guitar, landscape paintings, and macramé yarn. Sara's father was also a schoolteacher—he taught history at Wenniway South. School teachers didn't earn much money. They didn't build anything was why, I guessed. Also, they got summers off and they got to be home at three-thirty in the afternoon, which kind of cramped a guy's style when he was trying to make time with their daughter.

I had walked Sara home after cross-country practice, and when we entered the front door—which opened right onto a living room crowded with bookshelves rising from the floor and spider plants dangling from the ceiling—both her parents were sitting on the couch, listening to a Joan Baez LP and reading books: for him, *A People's History of the United States*; for her, *The Moon is Always Female*. Mr. Coonley sure looked like a schoolteacher: he wore aviator glasses, a wispy blond mustache, hair parted in the middle and brushing the tops of his ears, and, of course, a blue crewneck sweater. He rose from the couch. Mrs. Coonley just waved.

"Nice to meet you," Mr. Coonley said, offering his hand. "I hear you do a lot of running."

"I'm on the cross-country team," I said, although, of course, he knew that, since that's how I'd met his daughter.

"If a guy ran the 5K in twenty-five minutes, where would he be on your team?"

"Well, not on the varsity; but we let anyone run."

"Ouch," Mr. Coonley sat back down, setting the book on his lap. "That's what I did at the hospital fun run. I guess there's a time and place for everything in life, and forty is not the time for running fast. I just wish I'd discovered it in high school. Back then, you were either a jock or a bookworm, and I was a bookworm. Now you can be both—like Sara."

After an awkward pause, Sara said, "We're going to listen to records."

"Leave the door open," Mrs. Coonley ordered.

"But then you'll hear my music, and you hate my music."

"I'll make a point not to listen."

The walls of Sara's bedroom were decorated with posters of musicians. Pale, gaunt musicians. David Bowie. Iggy Pop. Johnny Rotten. I wondered whether she thought I resembled them, and then I wondered whether she had joined the cross-country team to find a pale, gaunt boyfriend. A lot of runners looked that way.

"What kind of music do you listen to?" Sara asked me.

I didn't know what to say. I didn't listen to music. The clock radio on my nightstand was always tuned to sports from Frontenac: baseball in the summers, hockey in the winters. I mentioned a couple bands I'd seen on MTV.

"Rush. Ozzy."

Music was so integral to Sara's life and identity, and so peripheral to mine, that no band I could name would impress her. I hoped my running was enough.

"Those are such guy bands." Her features squinched, either in distress or distaste. I couldn't tell. I was quickly figuring out that Sara knew more about everything than I did, except for the one thing I knew everything about, and could do better than I did any of the many things she was interested in.

"Well, what kind of music do *you* listen to?" It wasn't a challenge, despite my tone of voice. I wanted to know what she knew.

Sara's stored her record albums in a milk crate on the floor. The jackets bore the names of bizarrely-titled bands I'd never heard of: The Buzzcocks, Elvis Costello (I had heard of Elvis Presley, of course, but not this little guy with big glasses), the Cramps, The Damned, Devo, Joy Division, The Psychedelic Furs, the Sex Pistols, the Stooges.

"Where did you get all these?"

"Campus Vinyl. In Auburn. My parents met at the U, so we go there at least once a month. They go for the bookstore or a folk concert and they drop me off to shop for records. You can put one on, but don't play it too loud. My parents," she glanced at the wide-open door, "they like *soft* stuff. My mom listens to folk and my dad is Mister FM Lite Rock. I mean, he's into *Seals and Crofts.*"

Sara's face was not what I would have considered beautiful: round, with a blunt nose and widely spaced eyes. Before she asked me to the movies, I had thought of her only as another slow runner on the girl's team, with a face not worth remembering because it was neither pretty, nor did it figure in the scoring. The more I looked at that face, though, the more I found to look at, because so much happened there: her eyes expanded in exasperation as she described her mother's musical tastes, her lips clenched in dismay at her father's. Twitching nose. Blushing cheeks. Eyebrows marching in place. I had never seen such dramatic range on a set of features. I couldn't stop watching her talk. Perhaps a face could be beautiful because of what the person behind it made it do, not just because of how it had been composed by nature. Of course, I wanted to kiss her again, but my junior high school English teacher was in the next room.

"What do you want to listen to?" Sara asked.

"Anything you want." Having no musical interests of my own, I was willing to adopt Sara's. She pulled an Elvis Costello LP out of its sleeve and set it on the turntable atop her dresser. The first song was a sad number about a guy who was in love with a woman who didn't love him back. It dragged much more slowly than the original Elvis.

"I've got all this on tape too," she said. "I taped my whole record collection. I made mixtapes for running. I always listen to my Walkman when I run by myself, but they won't let me do it on the team. When I brought it to practice, Coach Funkhouser yelled at me to put it away."

"I never listen to music when I run," I said.

"Not even when you run ten miles?"

"Uh-uh."

"Don't you get bored?"

"Running is the only thing that *doesn't* bore me."

I stayed for dinner. Mrs. Coonley served a recipe from her cookbook, *Diet for a Small Planet*: falafel, hummus and pita bread. This was not exotic for Wenniway. We had a lot of Lebanese. Most were lawyers, politicians, and real estate developers, but a few Old World immigrants operated lunch counters where they argued with each other—and their Lebanese customers—in Arabic. I'd eaten falafel sandwiches for two-fifty apiece at Farhat's, on the other side of the plant from Pete's.

"Are you doing any drama at Central?" Mrs. Coonley asked me.

"No," I said. "Just running."

"I knew you'd find a passion," she said. "Yeats said that education is not the filling of a bucket, but the lighting of a fire."

I nodded.

Before I left Sara's house, I kissed her on the front porch, a real kiss, a tongue kiss. (It wasn't my first kiss. That had been with a sprinter on the girl's track team, at a post-meet party sophomore year. I never kissed her again. She told me she'd just wanted to find out how white boys did it. I guess we didn't do it well enough, or at least I didn't.) I jogged the mile and a half home, keeping my mind occupied the entire way by imagining Sara naked.

Six

The Wenniway Central Warriors won the Mid-State Conference Championship meet at the Shady Oaks Public Golf Course. Joaquin and I ran one-three, with Steve Schaden in between us, just as it should have been in our first race together. Then we finished second at regionals. That qualified us for the state meet, which was always held at the arboretum of the state university in Auburn: The Arb at the U. The course never changed. Neither did the course record, which had been set in 1971 by Matt Ledesma, the greatest long-distance runner in our state's history: he ran at the U, winning the NCAA cross-country championship; he ran in the Montreal Olympics, finishing fifth in the 10,000 meters; then he won a bronze medal at the world cross-country championships. No one had finished within twenty seconds of his time at the Arb. As we jogged the course the morning of the state meet, I could tell I wasn't going to come nearly that close. The Arb was laid out on a bluff that declined to the Ottawa River, at what felt, as we ascended it, like a forty-five-degree angle. I leaned forward and labored up its half-mile length with pitty-pat steps. Reaching the pinnacle with heaving lungs and aching legs, I wondered what I would have left for the race. Coach had never trained us on hills. There are no hills in Wenniway. I had never been in an airplane, but those who flew over Wenniway described it as looking like a tostada sprinkled with lettuce—flat and forested. I didn't know who in our state could run fast on this course, except for guys who lived near the U, and could train at the Arb, or guys who trained on the dunes overlooking the Big Lake (which is where Matt Ledesma learned to run).

I rarely got nervous before races, but before the state meet, I sat down in a Porta-john, waiting in a long line of similarly anxious runners, still swaddled in sweats against the thirty-three-degree morning. I wasn't afraid of the agony awaiting me on that hill. I was afraid because Sara was waiting at the finish line. Sara and her father had followed the team bus the hundred miles from Wenniway to Auburn, in a caravan of boyfriends, girlfriends, and parents that gathered in the school parking lot at six in the morning. In a conference meet, I knew I was going to finish near the front. Where would I finish here, racing up hills against the fastest runners in the state? What if I finished last? I tried to tell myself that wouldn't matter to Sara, as long as I crossed the line looking haggard, drawn and *in extremis*—all the qualities she liked to see in musicians and athletes.

Coach gathered the seven varsity runners in a circle and gave us—well, it wasn't exactly a pep talk. More like a pre-race excuse. I never made pre-race excuses, but some runners found them as essential as a pair of shoes: "I don't do well in the heat"; "I'm just gonna use this race as a training run"; "I'm gonna have to baby my knee a little bit this time." Loser talk. Guys who said stuff like that never won, or even came close.

"It's pretty amazing we've gotten this far," Coach said. "We're a track school. We do this to keep in shape for track, but we made it all the way to State, even though we lost three of our best guys thanks to their idiotic behavior. I'm looking at some of the best distance runners in the state right here, and next spring when I get you guys together with our sprinters and our hurdlers, we're gonna be unstoppable. This is a tough course. We're not used to hills. Just go out there and run your best race."

So, Coach wasn't expecting us to win the state cross-country championship. Neither was I. Cross country is a sport for white dudes and Mexicans. That was only half our student body. We didn't have a chance against those big schools in the Frontenac suburbs.

More than two hundred runners stood tensely behind a white stripe painted on the meadow at the bottom of the hill. Our freshly exposed arms and legs reddened and pimpled to gooseflesh. Some guys wore long-sleeved shirts under their singlets. Not me. I could stand the cold for sixteen minutes, as long as I kept moving. Distance running is an endurance sport. The more you learned to endure, the faster you'd run. When the gun cracked the air, the line collapsed forward, a surging, jostling herd of singlets in a confetti of colors. Ahead of me, the dozen fastest runners flowed around the first flag. I wasn't going to catch them. The distance between us would only expand. But if I was only trailing a dozen runners, I was near the front of the pack. I keyed on a guy just ahead of me in a black jersey—from which school, I couldn't tell, since I was looking at his back. I stared at his shoulders. "Hold your spot, hold your spot," I commanded myself. "Don't lose him. Don't lose him." All around me, rubber soles pounded frost-hardened dirt. I ran with a desperation I never felt in dual meets, when I knew where I was going to finish, and rarely worried about anyone catching me. For the first half mile, my legs felt weak, lighter than air, powered more by fear than muscle. After half a mile, the field strung out, and I settled into a rhythm behind my pacer. "Everyone else here as frightened as I am," I told myself.

But ahead was the hill. A mile into the race, we began our climb. This was not our Mickey Mouse Hill, which could be conquered with a ten-second burst of stutter steps. This was a campaign. An ordeal. An alpine expedition. With every stride, as I planted a toe in the dirt and launched myself forward and upward, my thigh muscles tightened, my breath became shallower. I could see the top of the hill, but the moment when I would again tread level ground seemed as distant as another lifetime. The pain of this ascent felt like all my existence was, or ever would be. I thought of the Olympic motto: *citius, altus, fortus*. Faster, higher, stronger. I was, incrementally, climbing higher, but I did not feel fast, or strong. Everyone else in this race was climbing the same hill, though, and some of them were hurting worse. I passed the black singlet. The next runner ahead of me was...Joaquin. As the number 1 on his back grew larger, I thought, *He can't handle this hill; I can beat him today*. I dug harder, even though I knew I was going to pay for that burst later in the race—or later on this hill. When I drew alongside Joaquin, he looked spent, helpless, exhausted. His eyes darted toward the side of his face, as though he was searching for someone to rescue him from a beating. We were both too tired to speak, but he nodded to urge me on. I did the same to him. When at last I reached the summit, I turned right at a yellow flag, stumbling a step on the suddenly flat ground. I ran half a mile along the top of the bluff, hit the two mile in 11:20, then turned at another yellow flag, where the course descended down an oiled service road.

At the bottom, I turned left at a red flag, and sprinted through the meadow to the finishing chute beside the river. I only looked back once, in the last hundred yards. Joaquin was gaining on me. He was faster on this flat homestretch, but too far back to make up the ground he'd lost on the hill. As I crossed into the roped-in chute, a race marshal handed me a popsicle stick inked with the number 14. Fourteen? I was the fourteenth-fastest cross-country runner in the state? I handed the stick to a marshal at the end of the chute, who recorded my bib number. Every time a runner crossed the line, a man sitting at a folding table hit a button on a device that looked like an adding machine. It printed the finishing order and time on a receipt tape. The race officials would match the tape to the list of finishers, type up the results, and mail them to our coaches on Monday.

Joaquin caught up with me in the chute. He put his hand on my shoulder.

"What'd you get, buddy?"

"Fourteenth," I said.

"I got sixteenth. You got me on that hill."

"That was the toughest…mofo I've ever run in my life." Even though I was Varsity One, at least for a day, my churchgoing parents restrained me from swearing.

"You did great on it, buddy! I'll get you on the track, though. There's no hills on a track."

Coach ran up to us, carrying our gray sweats and the school-color thermal jackets and pants—the "Greens"—we wore in seriously cold weather.

"Great run, guys. Fourteen and sixteen. That's fantastic in a race this big."

"Who won?" Joaquin asked.

"Some kid from Frontenac Catholic Central. They got fourth, too. They're gonna win this thing."

I dressed and sought out Sara. When I found her inside the warming tent, I handed her the popsicle stick.

"I didn't get a medal," I said. "I got a popsicle stick."

She examined the inscription.

"Fourteenth is great!"

"I'm the thirteenth loser." Fourteenth *was* pretty great, just not great enough to brag about.

Wenniway Central got seventh in the state, which didn't come with a trophy. We still had to hang around for the awards ceremony and watch the U's cross-country coach hand out trophies and hang medals around the necks of runners from Frontenac Catholic Central. The coach was a wiry old man named Harry "Red" Deane, after the color of the hair that had once grown atop his head. When the ceremony was over, instead of riding home on the team bus, I went to breakfast with Sara and her dad, still sweaty, still wearing my Greens.

"You're going to see where my parents *met*," Sara exclaimed as we walked through the U's Quad, a grassy commons enclosed on all four sides by gray Gothic buildings that looked like the campus in *Chariots of Fire*. (I saw all the running movies. There weren't too many.) I recalled the scene when Harold Abrahams sprinted over the flagstones, trying to complete a circuit of his college before the clock struck twelve. The U had its own clock tower, with its own profound bell. Could I have run the Quad in a dozen strokes? Probably not. I wasn't a sprinter, let alone an Olympic gold medalist.

"Your mother and I first talked to each other at Waldo's." Mr. Coonley was adding detail to Sara's story. "That wasn't the first place I *saw* her, though. The first place I saw her was in Professor Dunning's poetry class. Then I walked into Waldo's just as her bridge game was breaking up because her partner had to go to class. So I volunteered to take his place. I was not a great bridge player, so we lost. She must have felt sorry for me, because she invited me to hear her sing at a hootenanny that weekend. It was at a coffeehouse. They used to have these places where you could just sit and drink coffee and play chess and read magazines. Anyway, when I heard her sing 'Barbara Allen,' that was it for me. She sang it even more beautifully than Joan Baez."

"He *still* makes her sing it every week," Sara said.

Waldo's was a diner, still looking as it must have twenty years before, in the early 1960s. Sara's parents had probably played bridge on these same wobbly Formica tables, or in one of the hard wooden booths we now occupied. Only the prices had changed: they were pasted on the laminated menu, atop the originals. I ordered a three-fifty omelet. It turned out to be proof that, as Pete knew, bad food at low prices is a business plan for the ages. While we ate, Sara began talking about following her parents to the U.

"That's why I'm doing the play," she explained. "So I can get as much on my resumé as possible. I mean, if your SATs are high enough, you can get in anywhere, but who knows how I'll do on my SATs. I'm not that good at math. So, I have to be well-rounded."

Sara looked over at me. We were sitting on the same side of the booth.

"*You* could probably get a scholarship now, as fast as you ran today."

"I was fourteenth," I said. "There's only seven guys on a varsity cross-country team. This is a big-time Division I school. The U recruits guys from all over the country."

"You're only a junior," Mr. Coonley said. "You'll finish higher next year."

"I just want to go somewhere I can run, not too far from home. My dad's getting transferred to Tennessee, so my mom and my grandfather are gonna be on their own most of the time."

"Does your dad work at Empire?" Mr. Coonley asked.

"Yeah."

He sighed over his banana pancakes. "We may all end up getting transferred to Tennessee, after that place closes. They pay the taxes that keep the schools open. Sara's mom and I got hired in Wenniway after they expanded that plant. So of course, they built more schools for the kids of the people who were going to work there. We saw the best of Wenniway. I keep telling Sara, 'Go to the U, and don't look back.'"

Before we left Auburn, Mr. Coonley took us to the Campus Spirit Shop. He bought me a maroon and gold t-shirt with the U's logo across the chest.

"Run in that," he told me. "Someday, they'll give you the real thing."

"He wants everyone to go to the U," Sara said.

"The very first class I took, my professor said, 'Welcome to one of the world's great universities.' I came in here from a small town Up North. I didn't know how to pronounce 'unique.' I thought it was you-ni-kyoo. I read a lot, but I'd never heard anyone use a five-dollar word like that. I left with a great wife and a great job, and I've still got both. I'd recommend it to anybody."

We walked beneath the Engineering Arch, the entrance to a tunnel that would return us to the Quad. Inscribed on the keystone were a compass and a ruler.

"The legend was, if you kissed a girl here at midnight, you'd get married."

Mr. Coonley stared at Sara and me.

"Midnight is a long ways off." He checked his watch. "All the way on the other side of the clock."

I rode home to Wenniway in the back seat of the Coonley's Volkswagen Rabbit (more about that un-civic transportation choice later). One hand held Sara's. The other hand bunched up the maroon and gold t-shirt in my lap. Everyone in the state cheered for these colors. Who wouldn't want to wear them? And Auburn was only a hundred miles from Wenniway.

When Mr. Coonley dropped me off at the house, I learned that my fourteenth-place finish in the state cross-country championship had been upstaged by an even more impressive family achievement.

"Your sister's in labor," my Mom said. "We're going over to the hospital now."

"You have a good race?" my father asked, as he pulled on his coat.

"Pretty good," I said. I could tell they were less interested in what I had just done than what my sister was about to do. As my parents hastened down the driveway to the car, my father called back, "I hope you beat that Mexican kid!"

I wanted to shout, "I did!" but I thought I'd save it for a time when he cared.

SEVEN

We were southbound on the Interstate, headed for Tennessee. I was in the backseat of the car, reading again one of my Christmas gifts: *Best Efforts* by Kenny Moore. He ran with Pre at Oregon, then finished fourth in the marathon, which, he wrote, is the worst place to finish at the Olympics. The three guys ahead of you get a medal, and you get…an acknowledgement of your participation. (Still, it was better than fourteenth at a state cross-country championship. Kenny Moore got to keep the USA track uniform. I had to turn in my gear to Coach Funkhouser.)

Dad was driving the Durant station wagon. Riding shotgun was Denny Earl, an Empire co-worker also doing the Tennessee Shuffle, as the guys in plant callied the transfer. Dad and Denny were planning to room together, and carpool home every weekend. Before they moved, they had to rent a trailer. It was spring break, so I agreed to come along, as long as I got to run every a.m. and p.m. Track season was starting as soon as I got back. I had run a 4:39 indoor mile and didn't want to lose a step.

"Since you've got your learner's permit, we could use an extra driver," Dad had said, in trying to persuade me to make the trip. "And I'm not gonna get to see you as much once I start working down there. I'm gonna miss your senior year. You're gonna be the big running star."

At the state line, I wished I were Mister Fantastic, from the *Fantastic Four* comic book, so I could stretch my arm across the dashboard, beating everyone else in the car into the next state. I had crossed the Frontenac River into Canada, so I had been to another country, but never another state. Our tires clicked across a groove, and the gray, tar-patched highway suddenly smoothed out into a bed of fresh black asphalt.

"Well, what are we gonna do in Nashville?" Denny asked my dad.

"We're not goin' to Nashville. We're goin' to this little flyspeck on the map an hour away. That's where they're buildin' this plant in a—I don't know what they got down there—a cotton field."

Dad sounded irritated, although I couldn't tell whether he was irritated by Denny's question, or our destination.

"My wife is a huge country fan," Denny said. "She told me to check out Conway Twitty's house on Music Row."

"If you want to take the car one night and go into Nashville, that's fine with me," my dad said, with a finality that suggested he was done talking about Nashville.

"It's the damnedest thing," Denny said. "My mom and dad moved up from Missouri to work in the plants during the war, and here we are moving back down South again. It ain't all bad. I used to come down this way to visit my grandparents, before they passed, and I've got some cousins down there. I ain't seen 'em in a while. We just send Christmas cards. I've got to put in ten years down there before I can retire, so I might as well have some fun. There's some good barbecue, good music and good fishin' down south."

My dad spotted a rest stop and pulled over.

"I'm gonna call your mother," he told me, looking over the headrest. "Do you want to talk to her?"

"We just talked to her this morning," I said. "We've only been gone two hours."

"I like to keep up with her during the day. I usually call her from work when I'm on break."

"Sure," I said, mainly because I didn't want to sit alone in the car with Denny. I was already worried he wouldn't get along with Dad; unlike my father, Denny seemed to be looking forward to spending time away from his wife.

Carrying a zippered pouch stuffed with quarters, my dad sought out the pay phones. The day before, at the bank, he had withdrawn enough money for a week's worth of long-distance phone calls.

"Jo Anne," he called into the receiver. "Yeah, we're in Winnemac now. How's everything going there?...Yeah, well, I know Garrett had a little croup last night, and I wanted to see whether that had cleared up...OK. Well, I'll call you again in a couple hours, and you can let me know if you've talked to her then. Do you want to talk to Kevin?"

Dad handed me the receiver.

"Hi, Mom."

"Hi, Kevin. How's Winnemac?"

"Pretty much the same as home. Gray, chilly. I guess Tennessee will be warmer."

"You'll have that to look forward to."

"Yep. Here's Dad again."

"I love you, sweetie," Dad signed off. "I'll call you the next time we stop."

Dad called Mom twice more from highway rest stops, and again from the motel in Kentucky where we spent the night. (Dad had promised me we would be off the road by six, so I could get in my evening run.) When I left the room, he was lying atop the floral print asbestos blanket, holding the phone in both hands. Denny, who had the room next to ours, was standing in the breezeway, with a cigarette in one hand and a can of Budweiser in the other.

"You're one of those masochists, huh?" he said.

I nodded.

"Well, enjoy yourself. You couldn't pay me to do that."

I couldn't imagine anyone paying a pot-bellied smoker to run. (Actually, Denny's belly was bigger than a pot; it was closer in size to a double boiler.) Instead of pointing that out, I bounded away, spending the next hour running back and forth along the frontage road between the highway and the motel parking lot. When I returned to the room, Dad was still on the phone. The TV was tuned to *Happy Days*.

"How long were you and Mom on the phone?" I asked.

"About an hour and a half. We were watching TV together. You know we both like *Happy Days*. That's how it was when we met. I was a greaser, like Fonzie, except I had a '54 Corsair, instead of a motorcycle. I called it The Humper...until I met your mom."

My father was still car crazy. We always parked the station wagon in the driveway because he was restoring a World War II jeep in the garage.

"The car's gone," I said.

"Denny wanted to go to the Grand Ole Opry. I'd rather watch *Happy Days* with your mom. This is the first night we've spent apart since we got married." Dad looked longingly at the telephone on the nightstand.

"Why don't you get her to move down with you?" I asked.

"She's got a job, and she wants to be a grandma now. And you've got to finish up at Central. We're just gonna have to suck it up for five years, and then I can retire back home. A lot of guys have to go off to support their families. What if I was a soldier or a sailor? I could die doing those things. I'm not gonna die in an auto plant. I was lucky to be with your mom every day for twenty-five years, and hopefully, I'll be lucky for another twenty-five years after this is over."

My father's workplace-to-be was a shell alongside the highway, awaiting equipment from the Wenniway plants. Hanging from its roof, sagging and billowing atop the corrugated skin, was an enormous mylar banner declaring, FUTURE HOME

OF THE EMPIRE MARQUETTE. OPENING THIS FALL. The plant was twice as large as Empire Body and was the only man-made object along this stretch of highway (except for the highway itself), which meant it could grow, if people bought enough Marquettes. But we had not come all this way to see the plant. My dad couldn't go inside, even though he carried an Empire Motors ID card. We were here to see the trailer park, or "Auto Acres Mobile Home Court," as the development was identified on a billboard outside the entrance. Located across the highway from the plant, on the opposite end of the overpass leading the gate, it had been built for autoworkers like my dad and Denny, who were only moving their bodies down here, not their lives, and just needed a cheap place to crash between shifts. As they sat in the car, waiting for the leasing agent, Denny looked down the rows of rectangular trailers and wondered, "Which one of these shoeboxes are we going to be stored in?"

Their shoebox was a model named the Marquette, after the Empire sedan. "Marquette" is synonymous with "quality" ("the Marquette of lawnmowers," "the Marquette of running shorts"), so it must have been their most exclusive model. The leasing agent, a young man in a short-sleeved dress shirt and a brown striped tie (you couldn't wear that Up North in March), unlocked the door. As my father mounted the single step into the living room/kitchen (sink, stove, refrigerator and Formica countertop on right, thin acrylic carpet on left), he exhaled and sagged as though emptying himself out was the only way to confront the emptiness he was facing. Dad and Denny walked through the cubicle bedrooms and the plastic bathroom, pretending to inspect each room for their own satisfaction. We all knew, though, that they had as much choice in their living quarters as a prisoner did in his cell.

"How much is the rent on this one?" my dad asked the agent.

"Three thirty-three."

"Don't you offer a ten percent discount for Empire employees?" Denny put in.

"Yes, we do," the agent responded. "So, it'll be three hundred for you."

"We'll be looking to sign a lease for September," Dad said.

"That's when we're opening. If you want to put down first month's rent deposits, we'll hold it for you."

Dad and Denny wrote checks.

"Hell, that's just a three-hundred-dollar trailer," Denny exclaimed on the drive back to the motel. "They priced it at three thirty-three and said they're giving Empire employees a ten percent discount. Who the hell else is gonna live there? They want us to think we're getting a deal for that sensory deprivation tank. I may just be a shop rat, but I took enough high school math to figure that trick out."

When I got back to the motel after my run that evening, Dad was on the phone with Mom again. This time he was watching *Real People*, laughing at a segment about a man who had dressed his dachshunds in ballerina tutus and trained them to walk on their hind legs.

"Oh, those poor animals," he was saying. "How can they hold their heads up at the park anymore? All the dogs are gonna see 'em coming and say, 'Hey, those are the ones in the tutus from the TV show.' We never did that to Scooter. He was always so friendly to you, remember? I think he was trying to tell me you were the one...Uh-uh...Oh, no!...Ha ha ha...I'm not going to buy you a dog just so you can dress him in your homemade clothes like you did the kids. You've got Garrett now if you want to get your sewing machine working again...Mmm...Maybe I will need to get you a dog to keep you company and protect you while I'm down here...Seriously, Jo Anne, do you think you'll need that?"

I stepped into the bathroom to take a shower. When I stepped out, Dad was staring silently at the TV smoking a cigarette, dribbling ashes onto the tray beside the bed. Dad had vowed to quit smoking after Gram died, but he had purchased a pack of Marlboro Lights at a gas station, which he still did whenever he was feeling nervous, stressed, or agitated.

"You and Mom talk a lot," I said.

"You'd think after you've known someone twenty-five years, you'd run out of things to say, but the more time I spend with your mother, the more I have to say to her, because we've been through so much together."

I wanted to ask my dad to put out his cigarette, because smoking in bed was a good way to burn down the motel, because secondhand smoke was bad for my wind, and because he was supposed to have quit. He was paying for the room, though, so I just sat on the edge of my bed, as far away as possible from Dad's cigarette.

"Have you thought much about what you're going to do next year?" Dad asked.

"What do you mean?"

"I mean, are you going to college, going to work? What?"

"Well, you know I want to keep running."

"In college?"

"Yeah."

"Which one?"

"Whichever one will let me."

"What does that mean? UCLA? Alabama?"

"I'd like to get a scholarship, so you don't have to pay for it."

"That would be good. If you go someplace that costs twenty grand a year, I may have to work the rest of my life down here to pay for it. And I'm not saying that to be cheap."

"I know."

"I'm saying that because the less time I have to spend in this place, the better it is for our family. I got four generations to look after now: your grandfather, your mom, your sister, your nephew. I'm gonna need you to step in. I'm hoping you can stay in Wenniway, or close by."

There were two colleges in Wenniway: Wenniway Community College, a two-year school, and Wesley College, a little Methodist school. Neither, however, had a Division I track team, and after that trip to the U with Sara and her dad, I wanted to run Division I. Suddenly, I understood what Empire Body's closing meant for me, my father, my family, all the thousands of people who worked in that plant, and the families they supported. My dad thought he could work five years in Tennessee, qualify for a full pension and lifetime health benefits, then come home to Wenniway and resume his old life. But life in Wenniway was never going to be the same once those plants stopped running. I know my dad wanted nothing more than to live out his life as the patriarch of a big family with summer weekends at the cottage Up North, grandchildren at Sunday dinners, baptisms, picnics, school plays, and Central football games. That would have been easy to do when there was a job for every patriarch. But now those jobs were leaving Wenniway, and, as Mr. Ewing had said, we were going to have to go to college if we wanted to earn a living. Which meant that some of *us* would have to leave Wenniway. My taking a track scholarship at an out-of-town school wouldn't be a big deal for my dad if he could stay close to the family. Empire Motors was messing with everyone in Wenniway, not just its employees.

"Sara and her dad want me to go the U," I said.

My dad sat up, stabbed out his cigarette.

"Well, that's a good school," he said. "With in-state tuition."

"It's not in Wenniway."

"It's two hours away. You could come home on weekends."

"Sure. I have to get fast enough to run there. It's Division I. They finished third in the NCAA cross-country championship."

"You beat that Mexican kid, didn't you?"

"Once. In cross country. I've never beaten him on the track."

"There's another track season coming up. How fast do you have to run to get a scholarship anyway?"

"I dunno. I'll have to find out."

I'd always wondered what had driven anyone to train as hard as Gerry Lindgren did—waking up in the middle of the night to get in three workouts a day, running two hundred and fifty miles a week. Later, when I found out how fast I'd have to run, I had my answer.

EIGHT

Our first meet of the outdoor season was at home against Oak Rapids, one of the country schools where everyone raised corn or cows and had the same last name. All their white kids (which was all their kids) were afraid to come to Wenniway Central, because they thought they'd get knifed, and all our black kids were afraid to go out there, because they thought they'd get lynched.

"You know what's gonna happen when they see us get off the bus?" James, our fastest sprinter, said to me while riding the bus out to their cinder track the year before. "They're gonna start hearing banjos in their heads, and then they're gonna look at each other like, 'Who brought the rope?'"

Oak Rapids didn't have a runner who could break five minutes in the 1600. This allowed me to make a proposal to Coach.

"Let me go out with Joaquin again," I begged after we finished our warm-ups on the track.

Coach glared at me.

"Last time you went out with Joaquin, you cost us the meet."

"That was cross country, against East Wenniway. No matter how hard I bonk, I'll still beat all these guys. I gotta get used to running that fast if I want to step up."

Coach's hollow cheeks puffed like a frog's throat, then deflated as he exhaled a sigh.

"I don't want you going out any faster than sixty-seven," he said. "EVEN IF HE DOES!"

I didn't tell Joaquin I planned to race him. If he knew, he might have pushed the pace from the start. We lined up behind the distance stripe and from the gun, I ran outside Joaquin, allowing him the rail.

"SIXTY-SEVEN!" Coach shouted as we finished the first lap; it felt like jogging. I imagined a PR and another victory over Joaquin awaited me three laps ahead. We passed the half-mile in two-fifteen, still in perfect sync, a pair of identical video game characters racing across the same screen, not a pixel separating our progress. And then...there's a saying among runners that the third lap of a mile is the longest four hundred meters in track. You've burned through all your cockiness and adrenaline, but it's too soon to sprint for the finish line, that invisible plane where all your exertion will suddenly, blessedly end. As we launched into lap three, I heard Joaquin sucking wind, but I was sucking even more wind. On the first turn, I told myself, "Just dig in and hold this pace; the last lap will be easier." By the backstretch, I was telling myself, "Maybe just relax and gather up for the final push; maybe lose a few seconds on this lap but make them up by kicking in the last two hundred."

Joaquin began edging away on the far turn. Once I was trailing, I sidled to the inside lane, hoping to save a few decisive steps. Three laps in three twenty-five. I was slowing down, but as predicted, the fastest Oak Rapids runner was nearly half a lap behind me. I could see him out of the corner of my eye as I glanced across the football field. To give you an idea of the pain I was feeling, a hard mile feels like being trapped in a hydraulic press. Every revolution around the track tightened that press around my chest, until I was gasping through oxygen debt. My clenched fists were swinging all the way to my chin, to provide the propulsion my lactate-flooded legs could no longer muster. No matter how fast or slow we ran, we were all equal in weakness on the final lap of a 1600. We had pushed against our limits, and now they were pushing back. In the home straight, I lapped an Oak Rapids runner who was struggling even more direly than I was (probably a freshman out too fast in his first race). I stumbled across the line in four minutes and thirty-six seconds—eight seconds behind Joaquin, but a new record for me. I had run the last lap in seventy-one.

Once I stepped off the track, Coach slapped me on the shoulders.

"Good run, Ward. Now go rest up for the 3200. I want you running your own pace in that one."

The letter arrived in a heavy-grained envelope bearing the U's logo, and the return address of the Track and Field Program. As soon as I got home from Tennessee, I'd written the U's track coach, to find out how fast I would have to race to qualify for a scholarship.

Dear Kevin,

Thank you for your interest in the U's track and field program. Enclosed is a list of standards for scholarships, partial scholarships, and walk-ons. These are not hard and fast times, but if you meet them, you will be given every consideration by this program.

Sincerely Yours,
Coach Harry Deane

Harry Deane had signed his name at the bottom, in black ink.

I scanned down the list to my events, the 1600 and the 3200. For the 1600, a full scholarship required a time of 4:06, a half scholarship 4:14, and 4:22 to walk on. For the 3200, the times were 8:54, 9:10 and 9:26. I was fourteen seconds too slow to walk on to the U's track team, but I still had nearly two seasons to get fast enough. I was running more miles. All the running books said mileage made you faster, but they also said to increase it no more than 10 percent a week. So, every week, I was adding 10 minutes to my morning run, leaving the house at six-twenty, then six-ten, then six o'clock, emerging into the dawn from deeper and deeper in the night. Sunrise is long in coming in our part of the country, even in the spring. We're far to the north, and close to the western edge of our time zone. I did most of my morning runs in the damp chill and the darkness. Now, I never ran along the railroad tracks or through the power station coal yard before the sun came up, because I could no longer see my way along that treacherous ground. Instead, I ran up Marquette Boulevard, across the arched bridge that overlooked the doomed assembly plant, past the locked and lightless storefronts of downtown Wenniway, the shopping strip where the pavement gave way to brick—Kinney Shoes, the Shamrock Lounge, Golden Horn Men's Fashions, the Popcorn Shoppe, Jack Robbins Pawn, Bob and Gary's Music Store. Above their flat roofs, the floodlit dome of the county courthouse glowed like a permanent full moon. Leaving downtown, I crossed an expressway that segregated the respectable merchants from Wenniway's red light district. I ran past the St. Vincent DePaul thrift store, the Wheel City Rescue Mission, and the Danish News, an adult bookstore with a hand-lettered marquee above its darkened windows and doors advertising MARITA AIDS. Then over the old flat bridge that spanned the downstream arm of the Oak River's semi-circular journey through Wenniway. Beyond that, the city limits and the sidewalk both ended, so I ran on the dirt shoulder of what was now known as State Highway 17, always facing traffic so I could see oncoming headlights. Once I extended my morning runs to six miles, I turned around at the gates of a trailer park that occasionally expelled a resident headed for a seven a.m. shift somewhere.

*   *   *

I didn't show the letter with the qualifying times to
Coach. I was afraid he might discourage me from burning
myself out in pursuit of a goal no Wenniway Central runner
had ever achieved—a scholarship at the U. Instead, I showed
it to the fastest runner I knew: Mark Molenka, a clerk at the
Athlete's Foot store. Mark had run a 4:10 mile at Great Lakes
State University, a Division II school Up North. Instead of
getting a real job after college, he started racing marathons,
hoping to qualify for the Olympic trials. Mark worked at
the running store so he could get a discount on shoes. He
shared a house downtown with two other ex-college runners. They called it the dormitory of the Wheel City Racing
Team. Mark had finished eighth at the Frontenac Marathon
and thought he could get his qualifying time in Chicago that
fall. In between now and then, he would probably win all the
5Ks and 10Ks in Wenniway: his name and race times were
always in the sports section on Sunday or Monday mornings, on page three, in agate type, under "Local Running,"
between the baseball standings and the bowling scores. Mark
probably weighed a hundred and twenty-five pounds, and he
was a few years past the age when it was natural to be so
skinny, so his face looked whittled and bony. He would have
looked better if he'd gained some weight, but he wouldn't
have run as fast. You can't have everything. Besides looking
like a day 23 hunger striker, Mark was always running, and
always broke, so I'm not sure he could even have attracted
a girl like Sara, who loved sharp, lean faces that presented a
profile no matter which way they turned.

"You want to run four-oh-six?" Mark asked when I
presented him with Coach Deane's mimeographed sheet
one afternoon in the empty store "You'd be state champion if you did that."

"Four twenty-two," I said. "That's fast enough to get
on the team."

"What are you at now?"

"I did four-thirty-six at a meet last week."

"You could take another twenty seconds off. But don't just run with those clowns from your high school. If you want to get fast, come out and run with us. We'll kick your ass. We're doing twenty this Sunday."

I told Mark that Sunday was my rest day.

"Fuck that day-off shit," he said. "How many days do you have left between now and when your legs start slowing down? Use 'em all. God could afford to rest on Sunday because he's immortal. We've gotta get it in while we can."

Then I told Mark I had never run more than twelve miles.

"Fine. That I understand. You're still a track guy. You're too young to run a marathon. We're doing twelve on Saturday, seven a.m. Six-oh-eight North Walnut."

On Saturday morning, I jogged the mile to 608 North Walnut Street. All three members of the Wheel City Racing Team were stretching their legs on the deep, sagging porch. Mark introduced me to Zack, who had run at Northern, and Phil, who had run at Eastern.

"We got a rookie here!" Zack shouted. Then he said, "We'll take it easy on you. We're just gonna do five-minute miles."

Phil pointed at Zack. "This guy's never broken five minutes in the mile in his life."

Zack glared at Phil. "He keeps forgetting the 1980 conference championship: 'Stride for stride on the final lap, and it's Zack Wade from Northern!'"

We ran the first mile in what felt like six-and-a-half, down city streets declining toward the river. For Zack, Phil and Dave, that was slow enough to carry on a conversation about an upcoming race.

"Did you get the race director to comp us?" Zack asked Mark.

"Nah. We gotta pay."

"How much?"

"Ten apiece."

"We got that?"

"Yeah. We'll have to put off the phone bill, but it'll pay off if we win the prize money."

"How much is that?"

"Hundred for first, seventy-five for second, fifty for third."

"Let's try to go one-two-three. Then we can pay the rent, too."

"Let's make this workout count, and hope Greg Meyer doesn't show up."

"Greg Meyer's running Boston next week. He's got better things to do than run a dinkwater 5K in his hometown."

We turned onto the Riverwalk, a path that reproduced the course of the Oak River in asphalt. There, the pace increased, to something like six minutes a mile. Running two abreast, we stormed past a jogger in a terrycloth running suit, and a middle-aged couple dawdling on matching Schwinn bicycles. Our shoes pounded the slats of a wooden boardwalk that conveyed us beneath a dank bridge. Mark, Zack and Phil were talking less. I was talking not at all. Despite my shallow breaths, I knew I could hold this pace for another seven miles, but I also knew that to do so would require the dedication of every cell in my brain. If I spoke even a word, I might stumble or slacken. This felt like racing, probably as much for them as for me. I was getting the impression that the members of the Wheel City Racing Team were not exactly a team. They didn't wear uniforms. I doubt they could have afforded uniforms. They needed each other as training partners, but during the races, they were rivals. Only one could win the hundred-dollar first prize, even if it would be spent on the phone bill and the rent.

"You doin' all right?" Mark asked me at around the six-mile mark. Too winded to form a word, I nodded. I wasn't going to say no. They wouldn't slow down if I did. This was business, not a friendly jog. I glanced at my watch. *I can run this hard for another ten minutes*, I told myself. Then I tried to discipline myself not to look at my watch for ten minutes. My resolve lasted eight minutes and forty-three seconds, but after that time, I was still running with the Wheel City Racing Team and recognizing landmarks we had passed on the way out. *Make it to the next bridge. Made it. Another bridge. Made that one.* Once we left the Riverwalk and began ascending to downtown Wenniway, I knew I was going to finish the workout. (Please do not imagine that Wenniway is a river city of dramatic bluffs. Its avenues ascend at angles barely measurable by geometry.) When we halted in front of The Dorm, feet slapping pavement after a final sprint, I bent over, clutching the hems of my shorts, heaving out tattered breaths. I felt Mark's palm on the sweat stain consuming the back of my t-shirt.

"You made it, rookie!" he said. "Good run. Come inside for breakfast."

Phil cut potatoes into thick slices, frying them in the household's only pan, set atop a grease-speckled stove. Once the potatoes browned, he wiped the pan with a paper towel, and cracked a carton full of eggs into its depths. Mark reached into the refrigerator for two cans of Stroh's. He handed me one.

"Always drink beer after a hard workout," he said. "It's healthier than Gatorade because it doesn't have all that sugar. Steve Scott drinks beer by the case."

I had sipped beer out of my father's glass at Pete's, when no one was looking, but never drunk an entire can. I cracked the top and tried to pour it down my throat, like any thirsty runner after a hard workout, but the sharp taste made me tentative.

"Mark, you're corrupting this kid," Zack shouted.

He asked how old I was.

"Seventeen," I said. That would be true in June.

"If you're old enough to keep up with us, you're old enough to drink that beer," Zack said.

We sat down to eat at a kitchen table with a mismatched chair in each corner. Halfway through my beer, I excused myself to go to the bathroom. I took the can with me. Mildewed running shorts and t-shirts drooped over the shower rod. The chipped lid of the toilet tank was piled with Ace bandages, wrinkled tubes of Vaseline, and a box of Breathe Right Strips. As I pissed in the bowl, I poured the beer in too, hoping the splashing of urine would cover up the fact that I couldn't hold an entire can.

"Hey, guys, I gotta get back," I told the Wheel City Racing Team when I emerged. I set the half-empty can on the refrigerator, where no one would look at it until I was gone. "I have to help my dad work on a car he's rebuilding."

This was a half-truth. My dad was working on his World War II jeep. He worked on his jeep every Saturday. I didn't have to help, but he would be thrilled if I offered. Since he was going to miss my senior year of high school, he wanted any father-son time he could get. The real truth was that I was feeling woozy with fatigue and alcohol. I didn't want to run anymore, and I didn't want to drink anymore. I walked the mile and a half home in my sweat-crusted t-shirt, wishing I had a quarter so I could buy a pack of Wrigley's Spearmint Gum to sweeten my beer breath. My father was indeed working on his jeep, but I dragged my ass up to my bedroom and clutched the mattress. I didn't move for 45 minutes.

That night, Sara and I went to the movies. We saw *The Outsiders*. I'd read the book in Mrs. Coonley's eighth grade English class. I should have enjoyed the movie. My dad had been a "greaser," way back when. The greasers smoked, they drove sweet muscle cars, they got into fights with rich kids they called "Socs," but we would have called "preppies." (I think Mrs. Coonley expected us all to identify with the greasers, since Wenniway was an industrial town, but she herself was more of a Soc, because she'd gone to the U. So was Sara, for that matter, since her whole life was about getting into the U.) I followed the movie up until the first rumble between the Greasers and the Socs...and then I fell asleep. I don't know how long it took Sara to notice, but I felt her prodding my shoulder. I woke up long enough to see Johnny stab a Soc, then was dragged back into unconsciousness by the lingering exhaustion from the morning's run. Sara did not attempt to revive me again, but when the lights came up, she was miffed.

"Did you think it was boring?" she asked as we walked through the lobby. "It was really important to me because my mom made me read it, like, five times."

"It was amazing. It was like someone made a movie about Wenniway, back in my dad's day."

"I know!" Sara seemed excited that I had made the connection. "That's why she teaches it in her class."

"Except my dad's never been in a fight in his life, and neither have I. We'd both get beaten up."

"How come you fell asleep?"

"I got up early and ran with these...really...fast...guys. These guys are pros. Or semi-pros. They race for money. I managed to hang on for ten miles, but I've been wiped out all day."

"Are you OK to drive?"

"I'm OK." I was not going to surrender that male prerogative. "I just had a nap."

In the car, driving home, Sara told me, "I think you're a real athlete."

"I'm not that fast," I said. "I might be able to get a scholarship, but I don't know if I can turn pro, or go to the Olympics."

"I don't mean your ability. I mean your outlook on life. You're dedicated to your sport. You're willing to make sacrifices to be the best you can be at it. Like a real artist."

I had noticed my resemblance to the musicians on Sara's bedroom wall; I wondered again whether she really wanted an artist. Maybe my obsessive running was the closest she could find in Wenniway.

"Come over tomorrow," Sara said, before getting out of the car. "My mom and dad went to Auburn this morning, and I went to the Black Platter."

The Black Platter was Sara's favorite record store; its bins were full of music hipper and more obscure than anything at Recordland in Wenniway Mall. I actually liked some of the stuff Sara was playing for me, especially the fast-paced punk rock: The Clash, the Buzzcocks, Dead Kennedys, Flipper. The song about the kid who only wanted a Pepsi. I could imagine myself running to the rhythm of those bands, had I been the kind of jogger who needed music as motivation. Finding the Edge, the Red Line, the maximum exertion I could maintain for many miles, that was my motivation. I'm sure that would have impressed her if I could have found the words then to explain. I appreciated bands who pushed their instruments to similar extremes, but their music would have distracted me from my own quest. So, I never ran with a Walkman. Sara also loved the slow New Wave bands—Elvis Costello and the Attractions, the Psychedelic Furs—but their music bored me. It tried to make me feel things—sadness, self-pity—a competitive athlete should not allow himself to feel.

"And guess who's coming to Auburn in June?"

"Who?" I hoped for a punk band, but I wasn't going to hear about one.

"Elvis Costello!"

Sara sat in the bleachers at all my track meets; I guessed I could spend one evening at an Elvis Costello concert.

"If you go, will you promise not to fall asleep?"

"Track season will be over by then. I won't be working out as hard." By then, only Elvis Costello's music could put me to sleep.

Sara had probably been right to compare me to an artist. As much as I wanted to win races, as much as I wanted a scholarship to the U, I would have run even without those goals. I ran because I was a runner, because running was my nature. I believed the fastest form of myself was the most perfect form of myself. I couldn't take a vacation from running any more than a dolphin could take a vacation from the sea. I knew that Sara was attracted to my obsessiveness, even if it caused me to fall asleep at the movies.

"I won't fall asleep if he doesn't play that song about Alison."

"He always plays that song. Everyone wants to hear it. Everyone has someone they felt that way about."

"Even you? I didn't shoot you down when you asked me out. I was easy."

"Maybe you're not the only guy I've ever asked out."

"Even if I'm not, that song is so dreary," I said, without pausing. I didn't want her to think I was jealous of her frustrated passion. "Why did he write a song about a girl who doesn't even like him? He's kind of a dorky-looking guy, with those big glasses, but he's also a rock star, so I'm sure there are plenty of girls who do like him."

"That's not the point of Elvis Costello," Sara said. "He sings for people who aren't rock stars. If you want to hear about what it's like to be a rock star, you can listen to Van Halen."

"He's just trying to make everyone feel sorry for him," I said. "I know guys like that. I'll bet he gets more girls than Van Halen that way."

"Just come to the show with me. Maybe you'll get it then." Sara kissed me on the mouth, then ran up the walkway, waving once her key turned in the lock.

*   *   *

That Tuesday, we ran a home meet against Wenniway South, our crosstown rival. I got through the 1600 all right, finishing behind Joaquin in 4:38, only two seconds slower than my PR. In the 3200, though, the asphalt track felt as firm and inflexible as a sidewalk. My muscles were wet concrete, hardening with every step. On the final lap, South's fastest runner caught me. I couldn't go with him and was relegated to third place. After the meet, Coach asked me to stay behind in the locker room.

"You looked sluggish out there," he said.

I nodded.

"You got a bug?"

I shook my head.

"What's wrong?"

The Wards are not Catholic, but we believe that confession is good for the soul. Trying too hard to be fast had slowed me down and cost the team points (although not the meet).

"I think I overdid it last weekend."

"What'd you overdo?"

"I ran with a guy from The Athlete's Foot and a couple of his friends."

Coach dropped his head and clapped his hands over his ears, as though trying to trap the steam in there.

"Those running bums!" he shouted. "I know those guys. They were just good enough in college to fool themselves into thinking they can win the Boston Marathon. They think if a slacker like Bill Rodgers could do it, they can do it, too. Lemme tell you something: it's better to either be super-talented, or to totally suck. Those middling guys are wasting their lives. I ran the same times they did in college. I wish I could have spent a few years finding out how fast I could get. Luckily, I got married, so I had to get a job. Coaching a track team and worrying about running bums messing up one of my best runners."

Coach stood up and glared at me.

"If one of my no-talent runners had a bad race, I wouldn't be here with him," he said. "So, consider this chewing out a compliment. Number one," he lifted an index finger, "I don't want you running with those guys again until track season's over. Number two," he lifted his middle finger, forming a Cub Scout salute, "for the next week, I don't want you running more than three easy miles a day. No morning runs, no track intervals."

Coach saw my mouth tighten. Before I could speak, he launched into a story: "Roger Bannister, let me tell you about Roger Bannister. He was having trouble with his training. Feeling sluggish. Couldn't do a quarter in less than 61. So, he took a few days off. Went hiking. When he came back, he was doing 59s. Do you know how many days he took off before his four-minute mile?"

I shook my head.

"Five days! Rest is part of training, too. Just tell the other guys you have to take it easy because you've got a little injury. Your foot. I won't embarrass you."

NINE

I walked home from school, instead of running home as I usually did after a meet. If Coach told me to rest, I'd rest. When I unlocked the front door, the house was empty, and the telephone was ringing. The ringing stopped before I reached the kitchen, where the phone was mounted on the wall beside the refrigerator. A moment later, it started again. I picked up the receiver.

"Hello?"

"Kevin…"

It was Gramps' voice, thinner and softer than I'd ever heard it. Something must have been terribly wrong for Gramps to call our house. He hadn't spoken to my father since their argument about the union the previous autumn. I still went over to Gramps' place, and Mom sometimes brought him leftovers from Sunday dinners, but he was refusing to see my father until he apologized to the Wildcat Strikers. Gramps still led a group of strikers in monthly anti-tax break protests at the courthouse. I'd been to one, at Gramps' invitation. The half-dozen old men standing beside the bronze Civil War soldier on the lawn looked like living monuments to another moment in Wenniway's history. They held signs reading EMPIRE SCREWS OVER WENNIWAY and NO TAX BREAKS FOR EMPIRE, and handed out flyers with the same message, but they were too dignified, or too few in number, to chant like other courthouse lawn demonstrators. Every time I saw Gramps, he told me about another striker's funeral.

"Kevin," Gramps whispered through the phone, "is your mother home?"

"Uh-uh. She's at work. I'm here by myself. What's wrong?"

"I can't move…my right arm and leg. I can't get out of this chair."

"I'll be right over, OK?"

"Come soon."

I had just raced an agonizing 3200, then promised Coach I wouldn't run hard for another week. As soon as I hung up the phone, I broke that promise. Still in my sweats, I sprang down the front steps and ran the three miles to Gramps' house as fast as my leaden legs would carry me. When I got there, the front door was locked. Gramps had been shot at in his youth, so he was big on "security." I found an unlatched kitchen window just wide enough for a high school miler to crawl through.

Gramps was sitting in his TV chair, with the set tuned to *People's Court*. The remote lay on the floor, out of his reach. His still-agile left hand held the cordless phone on which he'd called me.

"Turn it off," he ordered, glaring at the television and scowling. "Judges."

I tapped the red power button with the toe of my shoe.

"What happened?" I asked. "Are you OK? What can I do?"

Why hadn't Gramps hadn't called an ambulance? Maybe he didn't understand the severity of his condition. Maybe he thought he just needed someone to help him out of his chair. It was obvious even to me he needed more help than that. I asked Gramps for the phone and called Mom at work. She was a medical transcriptionist at a hospital, so she would know exactly what kind of help.

"Mom, I'm over at Gramps'," I said, still panting from my third hard run of the afternoon, "He's sitting in his TV chair and he can't get out. He's talking real soft, and he can't move his right arm or leg."

Gramps glared at me, his expression both angry and plaintive. He didn't like hearing me describe this infirmity that had stolen his ability to walk and speak.

"For God's sake, Kevin, your grandfather just had a stroke!" Mom shouted. "Have you called an ambulance?"

"I just called you. He called our house, and I ran all the way over here."

"Well, I'll call an ambulance, and I'll be right over there myself. Just stay with him. Give him a glass of water. He's probably been sitting there for hours."

I went into the kitchen and returned with one of the Mason jars in which Gram had served drinks. When I placed the jar in Gramps' good hand, I noticed a stain on his khaki trousers. He hadn't been able to get to the bathroom.

While waiting for Mom and the ambulance, I called home again, hoping to reach Dad. No answer. So, I looked up Pete's in the phone book and called there.

"Who wants to know?" Pete asked jovially when I asked if Gary Ward was there.

"This is Kevin," I said, trying to sound as serious as I could. "I'm at my grandfather's house. He has to go to the hospital."

"Oh, Jesus and Joseph."

Pete handed the phone to Dad. I told him that Mom thought Gramps had suffered a stroke, and that an ambulance was on its way to take him to Wenniway Memorial.

"Meet you at the hospital," he said. The next sound I heard was the receiver clunking on the bar. Among the Wards, bygones are bygones once someone is in trouble.

Mom arrived at Gramps' house at the same time as the paramedics. We watched them lift Gramps onto a stretcher and roll him into an ambulance. He grimaced the entire time, not because he was in pain, but because he had suddenly become an old man who needed young men to carry him.

"Do you really need to go to the hospital?" Mom said when we got into the car. "You're all sweaty from your track meet. I'll take you home so you can change. If we're at the hospital a long time, I'll come get you. You did a great job with Gramps. We're just so lucky somebody was home."

Gramps went directly from the emergency room into surgery. When I got to the hospital, around eight o'clock, he was still on the operating table. Dad was sitting in the waiting room with Uncle Dick, Aunt Sharon and some of my cousins.

"He just...he let himself get so worked up about Empire Motors leaving town," Dad was telling Uncle Dick. "First, we had that big fight about it and stopped talking, and then he was ranting and raving at those protests on the courthouse lawn. I just wonder if this happened because he got himself so worked up."

Uncle Dick had spent a few years on the assembly line after high school, but he didn't like working indoors, and he was just the kind of hothead who would rather punch a foreman than punch a clock. When he finally did punch a foreman, Gramps told him he'd dishonored the Ward family *and* the Autoworkers Alliance. Uncle Dick quit building cars and went to work as a carpenter's apprentice. He built houses, until Wenniway and its suburbs had all the houses they needed. Now he remodeled kitchens, bathrooms, and basements. The Ward and Son Remodeling van (Uncle Dick and my cousin Jimmy, who was such a burnout he could never hold a job with any company that could fire him) was parked outside the hospital, which meant they must have come straight here from a job.

"You know Dad's an extremist," Uncle Dick said. "He loved Mom so much that after she passed, he had nothing to live for, so he just sat in front of that TV. Then this factory closing came up and BANG," Uncle Dick smacked his hands together, "it's like he was thirty years old and fighting the company all over again. Dad is a passionate guy. He wasn't just gonna putter through old age playing golf and walking at the mall. He was either gonna burn out or fade away. You know how the song goes."

I was sure Dad didn't know how the song went. I didn't know either, until I quoted it to Sara, who told me it was by Neil Young. Uncle Dick was a rock-and-roll fiend. He dragged Jimmy to a Rolling Stones concert in Frontenac, then allowed Jimmy to drag him to a Judas Priest concert. Afterwards, he raved about the lead singer riding a motorcycle onstage with a microphone in each tailpipe. Uncle Dick liked life big and loud.

Sara showed up a few minutes later. I'd called her from home to tell her about running over to Gramps' house. She'd borrowed her mom's VW Rabbit to drive to the hospital. I wondered how Gramps would feel about me dating a girl who drove a foreign car. When Empire had started laying off workers a few years before, Gramps had blamed "the Japs, the Krauts and the Eye-ties. We rebuilt those countries after the war, and now they're repaying us by flooding America with their crappy little rice burners." When the Auto Workers Alliance organized a "Whack-a-Toyota" fundraiser for guys on layoff, Gramps paid his five dollars, hoisted a sledgehammer and smashed it through the windshield of a Celica donated by a junkyard. As a Wildcatter, he was given the honor of first swing. A unionist had noticed Mrs. Coonley's Rabbit outside the school and he called the principal to complain about a schoolteacher spending her publicly-funded salary on a foreign car, then parking it in a lot built with taxes paid by Empire and its employees.

(Mrs. Coonley told this story in class, imagining she was giving us a lesson about prejudice and tolerance. She explained that her Rabbit burned less gasoline than any Empire model, which was good for the environment, but we weren't buying it.) In every union hall parking lot was a sign warning "All Non-North American Nameplate Cars Will Be Towed at Owner's Expense." The Coonleys did own a Durant station wagon, for family vacations, so they were down with the town that way. Mr. Coonley drove the station wagon to his job. He went along with what Wenniway wanted. He also went along with what his wife wanted, even if those two conflicted. Mr. Coonley wasn't going to allow a car to cause hard feelings with anyone in his life.

Around nine o'clock, the doctor who'd been operating on Gramps came out to the waiting room. He had removed a piece of Gramps' skull, to relieve the swelling on his brain. It would be reattached when Gramps recovered. That sounded as gruesome as anything you'd see in a slasher flick, or the cover of an Iron Maiden album. Gramps was still sedated, so it would be a day or so before he could receive visitors. He would spend at least a week in the hospital, then go to a rehabilitation facility where physical therapists would teach him how to walk, speak, and use his limp left arm. All the stuff he'd learned as a baby, and now had to learn all over again in his seventies.

"It's rare to see a complete recovery from something like this," the doctor told us. He was a really young doctor, younger than Dad, with a full head of brown hair. Maybe doctors started out in Wenniway then moved on to bigger cities, like ball players. "It's likely he'll need to walk with a cane or use a wheelchair for the rest of his life. We just don't know yet."

"He's been living alone," my dad said.

"I'd think it would be difficult for someone who's suffered this kind of stroke to live independently. We'll have to see how he does in rehab."

Mom and Dad looked at each other. They had wanted Gramps to move in with them, but they hadn't wanted a stroke to make it necessary.

"We'll talk to him about that," Dad told the doctor.

*　　*　　*

Gramps didn't appreciate visitors. When I had discovered him in his easy chair, the look in his eyes told me he didn't want his grandson—or anyone else—to see him in such a helpless state. Gramps had been a Wildcatter, a 42-year man at Empire, an outdoorsman who rose at six o'clock on summer mornings to hike four miles in work boots around Agaming Lake, site of the family cottage. (During my early fascination with running, I circled the lake every time I visited my grandparents, trying to better my time with each lap.) Now, as he lay in a hospital bed, his useless arm and leg sunken into the mattress, he seemed like only half a man, the other half a puppet who needed a nurse to move his limbs. I wondered whether he wished the stroke had taken all of him, instead of just half. Maybe to be anything less than whole was to be nothing. I tried to imagine myself with a leg that would not fulfill my brain's command to walk, much less run. I wouldn't want to live in that body. The part of me that didn't exist to run...didn't exist. Dad, Mom, my sister and I stood awkwardly around the hospital bed. Gramps wasn't talking to us, and we weren't talking to Gramps. I wondered not only if Gramps didn't want *us* there, but if he didn't want *himself* there.

"Do you need anything from home?" my father finally asked.

Gramps' eyes shifted in my father's direction, but his head didn't move. He was back to being just a pair of eyes that absorbed TV signals, as he'd been after my grandmother's death.

"Turn the channel," he murmured, out of the side of his mouth that still opened. Talking that way made him look like Popeye, I thought. Then I thought that I shouldn't have thought that. I looked at the TV screen. Another one of the judge shows Gramps hated.

Dad picked up the remote off the nurse's stand.

"What do you want to see, Dad?"

"Something...funny."

Dad shuffled through the cable channels. Each time he settled on a new program, he turned to examine Gramps' expression. When the old man's face clenched in distaste, Dad moved on. Finally, he arrived at a *Get Smart* re-run. Looking placid, Gramps turned all his attention to watching Maxwell Smart and Agent 99 fight KAOS. The rest of us did, too.

TEN

We visited the hospital every evening, whether Gramps
wanted us there or not. With all the time I spent there, it
was just as well I wasn't running much that week. While
the rest of the distance guys sprinted 400-meter intervals
on the track, Coach relegated me to two "figure eights"—
mile-and-a-half loops around the baseball field and the
park behind the football stadium. Our next meet was a
five-school invitational in Auburn, where my usual time
might not be fast enough for second-place points, behind Joaquin. Maybe if Roger Bannister could break the
four-minute mile after a week of idleness, I could break my
mile PR after a week of jogging.

Auburn's track might help, too. Wenniway Central's was
six lanes of asphalt, its numbers and stripes faded and flaked
by decades of Northern winters. Auburn ran on a rubberized track eight lanes wide, its surface the chestnut color of
a racehorse's coat, just like the tracks I'd seen on the Olympics, or the NCAA championships. In Auburn's gymnasium,
an indoor track encircled a long jump pit. I'd heard it was all
paid for by the U, which was trying to develop hometown
talent for its own track team. Would Coach Harry Deane
scout this meet? My stomach clenched at the thought of
him sitting in the bleachers. I might disappoint him. Worse,
he might ignore a fourth place runner finishing in 4:45.

Before the race, Coach told me, "I want you to go out
with Joaquin again. You stayed with him until the last lap
last time. I think you can carry it further this time."

Fifteen guys lined up behind the distance stripe, three from each school. From the gun, I wasn't just racing Joaquin, I was racing every number one on the track. As we passed the quarter in 68, my legs flowed, they floated. As the second lap began, I dropped my eyes to the track, watching Joaquin's pinwheeling shoes. *Draw inward*, I told myself. *Focus. Breathe at a steady cadence. Withdraw your mind from the effort, and this will be painless.* The half in two-eighteen. Four remained in the lead pack. *Grit. Hold the pace. If you're still with the leaders at the bell, that will be today's victory.*

I was still with the leaders at the bell, but this time my legs didn't weigh me down on the final lap. They felt weightless, as though I were being swept along by an invisible hand. Auburn's runner broke away on the final turn. I matched strides with Joaquin. For a moment, I imagined I could beat him, but we were running second and third, so we'd get the points either way. No point in a sprint that would burn us both out for the 3200. We pushed our chests across the line together. The timer gave second place to Joaquin, 4:32.1 to my 4:32.3. That was far from the four-minute mile, but it was still a four-second PR. In the last week, it had taken effort not to expend effort (which sounded like one of Mrs. Coonley's mystical sayings). Relaxation was a form of self-denial for me, but minimum effort had enabled me to run with maximum intensity, harder than ever before.

"Good run, guys," was all Coach said when we sat back down on the aluminum bench and pulled on sweatshirts over our damp heads. In the 3200, I ran 9:48, another PE. Coach clapped me on the back and bellowed, "See, you just needed a little rest. Now you can go back to running three times a day. But stay away from those running bums while you're on my team!"

On the bus ride home I was elated. On that wing-footed final lap in the 1600 I had unlocked another level on a video game, a level that neither I, nor the designers, knew existed before.

"You're gonna be number one soon," said teammate Tim, sitting next to me on the bus.

"Maybe next year. When Joaquin graduates."

"Maybe this year. I seen how much you been running. I seen you running by my house in the morning."

"What street do you live on?"

"Schlee."

"Oh, yeah. I go down there on my way downtown."

"My alarm goes off at six-thirty, and when I get up to take a piss and look out the window, you're always there. Same time, same place."

"Come run with me. It's lonely. There's no one else out there except the paperboy."

Tim laughed. "I couldn't keep up with you."

"I don't run that fast in the morning. I'm just trying to get warmed up."

"I need my sleep," Tim shook his head. "If I got up at five-thirty and ran five miles, I'd fall asleep in class."

I had fallen asleep in class, during sixth period, on warm, drowsy afternoons. In our climate, air conditioning was not considered necessary for a three-season school. If I had to choose between a 4.0 grade point average and a four-minute mile, of course I would choose the four-minute mile. There's a 4.0 valedictorian at every high school every year. Only three high school boys had ever run a four-minute mile. I could, of course, name them: Jim Ryun, Marty Liquori and Tim Danielson. I wasn't going to achieve a 4.0, since I'd scored a B-minus in algebra and a C-minus in Mr. Ewing's chemistry class. I wasn't likely to run a four-minute mile, either, but 4:32 put me only ten seconds away from walking on at the U. I still had a year to close that gap.

*   *   *

Later, I told Sara about my mile PR. "If I get my time down ten more seconds, I can walk on at the U." I thought she'd be happy to hear we could go to college together. Instead, she said, "If you're just a walk on, you'll have to get in like everybody else."

We were sitting on the carpeted floor of Sara's bedroom, listening to *Public Flipper Limited*, a record she'd bought at the Black Platter. Sara knew I liked punk rock. It wasn't exactly make-out music, but Mrs. Coonley was always home, and Sara's bedroom door was always open. That was a disadvantage of dating a schoolteacher's daughter. The house was never empty between three and five, when every other Central couple enjoyed after-school trysts. Sara and I had only gotten as far as second base one night inside a climbing toy on a grade school playground.

"I'm going to apply," I said. "My dad wants me to go, because it's close to Wenniway."

"Well goody, goody!" Sara shouted, shaping her mouth into an O, widening her eyes—one of those Sara faces I loved to look at. "I want you to go, too, but the U has to want you to go. What's your GPA?"

I didn't know. My grade point average was on every report card, but I only looked at the letter grades. A mathematical rating carried out to several decimal points was too complex and technical to bother memorizing. Of course, I could recite my race times to the tenth of a second. (Not only my times, but the times of world-class milers. I could tell you the PRs of Sebastian Coe, Steve Ovett and Steve Scott to the *hundredth* of a second.) I told this to Sara. Her face hardened into a mock glare.

"You," she said, "have a one-track mind."

"Pun intended."

"Ab-so-lute-ly!" she shouted and laughed with all of that little body.

"I usually get A's, B's and C's," I said, omitting the C-minus in Mr. Ewing's class. A C-minus was still a C, right?

"And you're going to take the SAT and the ACT, right?"

"Sure," I said, although I had made no plans to do so, didn't know what those acronyms stood for, and had no idea how they would affect my chances of attending the U.

I told Sara about Coach Deane's time standards, and how I wasn't sure I could run fast enough to earn a full scholarship. Half of Sara's mouth bent into a frown—another of her facial tricks.

"I'm sure you can do it," she said. "You've got a talent, and you're the most single-minded person I've ever met. You can afford to put all your eggs in one basket."

Then she put on a Psychedelic Furs record and kissed me.

"Your grade point average," said my guidance counselor, Mr. Hart, inspecting a sheet he had withdrawn from one of his mismatched green filing cabinets, "is three point one seven five."

The students called Mr. Hart "Wimpy," because of the globular belly swelling inside his suit pants. It forced him to sit a foot behind his desk.

"Is that good?" I asked.

"It's average," he said. "You'll graduate."

"Is it good enough to get into the U?"

"Your GPA is only in the top fifty percent," Mr. Hart said. "The U admits the top ten percent of the graduating class of every high school in the state. That's not to say they *only* admit the top ten percent, just that it's guaranteed for them. If you have some impressive extracurricular activities, that might help."

"I run track," I said pointing at the winged-foot pin on my letterman's jacket.

"An athletic scholarship is a possibility. But the better your grades and your SAT scores, the more possible it is."

"What would my GPA have to be to get into the top ten percent?" I asked.

"Around three point eight."

Sara's was three point nine. She claimed it would have been perfect except that her English teacher, Dr. Wolcott, had dinged her down to a "B" for refusing to read an Ernest Hemingway story aloud because Hemingway was, in her words, "a male chauvinist pig."

"You're a junior," Mr. Hart said. "So, even if you got straight As from here on out, you wouldn't get into the top ten percent."

Mr. Hart's assessment was motivation to run faster. Soon, I had another. Three weeks after his stroke, Gramps was released from the hospital to a rehabilitation facility. The doctor told us he could probably regain some mobility in his weakened limbs, if he worked hard enough, but he would always need a walker. A wheelchair would be the most practical means of locomotion for trips outside the house. On the day Gramps was transferred, Dad asked Mom and me to remain at the table after supper. He went into the kitchen, returned with a can of Stroh's, popped the top, took a swig, and announced, still staring at the can, "I'm not going to Tennessee."

My mother glared at him. She looked—I've never used the word "flabbergasted" before, and I hope never to use it again, after seeing that scene at our dining room table, but it's the only word for the expression on her bloodless face.

"Gary, you've only got five years left before you can retire," Mom said, her voice as tense and high pitched as summer's cicadas.

"And how many years does my father have left, Jo Anne?" He glared right back at my mother. I knew they were angry because they were calling each other by their full names. Usually, it was "Gare" or "Jo" or "sweetie." "He can't

106

live alone anymore. I'm not going to put him in a nursing home and let him wither away because I'm down in Tennessee trying to add a few dollars to my pension. I'm not going to expect you to take care of him alone, either."

"You won't just be adding a few dollars to your pension. You'll be getting lifetime health benefits, like the ones that are paying for your dad's hospitalization *and* his rehab."

"You have health benefits through your job; you work in a...goshdarn hospital."

Suddenly, my father could not look my mother in the eye. As a man responsible for the well-being of four generations, he was finding himself trapped between the roles of loyal son and breadwinning husband. A man did not abandon his ailing father, but neither did a man relinquish the role of provider to his wife. Realizing that Mom might think he expected her to support the family, he said, quickly, "We won't starve. I'll get eighty percent of my pension. The house is paid for. The cars are paid for. We'll sell Dad's house and maybe the place Up North. Dick has always told me I should get out of the shop and into remodeling kitchens, and I've always wanted to go to work for myself, restoring old cars."

Dad picked up his napkin by the corners and held it in front of him.

"Do either of you know the story about the old man and the blanket?" he asked.

I shook my head. Mom was still staring incredulously at Dad.

"Well, an old man was nearing the end of his life. He didn't have any teeth, so he couldn't chew food, and he had to be fed with a spoon. His mind didn't work anymore, so he didn't recognize his family. He soiled himself. The old man's son decided he was too much trouble to take care of and told his own son to take him out to the barn, on a freezing night, and wrap him in a blanket. The boy did what his father told him, but he came back with half a blanket.

The father got angry and shouted, 'How can you leave your grandfather out there with only half a blanket? Don't you want him to be comfortable in his final hours?' The boy held up half the blanket and said, 'Dad, I'm saving this for you.'"

Dad's voice broke during the final sentence of the story. He dropped the napkin to his plate. His eyes were brimming, but a lifetime of repressing emotions prevented them from overspilling onto his cheeks. Ordinarily, Mom would have cried at that story, but still angry, her eyes only glistened with unfallen tears.

"That's not from the Bible," said Mom, which was her way of telling Dad she didn't want to hear his sentimental excuses for quitting his job.

"I don't think so," Dad said. "I heard it in a sermon, though. It just means that abandoning Dad isn't the kind of example I want to set for Kevin and his sister. That's not who the Wards are. We stick together as a family no matter what it costs. This could be the most time Dad and I have together since I was a kid."

"What about Kevin's college?" Mom said. "You said you'd send him to the U because it's the closest school with a track team."

Dad looked at me.

"Doesn't Wenniway Community College have a track team?"

"A...little one," I said.

In fact, I was already as fast as some of the runners on the WCC track team. By the time I got to college, I would probably be faster than all of them. I would win all the races, but no one would push me to run a four-minute mile.

"Maybe he can go there two years and then transfer somewhere else," Dad said. "We're all going to have to make sacrifices to keep this family together."

"Wait—" Mom interrupted him. I had *never* before heard my mother interrupt my father. She believed in the

Biblical admonition, "Wives, obey your husbands," which I had heard recited more than once from the pulpit of our church; but perhaps now that my father had just announced he was abdicating his position as our family's principal breadwinner, she felt she owed him a little less obedience, no matter what the Bible said.

"You're going to sacrifice your son's education and your son's future just because you don't want to go back and forth from Tennessee for five years?" she said in a hard, uncomprehending voice. She didn't shout. Mom never shouted. I think the Bible also says women aren't supposed to shout.

"I didn't want this situation," Dad said, breathing a sigh so long it seemed to deflate him. He slumped in his chair. "When I hired in at Empire, I thought I had a job for life. If Empire hadn't closed, if Dad hadn't had a stroke, everything would still be smooth sailing."

"Well Empire did close," Mom said. "And that means Kevin is going to have to go to college to get a decent job. He won't be able to just walk out of high school into the plant the way you did. Life isn't always smooth sailing. If it were, a ship wouldn't need a captain."

Mom started to stand up. I stood up, too. I wanted to end their argument.

"It doesn't matter," I shouted. "Even if Dad could pay for the U, I probably couldn't get in, anyway. My guidance counselor told me my grades aren't good enough. The only way I'll get in is with a scholarship, and if I get a scholarship, Dad won't have to pay anything. You're arguing over a mute point!" (Yes, I said "mute point." If Sara or her mother had been there, they would have corrected me.)

"There are other colleges in this state," Mom said. "Northern, Southern, Eastern, Western, Great Lakes. Every direction has its own college. If you go to WCC, you'll never graduate. It's just a place where people who don't know what they want to do with their lives kill time. You have a passion. You have a talent. I don't want you to waste it."

"Those direction colleges aren't much better than WCC," I said.

I wanted to train with the fastest runners in the state, at a Division I major. I wanted to compete for an NCAA championship. And I wanted to go to school with Sara.

I excused myself from my parents' dispute and went upstairs to my room. It was now my responsibility at sixteen to keep the Ward family in harmony. If I won a scholarship, my mother could never accuse my father of shirking his responsibility to provide for my education. I opened the drawer of my nightstand and withdrew an index card on which I had written 4:22—the time I would need to run to walk on at the U. I found a stubby pencil. Its eraser had broken off, so I crossed out the figure, and wrote down a new one: 4:06.

ELEVEN

We called it the Thousand Mile Summer. That's how far Dave, Tim and I planned to run between the last school bell of June and the first of September. It worked out to eleven miles a day, so every morning at six-thirty we convened in a rarely mown park, equidistant from our houses. The park was a swatch of shaggy grass enclosed by a chain-link fence browned with rust, looking too weak to sieve the wind. A powerful gust might have crumbled it. Not much remained of the park's playground. The frame of a swing set. A teeter-totter whose fallen end was hidden in the rising tide of grass. Sprigs of weeds pushed through a sandbox's silty dirt. At our latitude, summer mornings are slow to develop, so we ran in the damp, cool hour between the sun's orange rise and the white peak of its power. Rock doves cooed from their hiding places in lushly arbored Wenniway. The weedy park demonstrated that our city was always fighting back the forest in which it had been built.

We always ran the same route: over to the old rock quarry, then three laps of a three-mile circuit around a pond that had filled in the hole after the cutters emptied it of stone. We ran along a path worn by decades of teenagers who hid in these woods to drink, get high, and make love. (We kicked aside empty beer cans and stepped on withered condoms.) We ran on dirt because we were training for cross country, but we ran cross country to train for track. That spring, Wenniway Central had finished third in the state meet at St. Croix, behind a school from the Frontenac

111

suburbs, and a school from Frontenac itself. In the 1600, I finished tenth, in 4:25—not fast enough to score us points, but fast enough to set a personal record, and only nineteen seconds from my new goal. I even beat Joaquin, who was running his last race for Central, maybe his last race ever. No one offered Joaquin a scholarship. He was going to take the summer off from running while he worked at his dad's landscaping business, then take some classes at Wenniway Community College in the fall. "You the man now, buddy," Joaquin told me as we walked off the track (although he was still the man for one more race, because he beat me in the 3200). "You're gonna win this race next year. All the guys who beat you are seniors."

We finished our runs by eight o'clock every morning, giving me plenty of time to make it to my summer job, a ten-to-four shift at Harper Park, where I laid out bases on the softball diamonds, checked out bats, softballs, gloves, volleyballs, kickballs, kickboards and footballs, and broke up fights between eight-year-olds over bats, softballs, gloves, volleyballs, kickballs, kickboards and footballs. I wore a whistle dangling over a PROPERTY OF WENNI-WAY PUBLIC PARKS t-shirt, and blew it whenever I saw kids engaging in "horseplay," as the park supervisor put it. (The supe was an ex-minor league baseball player who'd been a huge superstar at Wenniway South, a .500 hitter. This was his first summer on the job, and his first summer out of baseball. He never smiled, and he yelled at the kids a lot.) I got paid three-fifty an hour, fifteen cents more than the minimum wage. I only spent my earnings to buy new Etonics, since I was wearing out a pair every six weeks, and to take Sara to the movies. Come September, my dad was going to be out of a job.

We were going to be OK for money for a little while at least, because that summer we put our house on the market and moved in with Gramps. Dad had planned it the other way around, but Gramps' could no longer walk up stairs, and he lived in a ranch, while we lived in a Cape Cod with the bathtub on the second floor.

"This is as good a time as any to unload this place," Dad said, after the realtor inspected the house and pounded a FOR SALE sign in the front yard. "Before that plant closes down and this town goes to pot. Who's gonna want to buy a house in Wenniway then? Everyone's gonna want a mobile home in Tennessee."

Ours was a pretty old house, built just after World War I by Empire Motors, for all the workers moving into town to build tanks and shells and army trucks. The house wasn't a suburban dream: it had four bedrooms, but only one bathroom. I kept a cup under my bed in case I woke up having to pee while my mom or my dad or my sister were in the shower. I emptied the cup by dumping the contents out my bedroom window. At some point, I decided to eliminate the middleman by peeing out the window. Since my bedroom faced the backyard, I figured nobody would notice. One morning, though, my sister stepped out the back door, and into my stream. Hearing her screech, I quickly stuffed myself back into my boxer shorts before she looked up and saw me. She never accused me of peeing on her, but from then on, I always used the cup.

Dad had bought the house for $19,500 the year my sister was born. He paid cash, saved up from all the overtime in his first few years at Empire. Not only had he accumulated a lot of money, at time-and-a-half pay, he hadn't had the time or the energy to spend it. Dad put the house on the market for $40,000, a price that would not only double his original investment, but replace most of the first year's wages he was sacrificing by refusing the transfer to Tennessee. (Take out the cost of gasoline for the drive back home, and rent on the trailer, and he'd come out ahead.) The house, however, did not sell for $40,000. Nor did it sell for $37,500, when Dad and the realtor agreed to lower the price. Or $35,000. By August, when we moved in with Gramps, our house was still on the market, and Dad was talking about renting it out.

"It's not going to be a buyer's market around here anymore," he reasoned. "It's going to be a renter's market. To buy, you've gotta have a steady job. Renters just piece a living together, month to month. So, they can only pay month to month."

In the meantime, we left the lawnmower in the garage, and Dad sent me over there once a week to cut the grass, "so the place doesn't look all seedy and abandoned."

Gramps' house was more spacious than ours, but it felt less personal and less private, with all the rooms were on a single floor. (My new bedroom had a full-height ceiling, which I only sort of liked, because I couldn't tape my Steve Scott poster to the roof slope and stare at it when I woke up in the morning. Instead, I taped the poster to the wall beside my bed.) Gramps had raised his family in an Empire-built house (which may have been why Dad wanted to do the same), but moved to this colony of long, low, brick houses set like blocks around the bulb of a cul-de-sac because "your grandmother and I got tired of walking up and down all those got-damned stairs."

(I suppose it was better for Dad that he wasn't moving back into his childhood home. Doing that, right after quitting his job, would have felt like giving up on adulthood altogether.)

The ranch house had witnessed my grandparents' transition from vigor to dotage and death. They had purchased it in the youth of their old age, right after Gramps retired from Empire and was still golfing twice a week. Since then, Gram had gone, dead of a cancer which so weakened her that by the end, with her flesh consumed and her locks shorn by the chemotherapy, she could only shuffle across the carpet on a walker cushioned by tennis balls. Now Gramps was in the same no-man's land between life and death, on a journey in which the only question was the duration, not the destination. As combative and cantankerous as Gramps had been before the stroke, he was now passive in equal measure. Just as after Grammy died, he spent his days in the La-Z-Boy, watching sitcoms. I usually got home from my job at the park in time to watch *The Andy Griffith Show* with him. My company was neither an intrusion nor an occasion for familiarity—his conversations was limited to commands to mute a commercial or change the channel to "something funny." He never laughed at anything on TV, although he smirked at *Car 54, Where Are You?* when the fat cop exclaimed "Ooh, ooh, ooh." My father helped Gramps into his chair each morning, and out of it each evening. Accepting our assistance and eating my mother's meals were his way of letting us know we were welcome to live with him.

Gramps was less tolerant of his physical therapist, a young woman who visited at one o'clock each Monday, Wednesday, and Friday, when he ordinarily watched *Mister Ed*. The therapist wanted Gramps to learn to use his walker, but he was indifferent to her professional goals. At this point, he felt there was nowhere to go. His wife was dead, his son, daughter-in-law and grandson had come to live with him, and the motivating cause of his own professional life—well-paying jobs for Wenniway autoworkers—had been wiped out by Empire's decision to close its factories.

Gramps allowed the therapist to lift, manipulate and massage his arms and legs, but he would not get out of his chair, or perform the daily exercises she prescribed him. After she left, Gramps made mordant comments about his physical condition.

"You ever heard the saying 'one foot in the grave'?" he asked me, pointing at his immobile leg. "Well, that's the foot!"

Another time, he told me, "I'm half dead. I'm just waiting for the other half now."

My dad finally got Gramps to take physical therapy seriously by using the only argument that would have worked on the old man.

"Dad," he told Gramps, "you spent your entire life fighting for the right to a good job. If you don't help this woman out, she's going to look bad to her supervisor. The last time she left here, she was nearly in tears because she couldn't get through to you. She's ready to give up on you, and that won't look good on her record. She might not get a raise. She might even lose her job. So why don't you help her out?"

After that lecture, Gramps at least practiced shuffling behind his walker when the therapist visited, as one final service to the American worker.

As much as I worried about Gramps, I worried about Dad, too—not his health, which would probably improve once he stopped inhaling paint fumes eight hours a day inside that windowless warehouse. I worried about his position in the family. A year before, he'd become the guy who led prayers at Sunday dinners, read eulogies at funerals, stood beside grandchildren at their baptisms, and started the applause at high school and college graduations. When Empire Motors announced it was closing, Dad had to make a decision: he could either remain the head of a family he saw a few days a month, or he could accept a diminished role in a family he saw every day. He chose the latter. He could not have borne a life apart from us, no matter how much money he earned. He was trying to set an example for me, too. He wanted me to stay in Wenniway, or as close to Wenniway as possible, so I would take care of him when he was old and sick, the way he was taking care of Gramps. That's what the blanket speech had been about.

Besides living in his father's house, Dad was working part time for his younger brother. Uncle Dick took Dad out on remodeling jobs in the evenings. Thanks to his years as a tradesman, Dad was handy enough to build cabinets and showers. Because of what Dad was doing for Gramps, Uncle Dick began talking about calling the business to "Ward Remodeling," to acknowledge the participation of brother *and* son. He would still be the full owner, though. And since they were independent contractors, Mom's job at the hospital would still provide benefits for our family. The plant wouldn't close until the end of September, so these changes were a ways off, but I wondered how Dad would deal with this sudden dependence on his younger brother, and his wife. At least he could still preside over the Gary Ward Memorial Euchre League.

TWELVE

Nothing Sara did or said could get me excited about the Elvis Costello concert in Auburn. Sara owned every Elvis Costello album. The week before the show, we listened to one every day, in chronological order: *My Aim Is True, This Year's Model, Armed Forces, Get Happy!!, Trust, Almost Blue,* and *Imperial Bedroom.* It was a seven-part symphony of cynicism and sadness. I listened because I wanted anything that important to her to be important to me, but I also wanted something important to me—OK, the *only* thing important to me—to be important to her, too.

"After we go to the concert, will you start running again?" I asked her, after the needle had risen on the last track of the terribly misnamed *Get Happy!!*

Sara had quit running after the cross-country season, when *Camelot* rehearsals consumed the dwindling daylight hours between the end of school and sunset. Since then, she had filled out a little bit, as housebound Northerners do in winter. I could barely squeeze my fingers between her belly and the waistband of her jeans. ("You maybe better unbutton them," she'd said, the first time I'd tried. That was something I could hear her say over and over again, even if I didn't exactly like the reason she'd said it.)

"You're going out for cross country again this fall, aren't you?" I asked, after she'd buttoned her jeans again.

"Yyyeeeaaah," Sara said. Had she been planning to could skip this season, because cross country was already on her college application? Did she now feel trapped by my expectations?

"You need to start running before practice starts. I showed up out of shape when I was a sophomore. Every day after practice, I came home and sat on the toilet for an hour."

Sara made another of her faces. Her eyes narrowed. Her lips drew back in disgust.

"That's nice to think about, Mr. Ward."

It was an embarrassing revelation, but worth it for a Sara Face.

"It's hot and humid in August."

"August is still two months away."

"How about if I come over on the nights you're not working at the library?"

Sara had a summer job shelving books and setting up chairs for author talks.

"Don't you already run in the mornings?"

"I'll do doubles. All the studs do two workouts a day."

Sara realized she wasn't going to get out of running cross country any more than I was going to get out of the Elvis Costello concert.

"We can start on Thursday," I suggested. "Do you work on Thursday?"

Sara's brow drew close to her eyes. Her lips thinned. I had said something wrong. I was about to find out what. Her face held its expression for an extra beat, just to build the suspense.

"The concert is on Thursday," she said.

I will always remember the night of the Elvis Costello concert in Auburn, not for the music, but for what happened afterwards, on the drive home, between Sara and me. Sara drove us to Auburn in her mother's Rabbit, freshly adorned with an EL SALVADOR IS SPANISH FOR VIETNAM sticker, on the opposite side of the bumper from VISUAL-IZE WHIRLED PEAS. The concert was in a theater with plush seats, a velvet curtain, a balcony, and a vaulted ceiling spangled with a map of the night sky. It was three times the size of our school auditorium, where I had heard Sara play flute for the Wenniway Central Thespian Society's production of *Camelot*. (To my disappointment, I could not hear the flute distinctly. That was all I'd come for. "We just kind of lighten the sound," Sara explained. "The horns and the strings hog all the attention.") It was the first play I'd ever attended.

This was the first concert. The moment Elvis Costello walked onstage—a little man made to appear even smaller by the remoteness of our balcony seats and the enormity of the venue—Sara gripped my hand. During "Alison," that song I hated about the man who loves a woman who doesn't love him back, she laid her head on my shoulder. I guessed I could endure an Elvis Costello concert. The romantic feelings his music evoked in Sara needed an outlet; she had brought me along to provide it. If listening to Elvis Costello made Sara want to get close to me, I would listen to Elvis Costello.

"Do you know how to drive a stick?" she asked, as we walked back to the car, hand in hand.

"Yeah, I know how," I said. Uncle Dick had taught me on his Ford F350.

"Can you drive home?" Sara asked, looking exhausted and beatific. "I just want to relax and remember every song."

In the car, Sara laid her head on my lap, facing the steering wheel. When my hand wasn't shifting gears, I rested it on her hip. Once I'd merged onto the highway, Sara shifted her body, so her head was facing my belt.

"Are you a good driver, Kevin Ward?" she asked.

"I hope so," I said, not understand why she would ask.

"You've never had an accident, right?"

"Uh-uh."

"Okay."

Then Sara's fingers and lips explained. Why had she chosen this time and place to introduce this intimacy into our love life? It must have been the music. I gripped the steering wheel to steady myself. At the ultimate moment, my foot pressed the gas pedal all the way to the floor, so the Rabbit's engine roared at the peak of its highest gear.

I had a story to tell Dave and Tim during our morning run, but how I could tell it without sounding like a…I guess "blowhard" is the right word, both figuratively and literally? I didn't want to sully Sara's reputation—whatever I said might be repeated. Nor did I want to brag about something Dave and Tim might not have experienced. They didn't have girlfriends, as far as I knew. So, I spoke in generalities, describing the aphrodisiac qualities of Elvis Costello.

"Have you guys ever listened to any Elvis Costello?" I ventured.

"There's an Elvis *Costello*?" Dave said. "I thought there was only one Elvis."

Tim thought so, too.

"My mom saw Elvis when he came to the Civic Arena," he said. "She said he was all fat and sweaty and wearing a jumpsuit."

"I'd sing 'Blue Suede Shoes,'" Dave offered, "but we're doing a seven-minute pace here."

The Elvis Costello after-concert story was going nowhere with my teammates—just as well for my good name and Sara's. We spent the rest of the run talking about what we always talked about when we ran: running. Specifically, the Dog Days 10K. We were racing it in August, to prepare for cross-country season.

"It'll be all hobby joggers," Dave predicted. "Kevin, you can win if none of the Wheel City guys show up."

There was no prize money for the winner—the race was a fundraiser for the Wenniway Policeman's Benevolent Association. The Wheel City Racing Team probably wouldn't bother, but I'd ask Mark the next time I replaced my shoes at The Athlete's Foot. I still hadn't won a race. Even when I'd beaten Joaquin at the state championship 1600, nine other guys had beaten me.

That evening, I mentioned the race to Sara. Sara hadn't raced since last fall's conference championship, when she ran with the JV. (I almost wrote "competed in a race," but Sara was not a competitor. She preferred music to sports because, she said, music was collaborative. When I pointed out that teammates collaborated by pushing each other to run faster, she responded, "Yeah, but when they run the race, there's still one winner and a bunch of losers. When a song turns out right, everyone wins—the musicians *and* the audience.") When Sara dressed for our jog, her legs were pale and soft in purple running shorts.

"TEN kilometers?" she burst out, when I described the distance. "That's twice as far as we run in cross country, and *that's* hard."

"A 10K is actually easier than a 5K," I said.

"How can it be easier to run twice as far?"

"You're not running as close to your aerobic threshold."

"Uh huh."

"It's less intense. I hurt more when I'm running a mile than when I do cross country."

"That's you," she said. "You're trying to win the race, I'm just trying to finish the race."

We jogged a mile, on the sidewalks. It took eleven minutes. In the last five hundred yards, Sara crept forward with tiny steps, fists balled beneath her chin.

"Lower your arms," I ordered her. "Your hands should never cross the center line of your chest. Then they're not propelling you forward, they're swinging you from side to side."

Back at Sara's house, she slumped through the front door and returned with a bottle of Gatorade.

"I got this at the party store for us to share."

"Oh. Thanks."

"I didn't think you'd want my mom's lemonade: too much sugar and empty calories. Athletes are fussy."

"Lemonade is fine," I said. I didn't like being called fussy, but I was glad to drink Gatorade.

"Do you really think I should run cross country again?" Sara asked. Although we had jogged only a mile, her cheeks were blotched red, and her blond hair was matted to her scalp with sweat.

"Yeah," I said.

"Why?"

"So I can see you in shorts every day after school."

I pinched the flesh of Sara's thigh, and was startled by how easily it yielded.

"Ha ha. But why should I want to do it? It's fun for you because you have a talent for it."

I had never liked the word talent because it implied that my times were the result of an inborn attribute inherited from my parents, rather than my own initiative. (I became a runner, you remember, because I lacked the size and coordination for sports like football.) Running is the most elemental sport, the original sport: before we wrestled, or hit balls with clubs, we ran to hunt game, to survive. The very first Olympic event, in 776 B.C., was a five-hundred-meter sprint. When I explained this to Sara, she said, "I know you train hard, but you've also got something to work with. If you were a big guy with thick bones and short legs, you wouldn't be fast."

"If I were a big guy with thick bones and short legs, I could play football. I wouldn't have to get up at six in the morning to run."

"It's not just your body, though," Sara said. "You've got the mindset for it. You're the most focused person I've ever met. What do you think about when you're running?"

"Running," I said.

Was thinking about nothing but running a good quality? It was good for my running, but was it good for anything else? Clearly, Sara was smarter than I was, in any way that could be measured numerically or expressed alphabetically. Her GPA was higher. And I was sure her SAT and ACT scores would be, too. I was just smart enough to run in circles for hours without getting bored. But I knew that Sara was complimenting me out of her own insecurity: she worried that her intellect and temperament enabled her to be good at everything, but not great at anything. All the musicians on her bedroom wall had carried their artistry to obsessive extremes—and probably their drug use, too— just as Sara thought I carried my training and racing to extremes. When I told her about running a track workout so hard that I temporarily lost my peripheral vision, she looked at me as though I had willed myself into an alternate reality. At the same time, she looked disappointed in herself, for lacking the will to follow me there.

"You should run because you can always run," I said. "Anytime, anywhere, for the rest of your life. It's not like football, where you get so beaten up you can't do it anymore."

"But what I'm saying," Sara replied, "is maybe there's something I can be great at, like writing poetry, or playing the flute, and I'm wasting my time on this thing I can only be average at."

Sara wasn't even average. She would never make the varsity. She was too short, too stocky. But I didn't tell her that. I wanted her to keep running for my own selfish reasons: so we could spend time together, because it was the only thing we had in common, because it was the one thing that I was better at than her, which I thought made me more of a man in her eyes.

"Maybe running can make you more creative," I said. "Like you said, you think about other things when you're running. People think athletes are shallow, but it's just as shallow to do nothing but sit around reading books and listening to records."

"That's what my dad says." Sara imitated her father's voice. *"Mens sana in corpore sana.* A sound mind in a sound body."

"Is that why we complement each other?" I asked.

"That's one way to put it."

Sara seemed satisfied that running was not a waste of her energies, that an activity at which she was not great might help her achieve greatness at something else. I had persuaded my girlfriend to keep running with me. And all I had to do afterwards was listen to the new R.E.M. and Echo and the Bunnymen LPs she had purchased at the Black Platter, before the Elvis Costello concert.

Thirteen

Before the Dog Days 10K, Sara wanted to cut my hair.

"Your hair looks too hot for running in the summer," she said. "Don't you want a hairstyle that will keep you cool?"

I had always parted my hair down the middle and let it flop over my ears, like every other guy. But Sara didn't want a boyfriend who looked like every other guy.

"It's shorter than your hair," I said. "Your hair goes all the way to your shoulders."

"But I don't run as fast as you, so I don't get so sweaty."

"Actually, you get sweatier, because you're out in the heat longer."

Sara pulled an album out of a milk crate and showed me a picture of a bug-eyed singer with orange hair growing on his head like unmown grass in the summer.

"What do you think of this?" she asked.

I thought I didn't want to look anything like that insane person.

"Who is that?"

"John Lydon. Johnny Rotten."

"You want me to dye my hair orange?"

"No. I just think it would look better shorter. And you'd be more comfortable. We could make it neater. Just short and spiky. If you don't like it, it will grow back."

I thought of Steve Schaden, that androgynous runner from East Wenniway. The one who'd beaten me in cross country junior year. Joaquin had called him a fag, but I couldn't slag a guy who ran faster than me.

"Why not just give me a buzz cut then?" I asked.

"No, no, no, no, no!" Sara squinched and shook her head rapidly. (Did she just practice cute facial expressions in front of a mirror, so she could try them out on me later? Probably not. They were spontaneous expressions of her Sara-ness, which just made me want to kiss that face even more.) "You don't want to look like you're in the army."

"*You* don't want me to look like I'm in the army," I said. Mrs. Coonley was always going on about imperialism, colonialism, Vietnam, El Salvador, and "the military-industrial complex." I was sure Sara had picked up on those attitudes.

"OK," she said. "I don't."

I submitted to the haircut. Sara spread a bed sheet on the floor and fetched her mother's shears from the master bedroom. A haircut from a girlfriend is an intimate act, and one intimate act often leads to another. Indeed, while she cut my hair, Sara squatted behind me, with her thighs pressed against my hips. I made only one request of her.

"Don't leave me with a rat tail," I said.

"Ugh, no. Those look so trashy."

When Sara was finished, she took me into the bathroom, dunked my head under the running tap, dried it with a towel, and ran styling gel through the nubs of my locks. I looked in the mirror. The haircut had turned out evenly, more or less. I've never been vain about my hair, or my appearance—only about my racing times—so I was actually looking at her in the mirror, rather than myself. Her eyes were shining. I didn't know whether she was proud of her handiwork, or proud that she'd finally transformed me into one of those rock stars on her bedroom wall. Either way, it seemed like a good opportunity to kiss her, so I took it.

"Got your ears lowered," was all my dad said when I got home.

"Sara did it."

"A girl who can cut hair is a keeper. She'll save you money and she can always get a job."

My mother approved, too.

"It's nice to see that good grooming is coming back for young men," she said.

By the Dog Days 10K, Sara and I had worked up to five miles. On the morning of the race, we stood together at the packet pickup tent, outside the police station on Marquette Street. Even at seven-thirty, my flesh was prickling in the damp heat that would soon burn off the morning chill. I pinned a race number onto Sara's new Violent Femmes t-shirt.

"You just got this shirt," I said. We'd seen the band play for about a hundred people at the Wenniway College Student Union the month before. "I'm gonna poke holes in it, and you're gonna get it all sweaty."

Sara began chanting the words to "Add It Up" while bobbing her head side to side.

"Why can't I get just one kiss?

Believe me, there'd be some things that I wouldn't miss.

But I look at your pants and I need a kiss."

She looked at my pants. I kissed her on the cheek, dryly. I didn't want to get excited in a pair of three-inch split running shorts, in public, before a race.

"I want that song going through my head the entire race," she said. "I figured this t-shirt could make it happen, since you told me not to carry a Walkman during a race."

I had told her that. I didn't understand why anyone needed music to run. Wasn't running entertainment enough? Now Sara listened to the Violent Femmes before all our runs. "It's got a great beat for running," she said. "I'm trying to appreciate music the way you might."

I kissed her again. Checked my shorts. OK.

"I'm gonna line up in the front," I said. "I'll come back out after I finish and run the rest of the race with you."

"If I beat you, I'll do the same!" Sara shouted at my back, as I weaved through throngs of joggers stepping out of warm-up pants, unzipping jerseys, stretching against light poles. The lines at the Porta-johns were five deep with anxious runners.

I lined up in the front row with Dave and Tim. We ran a few hundred-meter stride-outs while waiting for the starting gun. As I'd expected, the race was beneath the efforts of the Wheel City Racing Team, since the only rewards were a t-shirt and a trophy. I looked up and down the first rank of runners to see who might beat me: I saw a dude in a banana yellow singlet and blue nylon shorts cut so high his hairy legs looked like they reached all the way to his armpits. I recognized a tall, stringy guy shaking his spider monkey arms and ostrich legs. He was an assistant coach at East Wenniway, still young and fast enough to lead his runners through workouts. Dave, Tim and I had a plan: we would run the first mile together in five-and-a-half minutes. After that, every man for himself.

"I'd like to thank you all for coming out to support the Policeman's Benevolent Association," a cop in a well-filled windbreaker shouted through a megaphone. "And I want to assure you that even though I'm a cop, this is not a real gun in my hand."

We were all too anxious to laugh, especially at a joke about shooting people.

"I'm going to fire it in ten, nine, eight…"

"Good luck, Buzz," Dave said. That's what he'd started calling me after Sara cut my hair.

"…two, one."

BANG!

The three of us leapt off the starting line, with mirrored strides. Only the runner in the yellow singlet kept pace with us. I didn't know who he was. I'd never seen him before. A ringer from Frontenac who thought he could win a trophy in a small-town race? If so, I'd show him how fast we ran in Wenniway. Tim dropped off after the first mile. Dave dropped off after the second, panting, "Take him, Buzz!" Then it was just me and the yellow singlet, running together, silently, each waiting for the other to falter, so the survivor could run alone.

Since the Dog Days 10K had been organized by the cops, we ran behind a police escort: a black and white Durant, four-door sedan squad car, flanked by a pair of Harleys. I felt like I was winning the Boston Marathon. The course traced a letter G through the sagging neighborhoods surrounding downtown Wenniway, wood-frame rental houses whose paint was flaked and faded by years of sleet and snow. Every block or so, we passed a woman standing on a weed-scored sidewalk with her children. A man drinking a forty on a street corner, at eight-fifteen in the morning. He raised his bottle as we passed, out of respect for our efforts. Even these random gawping bystanders were a bigger audience than I saw at cross-country races, which took place in hidden parks and woodlots. At every mile marker, volunteers behind water tables smacked their hands together and shrieked at the two-man race for the lead.

"Come on, you two!"

"Looking good!"

"Two miles to go now!"

"Don't let him get away!"

I wished I had worn a Wenniway Central singlet so they could cheer for the hometown runner. Cross-country practice wouldn't start for another two weeks, so I had not yet been issued a uniform. Instead, I wore the shirt from my first-ever road race, the Pumpkin Fest 5K. I ran it when I was 14, in Essen, a small town outside Wenniway. I'd read about the race in the *Star* and asked my dad to drive me there.

"When should I come back?" he asked, when he dropped me off.

"Where are you going?" I asked, disappointed that he wasn't going to stay and watch me race.

"Home. I'll come back and get you when the race is over. How long is it going to take?"

"Twenty minutes."

"Oh. Marathons usually take two or three hours."

"This isn't a marathon,. It's a 5K. It's only three point one miles."

"Ah. I wasn't sure how long 5K was. I'll wait for you, then. A guy I work with in the shop lives out here. He says the diner serves a bottomless cup of coffee. I'll go over there until the race is over. Maybe I'll run into him."

The race actually took me twenty-one minutes and eleven seconds. That was fast enough for the first place ribbon in the 15-and-under age group. I located the diner in Essen's two-block business district, and showed my father the blue ribbon, his son's first athletic achievement. I'd made him wait longer than most dads. As we walked back to the car, he put his arm around me.

My dad hadn't attended a race since because he worked in the afternoons. The Dog Days 10K was on a Saturday morning, though, so he and my Mom were waiting at the finish line...which was still two miles away. Every runner trapped inside the agony of a race, miles and minutes away from the relief of the finish line, resents just a little bit the encouragement of the comfortable spectators on the sidewalk. By mile five, I was hurting badly. My only hope for victory was that Yellow Singlet Guy was hurting even worse. I glanced over at him, hoping to see a sign of weakness. His eyes were sliding back and forth. I imagined he was looking for someone to rescue him from his distress, but maybe he was likewise examining me. My brain tried to tell me that I could relax and outkick Yellow Singlet Guy in the last quarter mile. Just as quickly, my willpower stepped in to overrule my brain. If I slackened, I would never speed up again. I looked at my watch as the digits turned over from 26:59 to 27:00. Seven more minutes of this. I could do this for seven more minutes. I came up with a plan: with two minutes left, I would start to sprint. I was younger than my rival. I hoped that meant I was faster, too.

We wheeled around an orange traffic cone and onto Marquette Street, where the race had begun, and where, at the end of the empty straightaway before us, it would end. The Wenniway State Bank, the only building tall enough to be topped with an airplane warning beacon, loomed larger and larger on downtown's otherwise horizontal skyline. Five minutes until my sprint. I was trying not to look at my watch. I was trying to focus only on the effort of enduring *this moment*, but I needed to prepare for *that moment*—the moment of my final push. When it happened, I don't know whether I actually ran faster, or whether I held my pace while Yellow Singlet Guy slowed down, but suddenly, I was running alone. The finishing chute was distantly visible above the spinning lights of the police car. I had never led a race before. Hurling myself forward, to the brink of nausea, I tried desperately to close the distance between this sickening present and the respite awaiting on the other side of that CONGRATULATIONS RUNNERS banner. I didn't look back. I didn't need to. I crossed the finish line in thirty-four minutes and thirty-three seconds. A marshal handed me a popsicle stick labeled "1." Then I fell to my knees and threw up in the street, right where all the other runners could step in it. Delicate hands—nurse's hands?—lifted me from my crouch and guided me to the medical tent. I turned to see Yellow Singlet Guy bent over in the finishing chute, gripping the hems of his short shorts. I nodded. He nodded back. Maybe he felt even worse than

I did, since he'd lost. I wanted to lie down in a patch of grass. Instead, I prostrated myself on a cot and accepted a cup of Gatorade from a race volunteer. My first thought: *I won't be able to help Sara finish her race.* My second thought: *She won't feel stood up; she'll be impressed that I ran so hard I puked.* My third thought: *Maybe that's why I ran so hard.*

"Congratulations," said the volunteer, hovering over me as I sipped Gatorade. I felt like an empty vessel. This sticky drink would only begin to refill me, maybe from the soles of my feet to my ankles. "You left it all out there on the course."

"I did," I panted. "I hope no one's stepping in it now. I promised my girlfriend I'd go out and finish the race with her."

"You'd better stay here. I'm a nurse. You've done enough running."

In my passive state, that was all the permission I needed. My parents found me in the medical tent. When I was able to sit up, they helped me into my warmups. Half an hour later, Sara found me, too.

"You never came out to meet me, so I thought you'd gotten hurt or something," she said. "When I got to the finish I asked if anyone had seen a guy about seventeen, blond hair, yellow t-shirt, and they said, 'Oh, yeah, he won!'"

"I'm waiting for them to bring me my trophy."

"God, you look pale. Are you OK?"

I patted the canvas. Sara sat down beside me and held my hand. I looked into her blue eyes.

"I ran so hard I threw up at the finish line."

Those blue eyes got bigger, just as I'd known they would.

I finally stood, although queasily, for the awards ceremony. A uniformed police officer presented me a trophy with a brass runner balanced on its base and the inscription DOG

DAYS 10K CHAMPION. Sara won a medal for finishing third in the 15-19 age group. (Maybe that would convince her that running wasn't a waste of time.) We rode home with our hardware in our laps. When my dad stopped in front of Sara's house, she asked, "Can you come over later, we can listen to..." Looking anxiously at my mother in the front seat, she whispered "...the Circle Jerks."

"I thought they were too hardcore for you."

"Not for you. I got the record because I thought you'd like it."

I liked the Circle Jerks better than Elvis Costello, but not enough to get me out of bed the rest of the day. All morning and afternoon, I lay on the mattress, feeling nauseous and staring at my trophy, a runner captured in mid-stride as he crossed my nightstand. I ate a turkey sandwich for lunch, threw it up, and finally made it to the living room in the evening to watch *One Day at a Time* and *The Jeffersons* with Mom, Dad and Gramps. Too sick to laugh, I wondered whether it was worth sacrificing an entire day of my life to run six miles, no matter how fast, or to impress my girlfriend, cute as she was. But I had finally won a race. Cross-country practice started in two weeks. Everyone who'd beaten me the year before. I was going to win more.

FOURTEEN

The assembly line at Empire Body was scheduled to halt forever on the September 23rd—a Friday. The company was throwing a party, with a giant cake in the shape of a 1967 Corsair, the best-selling model ever produced in that plant. I guessed there would also be severance checks for everyone who lacked the seniority to make the cut for Tennessee, or, like my dad, refused the transfer.

"I thought they only let us in on Family Day," I said, when my dad asked me to stop by the plant after practice.

"Good grief, Kevin, what are they gonna do? Fire me? For bringing my son to the plant on the day it closes? When I've already quit?"

("Good grief" was the strongest oath that ever passed between my father's lips. He wouldn't even say "Jeez o'Pete," because, he said, it was short for Jesus and Peter, the founders of the church. In his mind, taking the Lord's name in vain was worse than the F-word, the S-word, or any of the other seven you're not allowed to use on television—although I never heard him use any of those, either. Once, Dad exclaimed "Jesus Christ" after cutting himself while pulling a screen out of a window. "There's no need to bring the Lord into this," my mother scolded. He never profaned Jesus's name again, at least not in front of the family, although I'm sure he had plenty of reasons to do so at work. I didn't know whether that was because he believed it was a sin, whether he wanted to avoid offending my mother, or whether he wanted to set a good example for me. It was hard to tell which of those motivations in-spired his religious behavior. I think my dad believed that doing what the Bible prescribed took no more effort than doing what it prohibited, so he might as well err on the safe side—especially if it made my mother happy.)

"They're gonna shut down the line at the end of second shift, so just come by after practice," Dad instructed me. "And wear your sweats, so everyone can see you're a superstar."

So far that season, I had won all five of my races, and broken the Wenniway Central cross-country course record. After that feat, the *Star* named me Mid-State Boys Prep Ath-lete of the Week, which was astounding, because in the fall, it was almost always a football player. A sportswriter called me at home to interview me. I told him my secrets were getting up at six in the morning, and running a thousand miles over the summer with Dave and Tim. (I felt safe giving away my secrets; because most people were too lazy to follow them.) Mom laminated the clipping so she could carry it in her purse and show it to people everywhere she went, except church. ("We put pride aside there.") Coach told me not to get a big head. We were running in an invitational that Saturday, where I was going to have to beat kids from all over the state, "not just those Wenniway mopes you've been clobbering."

Because of the invitational, our Friday workout was three miles of jogging around the school grounds and the park behind the stadium. Coach told me to run with the sophomores, "so you won't run too fast and waste your race, and so you can talk them out of doing anything stupid. They look up to you more than they look up to me." A sopho-more named Duncan told me he'd joined the cross-country team so he could train for a marathon with his dad.

"If I ran a marathon, Coach would kick my ass off the team," I told the kid. "He chewed me out once just for running with a bunch of marathoners. He didn't even like it when I won a 10K during the summer. After he saw my picture in the paper, he called me up and said, 'I hope you can win a 5K, too, because that's what we run!'"

When I met Dad at the Main Gate, across the street from Pete's, I wasn't even sweaty. We walked together through the metal doors. The windows above those doors were reinforced with chicken wire. The cops had busted those windows during the Wildcat Strike, so they could fire tear gas bombs at the strikers inside. Gramps and his pals had aimed a fire hose through the broken glass. The spray had driven the cops across the street, where they shot at the plant in retaliation. The guy standing next to Gramps was wounded in the leg. Gramps had told that story at, I think, every Sunday dinner he'd ever attended. It was why he'd protested the plant's closing: his union brothers had bled for the right to earn a decent wage there, but after today, no one was going to earn any wages.

Inside, the shop floor was crowded with workers, all gathered around the spot where auto bodies came off the assembly line and were loaded onto trucks and trains. Stretched above the line was a banner that read, simply, 56 YEARS OF QUALITY. My dad pointed it out to me.

"The union put that there," he explained. "Empire can never say we didn't do a good job here. We built the most reliable cars in America."

A lot of second and third shift guys had shown up to watch the final body come off the line. After the first shift workers welded the last quarter panel, hung the last door, bolted in the last seat, and draped the last upholstery, they abandoned their stations and gathered to see the finished product. Auto bodies are like mannequins: the shape of the car, but none of the life. That was added during final assembly at the riverfront plant, where these shells were lowered onto the chassis that contained the motivating organs of the automobile: engine drive train, steering column, and wheels. (The riverfront plant was closing, too. Down in

Tennessee, the entire process would take place under one roof.) Dad led me through the crowd to his buddy Denny, the guy he'd been planning to room with in Tennessee.

"You remember my son Kevin?"

Denny eyed my sweatshirt.

"Still a masochist, I see."

"He's a champion masochist," Dad boasted. "Prep Athlete of the Week in the *Star*."

"Well, if you're gonna suffer, you might as well get some recognition for it."

"When you goin' down?" Dad asked Denny.

"Plant's opening in November, so we're getting a little paid vacation."

"You find someone else to share that mobile home?"

Denny plucked a cigarette from his shirt pocket and hung it, unlit, beneath his moustache. Smoking was prohibited inside the plant, but just the suggestion of menthol apparently soothed him as much as inhaling it.

"Nahhh," he said, slumping his shoulders, "the whole family's moving down there. I guess my wife wants to keep an eye on me in Music City. She trusted me with you. It's still not too late to change your mind."

"I already cashed the buyout check."

"Pretty good?"

"Six months' pay."

"If I had as much time in as you, I might have been able to say, 'Screw it,' but I've still got ten years to go. I did three years in the Army, and then I came back here and spent a couple years ridin' my motorcycle until I had to get married. When you get married, you have to get a job, too, and Empire was always hiring in them days."

Denny looked at me and tapped his temple.

"Kid," he said, "always think with your head. This head."

"He thinks with his legs," Dad said. "He runs so much he hasn't got the energy for nothin' else."

"We're tryin' to sell the house," Denny said, "but Jesus, have you seen all the For Sale signs around here? Everyone who took the transfer is trying to sell. We'll be lucky if we get what we paid for it."

"I'm tryin' to sell, too. We moved in with my dad after he had a stroke, but we haven't even had an offer yet. I'm gonna give it another month or so, then I'm gonna rent it out."

"Well, good luck to you here. I guess it's just as well we're getting out. I don't know what this town's gonna be without Empire."

Denny lit his cigarette with the Bic he stored beside the hard pack in his pocket.

"I know you're not supposed to smoke inside a factory," he said, "but screw it, in fifteen minutes, this isn't going to be a factory anymore."

Indeed, the final Empire Body was making the turn toward the loading bay, jerking forward, with only empty space behind it on the assembly line. The endless procession of auto bodies issuing from this plant—my father's life work—was finished. When the last body reached the end of the line, the inspectors posed for photos. Disposable flashbulbs spangled the eternal gloom of the shop floor. Applause swept through the crowd, but it sounded faint and sparse. The room's vastness absorbed all but the most thunderous industrial racket. The clapping wasn't celebratory, but the reflexive reaction to the end of a function. Once the inspectors approved the body, the president of the AA local hoisted his hefty self onto the hood to make a speech. An Empire executive would not have been well received. My dad, though, had seen all he wanted to see and heard all he wanted to hear. Empire Body of Wenniway was dead. There was no reason to linger for the eulogy.

"Let's go over to Pete's before it gets too crowded," he said.

Pete's was already crowded with autoworkers eager to spend their final paychecks on booze. A TV camera beside the door filmed men drifting out of the main gate in twos and threes. Despite the crush, Pete had reserved a table for the Gary Ward Memorial Euchre League.

"You come in here every Friday for twenty years," Pete said. "I don't forget you on a bad day like this."

"Some of the guys are going to Tennessee," my dad said, holding up two fingers to signal he wanted two bottles of Stroh's, "but the rest of us will keep coming for another twenty years."

Pete shook his head. He pointed to a photograph behind the bar, of a cluster of chalk-white buildings beside a glittering sea.

"I'm going home," Pete said. "No plant, no bar. If someone wants to buy, they can buy. I been here twenty-six years. I save enough. Plus, no more winter. The weather in Greece is sincere. You always know what it going to do. Here, you never know. One day rain, one day snow. One day hot, one day cold."

Pete set the beer bottles down in front of my father. My dad pointed at one.

"I have a big race tomorrow," I protested. "Plus, Pete could get in trouble."

"He's closing the place down. He don't care if he loses his license. Just take a sip. I want to deliver a toast."

He raised the bottle and clinked its heel with mine.

"To Empire Motors. They paid for our house, they paid for our cars, and now they're going to pay me just enough of a pension to live on for the rest of my life."

"You're not mad they're leaving? Gramps sure is, and he got to put in forty years."

Dad shrugged and drew on his bottle. I took a sip, just as he'd asked.

"I wish they'd stayed here another five years," he said.

"But it's not like they fired me. They gave me a choice: my job, or my family and my hometown. They're still building cars; they're just not building cars where I want to build 'em. I just decided the job wasn't as important as keeping the family together. No matter how much money you make, if you can't keep your family together, you've failed at life. We'll have enough. We won't have an RV or a speedboat, but we can live in Gramps' house as long as we want and rent out the other one. The only thing I'm sorry about is I can't pay for you to go to the U."

"I told you the only way I'm going is if I get a scholarship, and then you won't have to pay," I said. "I don't want you to spend five years living in a mobile home and never seeing Mom just so I can go to the U. There's other colleges."

"Like where?"

"Wherever I can run. I know a guy who ran at Great Lakes. He knows the track coach there. Maybe they'll offer me something."

Dad took another drink when I mentioned Great Lakes.

"Great Lakes is two hundred and fifty miles away. We'd hardly ever see you. But what do you want to do after college? You can't run forever."

"I guess you go to college to figure that out," I said, because honestly, I could not imagine a life beyond running. I didn't want to join the Wheel City Racing Team, and work in a shoe store to pay my hundred dollar a month share of the rent, but neither did I want to get a full-time job and become a hobby jogger, just fast enough to win the Dog Days 10K. I wanted a shoe contract from Nike or Saucony, who would pay me to train for the Olympics. I could never tell my father that, though. Or my coach. Or Sara. Or Dave or Tim. Such a grand ambition was impressive if you achieved it, but if you talked about it and failed, you'd look like a fool. The best thing about an ambition like that, though, was that it could be accomplished right here in Wenniway. Unlike football, or hockey, or basketball, a runner didn't need to go to a big college to prepare for the major leagues. A runner didn't need to go to college at all. Bill Rodgers, who ran in the Olympic marathon that set me on this course, had been a scrub at a dinky, no-name college in the no-name state of Connecticut. Then he was a hippie draft dodger smoking a pack of cigarettes a day and riding his motorcycle to work in Boston. When someone stole his bike, he started running to work, Four years later, he won the Boston Marathon. The simplicity, the individuality of the sport meant anyone could do it, anywhere.

"If you don't get a scholarship," my dad was saying, "you could think about a trade. If you learn a trade, you'll always have a job. Look at your uncle: he still has a job, and I don't. I'm gonna be working for *him*. He can probably get you in the Builders. You'll have a more flexible schedule so you can do your running and racing. It might make sense."

"I'm going to run home," I said, standing up.

I wanted to get out of Pete's before my dad gave me more career advice, or encouraged me to drink more, and before I inhaled any more cigarette smoke. It was bad for my wind. Even on that mile-and-a-half run home, in the first hour after the last car came of the assembly line at Empire Body, I noticed a difference in Wenniway. As I passed beneath open windows of the plant, I smelled... nothing. Instead of inhaling the sweetish chemical tang of atomized paint, I inhaled...fresh air. That night, at the football game, when I looked across the street at Empire Body, the windows were dark, the balconies empty of the nightshift workers who watched our games during their smoke breaks. The plant was illuminated only by sodium vapor lights, triggered by dusk. The audience of autoworkers had always made Warriors football seem bigger than the school itself. The eyes of the entire city were on us. Now, the cheering was confined to our little chain-link fence and wooden-bleacher stadium. I left the game at halftime, with us leading South 20-7. When I got home, Gramps was watching *Dallas* with my mom and dad. It was his TV.

"You see the last car?" he asked.

I nodded.

"Well, those SOBs finally screwed us after fifty years, by God," he said.

Mom tensed at Gramps' language, but this wasn't her house, and Gramps wasn't her husband.

FIFTEEN

When I woke up Saturday morning, to make it to school for the six-thirty bus to the Invitational, I didn't hear the pounding of the drop forge stamping out dies for the auto plants. The drop forge had always sounded like God's hammer, pounding against the brass dome of heaven, but we slept right through it. (In fact, we couldn't sleep without it. When my sister and her husband first moved away from the neighborhood, she was so unsettled by the all-encompassing silence of the suburbs that she put a pair of tennis shoes in the dryer to mimic the industrial lullaby of our childhood.)

I almost won the Invitational. I lost the lead in the last twenty-five yards, because I made a tactical mistake. Except for the race in which I broke the course record, I never ran my hardest. I only ran to win. I went out with the leaders in the first mile, built a lead of fifty or a hundred yards in the second mile, and maintained that throughout the third mile. Since I was the fastest runner in the county, no one ever caught me. The Invitational, though, attracted runners from all over the state. It was our biggest race since the state championship in Auburn, and it included the team that won that meet: Frontenac Catholic Central.

The course was three laps around a golf course. (I've never liked golf: it's a boring game for boring old guys who are too fat to exert themselves but still fancy themselves competitive athletes. I do, however, love golf courses. All that grass in one place is great for cross country.) Five guys stuck with me through the five-and-a-half minute first lap. On the second lap, I broke away. By the time I hit the two-mile, in 10:53, I had a hundred-yard lead. I was so certain of winning I slackened my pace. I wasn't going to run my guts out, like I'd done at the Dog Days 10K. We had a dual meet on Tuesday. I wanted to save something.

In any race, the psychological advantage is with the pursuer: he knows where the leader is and knows what he has to do to catch his prey. The leader only knows where his pursuer is if he looks over his shoulder: a display of weakness no runner should show his opponents. So I didn't know my lead was shrinking until the final straightaway, a quarter-mile gantlet on which was gathered every coach, every parent, and all the girls, who had finished their race half an hour before we started ours. I sped past keening, screeching cheers. I heard my name, from our girls: "C'mon Kevin! Go, go!" "Don't let him catch you!" Then, an instant later, I heard an unfamiliar name from the girls in Frontenac Catholic Central's black jerseys. "You got him, Craig! You got him!" Sara was on her knees, pounding the grass. I didn't look back. I didn't have to. The voices told me that someone—someone named Craig—was close behind. I sprinted. I extended my limbs to their utmost. I squeezed every last breath from my lungs. Craig, though, had calculated exactly how fast he had to run to win this race. I heard his footsteps. I heard the flapping of his flimsy race number. His deep, desperate breaths. Surely, he was as exhausted as I was. But no, he was three steps fresher. I felt his presence at my shoulder. Then I saw his black singlet interpose itself between me and the finish line, just a few yards too far away. Three of my senses—hearing, touch, sight—registered defeat. As I stumbled into the chute and clapped Craig's shoulder in a show of sportsmanship, I understood why Olympic silver medalists always looked so deflated and dejected on the podium. At the end of that first Olympic marathon I'd watched with my mom, our American hero, Frank Shorter, had glumly shaken hands with his East German conqueror.

Like Frank Shorter, I had come closer to victory than anyone else, but still lost, like everyone else. Coach didn't see it that way.

"That was a great race," he said, as I was pulling on my sweats in the gear tent.

"I'm sure it was great to watch," I said, not making eye contact. "It wasn't great to be the guy who got caught at the end."

"No," he said. "*You* ran a great race. This is the toughest field outside the state championship, and you dominated almost all the way."

Almost.

"I got cocky," I said. "I'm used to controlling the pace, so I let up in the last mile. I could have run faster."

"Better to learn that here than in a race that really counts," he said.

If the race had really counted, I would have run faster. *Am I be willing to spend a day throwing up for a state championship? Yes, I am!*

"If we could find a hill for you to run on, you could do something special at state"

"Where are we going to find a hill in Wenniway?"

"There's a ski hill about thirty miles outside of town. It's built on an old garbage dump. They call it Mystic Mountain, but I call it Mount Trashmore. We'll make a team trip out there. I'll make sure you can run with those kids who train in the Arb, or on the sand dunes."

Coach wanted to train a state champion. That would mean as much to him as to me. Because I read everything about running, I had read a short story called "The Loneliness of the Long-Distance Runner," about a cross-country runner at an English bording school. He's about to win a race, but stops a few yards short of the finish line. He thinks it will just be a victory for the reform school where he's been imprisoned, and for its principal, who might become "a sir" as a result of producing a champion. Maybe if I won at state, Coach could get a college job. Maybe at Central. I was willing to run harder for that. I was even willing to throw up.

When our house fetched no offers, even at $30,000, my dad gave up on selling it and took out a classified ad in the *Star*, asking $400 a month in rent. We replaced the FOR SALE sign with a FOR RENT sign. As we made the switch, our old next-door neighbor, Mr. Ockenfels, addressed us from his porch, where he was listening to a football game on his transistor radio.

"This is a *homeowning* neighborhood, not a renting neighborhood," he shouted.

(When our old dog, Tuffy, burrowed under the fence, and into the Ockenfels' yard, they hadn't called us. They'd called Animal Control. My dad drove to the pound at eleven o'clock at night to rescue her. That was five years ago. This was the first time Dad and Mr. Ockenfels had exchanged words since, even though Mr. Ockenfels was always on his porch when the temperature was above fifty degrees, a one-man neighborhood watch, glaring at anyone who passed by on the sidewalk,.)

"You want to buy it then, Frank?" my dad snapped. "I'll sell it to you for thirty-six. That's a dollar for every year you've been in the neighborhood. You can tear it down and double the size of your yard. You'll have twice as much to keep an eye on."

"Just who are you going to be inviting in there?" demanded Mr. Ockenfels, leaning against the railing of his porch as though it were a battlement providing him the safety to launch any invective across his property line.

"Anyone who can pay four hundred dollars a month, plus a security deposit."

"No background check? No criminal check?"

"Nope. Just a check. I need the money. You may have heard that my place of employment closed down."

Mr. Ockenfels's face and scalp turned red with frustration, all the way back to his cropped fringe of gray hair. Even the hairy hands protruding from the sleeves of his flannel shirt seemed to redden.

"I'm going to have to live next door to your tenants," he reminded my dad.

"You lived next door to us for twenty years; it should be easier. They may not have a dog."

"You were homeowners and taxpayers."

"Do you know what's even worse than living next to someone you look down on?" my dad asked Mr. Ockenfels. "Living next to nobody. If this house stays empty much longer, people are gonna break in and get drunk or get high, or they're gonna try to steal the boiler and the copper pipes. And if they do that to my house, they're gonna try to do it to your house."

Realizing that his rights ended where his property ended, but not liking it, Mr. Ockenfels retreated from the balustrade and withdrew inside his house. He was back on the porch again, though, when we moved in our new tenants, a family with five kids and a Section 8 housing voucher. When Dad announced the lease signing at the dinner table, my mom wondered if he had rented to that family the house just to spite Mr. Ockenfels, for sending our dog to the pound all those years ago.

"If he feels like I'm spiting him, I won't mind," Dad said, "but that's not why I did it. If you've got Section 8 tenants, you know you're gonna get paid. That's why so many ads say, 'Section 8 welcome.' It's a guaranteed four hundred a month. That'll buy a lot of groceries."

My mother sighed. "Our house is moving down in the world," she said.

Sixteen

Sara wanted to see *All the Right Moves*, because it starred Tom Cruise, who played Steve Randle in *The Outsiders*. I was surprised, because Tom Cruise was so husky and wholesome, as opposed to Sara's usual lineup of underfed, self-destructive celebrity crushes.

"He's a really good *actor*," she insisted. "I should have hated him in *Risky Business*, but I didn't. Our next-door neighbor Michele Sundstrom goes to the U and she says *all* the out-of-state students are like that: total Ivy League wannabees from the suburbs. Gahhhd! I hate kids from the suburbs."

In the movie, Tom Cruise played Stef, a high school quarterback from a Pennsylvania steelmaking town that wasn't making much steel anymore. He didn't want to work in the mills like his dad and his brother. He wanted to win a college scholarship so he could study to be an engineer. He got kicked off the team for arguing with his coach about who was responsible for losing a game, and you thought, uh oh, he's going to end up just like his buddy who married his pregnant girlfriend and stayed in town. But his coach got a job at a school in California and took Tom Cruise with him. Big music. Triumphant finale. As each plot point unfolded, I caught Sara staring at me. Yeah, there were a few similarities between me and Tom Cruise up there on the screen. I was a high school athlete in a car-making town that wasn't making cars anymore, and I was trying to win a college scholarship.

"Did you identify with Stef?" Sara asked on the drive home.

"No," I said, curtly. "I thought the movie was insulting."

"To whom?" asked the English teacher's daughter.

"To places like this," I said. We were headed back into town from the multiplex, down a four-lane strip illuminated with the logos of every chain that set up an outpost on the outskirts of every small town in America: Rax Roast Beef, Jiffy Lube, Firestone Tire, Kentucky Fried Chicken, MC Sports.

"It's just the reality," Sara said. "If he had stayed in Pennsylvania and worked in the mill, he probably would have ended up getting laid off."

I tensed. "Like my dad?"

"Like a lot of people at Empire."

"OK," I agreed, "but the movie was saying that everyone should *want* to leave their hometown if they can't get a great job there. His friend is a big loser because he decides to stay and marry his girlfriend and Tom Cruise is a big winner because he goes to college in California. I'm sure the people who made the movie think that's the definition of success because *they* all went to California to make it in Hollywood. I'm trying to get a scholarship to the U so I can stay in Wenniway—or at least as close as I can get."

"So what if you just got offered a scholarship to, like, Stanford?" Sara asked. "You wouldn't go?"

"I mean—this doesn't seem like a good time to go all the way across the country. My dad lost his job because he didn't want to abandon the family and go to Tennessee. Now my mom has to keep working at the hospital, so we'll have benefits. My grandfather had a stroke, so he needs us around. My sister's going to have another baby. And *you're* going to the U. You and your dad are the reasons I wanted to go in the first place. Don't you want me to go, too?"

"Sure," she said tentatively. "But if you wanted to go someplace that was even better for you—better for your running—I'd understand that."

I stopped the car in front of Sara's house. I started kissing her, and she kissed me back. Even though we'd sort of had an argument—an argument that I would end up remembering in far more detail than I remembered the movie—I felt the same surge of affection and intimacy that I always felt when I kissed Sara. So much so that I pulled back and told her something I'd never told anyone. About hearing Howard Cosell's voice in my head when I ran in the mornings. about the Olympics.

"I would love to run in the Olympics and have them say, 'Look at that guy from Wenniway out in front.' We're going through a tough time here, so we should have the toughest runner, right? I want to represent what we stand for here, not just run away to some beach town where everything is easy. I don't run because it's easy; I run because it's hard. You know what I mean?"

"Yes," Sara whispered. She didn't leave my car for another half hour.

Seventeen

Every November, Dad asked if I wanted to go Up North to Gramps' cabin to hunt deer with him and Uncle Dick. Every year I said no, even though Dad offered to buy me a rifle and a camo suit and a bright orange hat. One reason I said no was that I knew they spent two hours every morning in their tree stands, and the rest of the time draining a case of Stroh's or drinking at various North Woods bars with antlers mounted on the walls. I was supposed to be the disciplined athlete, right? Another reason I said no was that the deer were just trying to run through the woods, and as a dedicated cross-country runner myself, I didn't want to spoil their fun by shooting them dead in mid-stride. Now that I was Wenniway Central's fastest runner, I had another justification: the state championship meet was the weekend after firearm deer season started.

"Well, shoot, we're gonna have to cut this trip short, then, so your mom and I can watch you run," Dad said, when I told him about the scheduling conflict. "That's too bad. This could be our last trip up there."

"How come?"

"I'm thinking about selling the cabin. I talked to Gramps about it. He's fine with it since he can't go up there anymore. I'll talk to your uncle about it when we go up there. I'm sure we could all use the money. A lot of Dick's customers were shop guys. His business is down."

*   *   *

On a morning run, a few weeks before the state meet, I descended the bridge that arches over the Oak River, alongside the assembly plant. Like the body plant, it, too, was scheduled for demolition. (When the plant was running, this bridge had been bumper-to-bumper with Empire automobiles during every shift change. From the top of the bridge, you could look down into a lot crowded with newborn automobiles glowing and gleaming even under Wenniway's weak winter sun.) I saw a runner moving briskly up the slope, coming from the plant side of the river. As the gap between us closed, I recognized the smooth stride, the oiled arms and legs that could make a four-and-a-half-minute mile look like jogging. Runners identify each other by strides, even more than faces. It was Joaquin. As I lifted my hand to wave, he wheeled around and ran beside me, back toward the factory.

"Buddy," he said, "I know you ain't gonna break stride for old home week. You don't stop runnin' for nothin'."

"You're out early, too," I said. In high school, Joaquin ran Coach's after-school workouts, partied all weekend, and still kicked my ass.

"Dude, I'm running for WCC. It's harder to beat those guys than it was to beat you, especially since I'm a freshman. So I'm doing two-a-days."

"Have they got a decent team?" I asked.

"It ain't the U. We got a guy who does a four-twenty mile. That's about it. But you don't gotta pay ten thousand a year to run there. All you gotta do is take one class. I'm taking computer programming, and the rest of the time I've been working for my uncle's landscaping business, saving up some money."

We ran nearly a mile along the railroad tracks between the assembly plant and the river. They were empty of boxcars. The river was clean and brown, without the rainbow sheen I was used to seeing on the surface. As we approached the next bridge, Joaquin pointed across the water.

"I'm gonna cross back over here," he said, "I've been seein' your name in the paper. Good luck at state this year. You were tough on those hills last year, man."

"Coach is taking us to run a ski slope this week."

"Man, I wish he'd done that when I was on the team. Maybe I would have beaten you in the Arb."

And then Joaquin turned to cross a bridge, back to Mexicantown, a neighborhood of narrow frame houses clustered on a flood plain enclosed by a loop of the Oak River.

Only the varsity seven ran up Mount Trashmore. That was all Coach could fit into his Durant, and the car of a fellow teacher who held the title "assistant coach" because he joined us on weekly ten-mile runs.

Mount Trashmore was a smooth slope, a quarter mile long, rising from the flat farmland at the angle of an isosceles triangle. (I had gotten a B in geometry. Numbers and angles made more sense to me than literature, or philosophy.) Local legend said the Ojibway tribe built the mound as a platform for ritual sacrifices and other religious observances. The real story: Mount Trashmore had been a dump, capped and abandoned when it ran out of room for garbage, then used as a ski hill, because it was the only high ground in this part of the state. We passed signs for Mystic Mountain, a name invented to make flatlanders feel they were skiing at a Walt Disney resort. I had never skied— only sledding and inner tubing—but like the golf courses where I never golfed, I happy glad Mount Trashmore eisted for my running. That was how I judged the usefulness of every natural and man-made feature: if I couldn't run on it, I didn't want to go there.

Coach walked up the hill, step by arduous step. At the top, he raised his arm, and blew his whistle, a shrill sound that reached our ears after we saw him drop his hand. We launched ourselves upwards, digging for every degree of elevation with the toes of our shoes. Coach pantomimed hauling us up the hill with a rope.

"Balls out, guys!" he bellowed. "Balls out!"

By the time we reached the peak, we were practically on our hands and knees, scrabbling in the dirt. We flopped to the ground, sweaty, exhausted, depleted of wind.

"How are you feeling?" Coach asked.

Nobody said a thing. We were all breathing too hard.

"Stand up," he ordered. "Don't get too comfortable down there."

Rising to my feet, I crouched over and panted.

"You're going to have to do this nine more times. We're not gonna get outrun at state because Wenniway is flatter than a pancake."

Wordlessly, we jogged back down the hill to await the next whistle: the same signal World War I soldiers heard, before climbing out of their trenches and attacking the enemy. (I learned that from watching *Gallipoli*, a movie about two runners who join the Australian army.) As every ascent weakened my legs, transforming muscle to rubber, I felt I would have been better off in the trenches. At least there, someone might shoot me, so I wouldn't have to run up this hill anymore. But it was never a good workout, or a good race, unless I wished for the sweet release of death at some point. At least I was leading all my teammates up the hill, a lead that lengthened with every rep.

After the tenth ascent, I hobbled slowly down the hill, step by aching step, feeling even hollower than I'd felt after the Dog Days 10K. I subsided into the back seat of Coach's car, allowing my limbs to flow over the vinyl upholstery. I wanted to go home, throw up, and go to bed. But some of Sara's friends had started a punk band and were playing their first gig that night in the drummer's basement. So, I had to go. I tried to nap beforehand, but I was so wired with exhaustion I couldn't sleep.

"What's the name of the band?" I asked Sara when I picked her up in my dad's car.

"Rumpledforeskin."

"Like Rumplestiltskin?"

"Yeah, except about foreskin. It's a play on words."

"I get that."

"You should," she said, making an observation only she, my parents and my gym classmates could make. "That's one of the bands."

"Who's the other?"

"Buttmuscle."

"How long is this going to go on?"

"I don't know. Late. It's Friday night. Why?"

"We had a really hard workout today. I'm wiped out. Coach made us run ten times up this really long hill, to train for state. Plus, I have to get up and run tomorrow, then help my dad and my uncle with a remodeling job."

"You don't have to stay for the whole thing. My friend Grace is going to be there. She can give me a ride home."

"I won't be so bad after state," I promised. "I'll be able to relax for a while…until indoor gets started."

Only five cars were parked outside the house—an Empire-built Cape Cod in my old neighborhood. There were scarcely more people inside. We descended a half-open staircase, to an unfinished basement with a drain cover fitted like a medallion in the middle of the concrete floor. An insulated pipe formed a pillar to the ceiling. In a corner was a cartoon sketch of a drum kit: bass, snare, cymbals, flanked by two black amplifiers, shaped like tombstones. In another corner was Carter, my old cross-country teammate, who had been kicked off the team for streaking the football game, then kicked out of Central altogether. His hair was short and spiky, with an electric blue crescent above his left ear, from which lobe dangled a gold ring. From the feet up, he wore combat boots, black stovepipe jeans running the length of his lanky legs, and a black t-shirt with a skull emblem. He had cut off the sleeves, exposing biceps looking softer than they had in a Wenniway Central racing singlet. (At least Sara's haircut made me *look* as though I fit in here.) Carter was also wearing an electric guitar. I say "wearing" because it wasn't plugged in, and he wasn't strumming any chords. The guitar seemed to be hanging from his lean frame only to complete the punk rock look. Even though he was, apparently, the lead guitarist of Rumpledforeskin—or Buttmuscle, I hadn't found out which—Carter greeted me first, loping across the basement, his guitar bouncing off his hip. Carter had always looked more like a runner than I did, even if he had never run as fast.

"Ward," he said, clapping my hand, "You been tearin' it up. I saw you were Athlete of the Week."

"You still running?" I asked, because it was the one thing we'd had in common. I'd heard a rumor that the school board had exiled Carter to South, but I hadn't seen him on their track or cross-country teams.

"Nah," he said. "That's ancient history. After I got kicked out school my parents sent me to Bishop Weber. We're not even Catholic, but they thought it would straighten me out. You see how that worked. There's way more drugs and punk rock there than at Central, 'cause everyone sends their fuck-up kids there, and we all get together and fuck up even more."

I was about to introduce Sara to Carter, but she stepped forward and introduced herself first.

"I was on the girls' team last year," she said.

Carter nodded. "Oh, yeah. Yeah."

I don't think Carter remembered Sara. I'd barely noticed her until she sat down next to me in the pizza parlor.

"I'm friends with your drummer, Grace."

"Right, right. Grace is...amazing. She can really pound the drums."

A heavy-limbed girl in a tank top and jeans, Grace squatted behind the drum kit, tapping the bass pedal. DOOMP. DOOMP. DOOMP. At that signal, Carter plugged in his guitar. He introduced the band as Rumbledforeskin. He didn't need to. Only five people were watching: me, Sara, and the members of Buttmuscle.

"This first song," Carter said, "is about some trouble I got into last year."

Carter clutched the neck of his guitar and raked the strings with a pick, creating a sluggish, dissonant under-tow of sound, dragged lower and deeper by the occasional pluck of a bass string, and the thumping of the drums.

"I showed them my aaaasss," Carter keened in a high-pitched screech that was a sonic counterpoint to the dark, heavy noise of the instruments.

"I streaked across the graaasss

Then I got kicked out of claaasss

'Cause I showed them my aaasss

Now every day I'm at Maaasss"

Then, Carter turned his back to the five of us, un-buckled his belt, and dropped his pants, showing us his ass. I'd seen it before, in the shower after practice, and at the football game. I guess after he'd displayed his ass to thousands of football fans, flashing it to his immediate cir-cle of acquaintances was no big deal. Even as he stood there in a state of semi-nudity, Carter continued to scrape his guitar strings. During this instrumental interlude, two more girls from the JV cross-country team descended the stairs. I barely recognized them. I was only used to seeing my teammates sweaty, flushed, and in shorts. Their hair was teased and sprayed into blond cowls. They wore long tweed overcoats over calf-length sweaters, narrow jeans cropped at the ankle, and fluorescent pink socks. It wasn't

a punk rock look, and they hadn't brought punk rock attitudes: halfway down the stairs, they halted at the sight of
Carter mooning the basement, gaping at his ass with open-
mouthed expressions on their pale, featureless sophomore
faces. Only Sara, who had invited the girls, could convince
them to complete the descent. First, she pulled up Carter's
pants, yanking the waistband of his boxer shorts before he
could stop playing the guitar. In a room this intimate, there
was no barrier between the audience and the performers.
Then she called out, "Kelly! Tess! It's OK to come down
now."

Kelly and Tess walked down the stairs, but they still
looked uncomfortable. Like me, they'd been promised a
concert, not this bohemian shindig. I glanced at my running watch. Eight-thirty. I could make it 'til nine. Rumpledforeskin's set would be over by then. They couldn't know
that many songs. They didn't, but they continued playing
nonetheless: a shapeless, timeless, free-form jam stretching
into the night. I guessed I was going to miss Buttmuscle.

"I'm gonna take off," I said to Sara, the moment the
digits turned to 9:00. She was watching the band raptly.
"You can get a ride home with Grace, right?"

"Yeah, but I wish you didn't have to leave already." She
pressed her hands against my chest and rubbed against me
as we kissed goodbye at the staircase. Music made Sara
more affectionate. That's why I went to concerts with her.

I thought she might still feel that way the day after, so
I stopped by her house after I finished working with Dad
and Uncle Dick, hoping to find her alone. Instead, I found
Mrs. Coonley alone, cooking squash and listening to James
Taylor. Mrs. Coonley invited me inside. The little house
felt warm, homey, autumnal, especially after the unheated
basement where we'd been hanging drywall. I wanted to
stay, but only if Sara was there, too.

"Sara's at the arboretum with her dad," Mrs. Coonley said. "They're tapping maple trees for syrup. Jim's been taking her there every fall since she was three years old. They both love it. You can stay until they get back. I'm making butternut squash and root vegetables, and we're going to drink mulled apple cider. A harvest meal. Jim and Sara are going to be chilly."

I excused myself. My mother was making pork chops smothered with cream of mushroom soup, and scalloped potatoes. After running ten miles and lifting drywall out of Uncle Dick's van, I needed something heartier than butternut squash and root vegetables.

"Tell Sara to call me later," I said.

Sara didn't call, so I went over to her house again on Sunday. I knew I shouldn't have. The ball was in her court. Knocking on the door of a girlfriend who was ignoring me looked desperate and pathetic. The Coonleys weren't home, so I suffered no loss of face. Still, my anxiety sharpened with every hour I didn't hear from Sara. She didn't call Sunday night. Neither did I, although I stared at the telephone in the kitchen, and once even lifted the receiver off its cradle, before setting it down again.

I wanted to go for a run, to take my mind off Sara, but Sunday was my rest day. Knowing when not to run was just as important—and required just as much discipline— as knowing when to run. Instead, I spent the evening in my room, re-reading old running magazines. I didn't want to watch TV with Mom and Dad and Gramps. They would see how restless I was.

While my eyes scanned a familiar story about the 1982 Boston Marathon, most of my mind was wondering why Sara hadn't called. Was it because I'd ditched her at the basement show on Friday night? Because I hadn't been able to conceal my boredom with the whole scene? I didn't share Sara's passion for music (although even I knew enough not to apply that term to the sounds produced by Rumpledforeskin). I didn't like to party, because partying prevented me from getting up early to run. I was a bore that way. And I was never going to fit into the punk rock scene, no matter how short Sara cut my hair. The punks rejected ambition and achievement. I was trying to win the state cross-country championship. A varsity letter wasn't punk rock. Maybe, just maybe, I wasn't the gaunt obsessive Sara really wanted.

Sara didn't show up for cross-country practice on Monday, so I asked Kelly and Tess if they'd seen her. They looked at each other. Just from that shared glance, I knew who, what, where, why, when and how. Two guys would have just shrugged. The Guy Code says you don't call out a player. Girls love to rat each other out for being slutty.

"Carter?" I asked.

They nodded.

That day's workout was five thousand-meter loops on our home course. We were supposed to run at race pace. I ran faster, and harder. I ran so hard Coach hollered, "Save it for the race, Ward! You're running like you've got the devil on your tail. What the hell's wrong with you?"

I didn't tell him. I hoped Kelly and Tess hadn't told anyone, either. Being the cheatee was just as shameful as being the cheater, especially for a guy. After we jogged back to school, I kept running to Sara's house, still at race pace, still in my sweats. This time, Sara answered the door. When she saw me, she jumped onto the porch and slammed the door behind her, even though she was wearing sockless slippers and a Misfits t-shirt in the stony chill of a mid-autumn afternoon.

"That was what you really always wanted, wasn't it?" I accused her. "A musician. A skinny musician. I just looked like one. Now you've got the real thing. If you can call that guy a musician."

I should have seen it coming. First, when she stepped forward to introduce herself to Carter. Next, when she pulled up his boxer shorts. She hadn't done that to spare Kelly's and Tess's sensibilities. She'd done it because she couldn't wait to get her hands on the lead singer. And she'd done it right in front of me. Then, like an idiot, I'd left the party, and left her to Carter.

Sara wouldn't look at me. She hung her head and clutched her torso against her cold, shrinking herself, making her already small body as small as her behavior.

"We weren't going to last forever," she said.

"Why not?"

"The U."

"How do you know I'm not going?" I said. "Why do you think I've been running my ass off this year? Because you wanted me to get a scholarship and go there with you. And even if I don't, it's only a hundred miles away. I've got a car."

"Even if you do, your life will always be here. You'll come back here after you graduate. Maybe you'll be the track coach someday. And that's fine. That's good. You'll probably be happy and successful here. Like you always say, you can be a runner anywhere there's roads."

"And where do you plan to go?"

"Somewhere else. New York, Chicago, Boston. I want to go grad school after the U. My parents don't want me to stay here. Now that Empire's gone, there's not going to be anything left for anyone—not just autoworkers."

"Some people don't believe in quitting when things get tough," I said. "You wouldn't know about that. You've never pushed yourself. You just jogged along with the pack."

"You don't have to be mean."

Sara's eyes and mouth popped open, and her face was suddenly the face of a scolded child, on the verge of tears. She could change her expression so quickly I wondered if she might have a future as an actress, instead of merely a member of the pit orchestra. It was a face that, in the past, would have drawn me to hug her. Now I just folded my arms. I had created that face, by attacking her most sensitive spot: her fear that she had no talents, and no drive to develop any.

"It's not going to make a difference how I act now," I said. "You've made up your mind. I just wish you'd told me before you went with that other guy." I couldn't say Carter's name. "You made us both look bad. Don't ask me if we can be friends, either."

"I'm not," she said. "But I do hope you can win the state championship."

"Mmm hmm. You weren't at practice today, so I guess you quit the team. You don't need us anymore, and we don't need you. You've got a sport on your application, and you're not going to get us any points."

"I always told you you're the one who can do something great, not me."

"That's because you won't commit to anyone, anything, or any place…and I will."

Sara rubbed her arms, to smooth out the gooseflesh. Suddenly, she stopped. I thought she was about to reach out towards me, so I stepped backwards off the porch, onto the walkway. Then I turned around and started running. Halfway to the corner, I heard the storm door slam, but I didn't look back.

Eighteen

All that week, my mother saw that I was out of sorts, but she never asked about Sara. The two of them had never had much to say to each other. My parents didn't even own a stereo. Mom had once referred to Sara as "kind of a hippie." That was her generation's way of calling someone flaky and unconventional. She had been right, even though punk rocker had replaced hippie as the identity of choice for countercultural types. I doubted Sara would go that far, though. She was too preoccupied with her resumé to drop out. I hadn't been able to turn her into an athlete. Carter wouldn't turn her into a punk rock moll. Sara had too much of a sense of who she was and what she wanted to subsume herself in any guy's passion. She was dabbling with a "musician," the way she'd dabbled with a runner. When it was time to go to the U, she would leave Carter behind in Wenniway…if they were even still together.

I'm pretty solitary and introverted, one reason running suits me so well. Running is a mental as well as a physical challenge. Being a runt isn't enough: you have to be a runt who's really into his own head. My parents were used to me hiding in my room, reading running magazines. The week after Sara and I broke up that was all I did. They say success is the best revenge, so I flipped through photo after photo of my heroes crossing finish lines with their arms raised in victory: Sebastian Coe at the Moscow Olympics, his joyful grimace looking as though his face had been pressed flat in a wind tunnel; Bill Rodgers waving his wool cap at the finish of a cold, rainy

Boston Marathon; and Steve Scott in his Sub-4 Running Club singlet, lifting an index finger as he set the American record in the mile. That was how I would commemorate my victory at the state meet in Auburn. Sara would be—well, she wouldn't be sorry, because she'd told me she wanted me to win. I was kind of sorry that she wouldn't be sorry, and even sorrier that our breakup, in the weeks before a big race, was fueling my motivation to win. Sara didn't deserve the credit.

Even though my mom knew how I felt, and why, and I knew she knew how I felt, and why, all she could talk about that week was…pantyhose.

"It's going to be cold at your race next weekend," she said one night at supper. "Maybe in the thirties. How do you run in that cold weather?"

"We wear long-sleeved t-shirts underneath our singlets," I explained.

"That keeps you warm, but what about your legs?"

"Our legs are always moving."

"Don't you get gooseflesh? Maybe you should wear pantyhose. That's how women keep their legs warm in the winter."

"Pantyhose!" my father exclaimed. "Men do not wear pantyhose. Especially not men who play sports."

Gramps nodded vigorously. It was one of the few times he'd participated in dining-room table discussion since we'd moved in.

"What about Joe Namath?" my mother pointed out.

"That was for a TV ad," Dad responded. "And he said right out front that he didn't wear pantyhose."

"But he *was* wearing them," Mom said. "They're warm, and they're flexible. They seem like they'd be perfect for running."

"Kevin would be a laughingstock." My father skimmed the melted cheese of his twice-baked potato and slurped it off his fork. He always ate twice-baked potatoes that way.

"Not if he wins. If he wins, all the other boys will wear pantyhose. And Kevin's been winning all his races this year. He could start a trend. The boys would be more comfortable. They might run faster if they were comfortable."

"I'm not wearing pantyhose," I declared.

"But you'd be so much warmer."

"That's a reason not to wear pantyhose. Cross country isn't supposed to be comfortable. It's about going out there in the cold and the mud and overcoming the elements. If I wanted to be comfortable, I'd stay home and listen to music."

"Well, I hope you don't get frostbite and have to have your legs amputated."

"I don't think that's ever happened in the history of cross country," I said. "If it was that cold, they'd cancel the race. You only notice the cold for the first mile, anyway."

On the morning of the sectional meet—the qualifying race for the state championship—at a county park in Grand Banks, the temperature was thirty-three degrees. We all waited until the last possible moment to strip for the start. Then a hundred runners lined up along the chalk stripe like a flock of pin-limbed birds, our legs flushing as warming blood flowed to the skin. Mercifully, the starter didn't give a speech. He just shouted, "Runners set!" then lifted his pistol and pulled the trigger, bursting a blank in the freezing air. As the field strung out on the sodden grass, I rushed to the front of the pack, intending to claim the narrow passage into the woods. Once I stepped across the threshold of the trees, alone in the lead, my run was transformed from cross country to...orienteering. The night before, rain and hail had fallen on Grand Banks. The heavy-bellied clouds above our heads were still pregnant with storms, ready to dissolve into sleet at any moment. I was running in spikes, for traction in the softened earth. When I splashed through the first puddle, needling water soaked through my thin soles and uppers. An eruption of mud streaked my calves. Maybe my mother had been right. Maybe I was going to get frostbite and lose my feet. Maybe I should have swallowed my masculine pride and worn pantyhose.

Through gaps in the woodland crown, I glanced up at the clouds. Their undersides were mingled shades of oatmeal, smoke, lint, and gunpowder. I hoped they could wait the sixteen minutes it was going to take me to finish this race to discharge their ballast. They couldn't. I had not even run a mile when the storm began. In the woods, the rain was a patter, but once I emerged from the trees for the first loop around the picnic grounds, it felt like someone flinging slush into my face, over and over again. No matter how painful and unpleasant this was, it was just as painful and unpleasant for every other runner. Heading into the woods the second time, I still led. Coach stood beside the fading white stripe wearing a rain poncho, holding a golf umbrella, shouting, "Thirty yards!" I was that far ahead of my nearest rival. On my next trip through the woods, with the trail awash in rain, the mud was thinner, more yielding. It splashed my shorts. I almost slipped and fell trying to negotiate a tight turn around a maple tree at eleven miles an hour. (Damn maple trees: Sara had hidden at a maple syrup festival to avoid facing me after making out with Carter.) Back on the picnic grounds, the lime stripe marking the course had washed away. A man in a poncho swung his arm to show me where to turn, like a cop directing traffic. The spongy grass could not absorb the rain. I stepped in a puddle up to my bony ankle. But I felt stronger than the storm. I saw all the movies about running, just like I read all the books and magazines. In the last scene of *Gallipoli*, as the sprinter is about to leave his trench to attack the enemy, he tells himself, "What are your legs? Springs. How fast are you going to run? Faster than a leopard." Unfortunately, his run is ended by a bullet to the heart. I repeated his encouragement to myself. My legs were like springs. I was going to run faster than a leopard. When I finally looked over my shoulder, in the finishing chute, the second-place runner was fifty yards behind me.

Dad left for the cabin early on a Monday morning, the day before deer season began. I saw him off before I started my run.

"I'll see you on Saturday at the state meet," he promised. "If you're gonna win, I want to be there."

"Is Uncle Dick going to the cabin?"

"Yeah, but he's driving up on his own because he's going to stay all weekend. He can do that now."

Uncle Dick and Aunt Sandy had recently separated, after twenty years of marriage, and ten years of barely speaking to one another.

"I'll be back Friday," Dad continued. "Your mom and I are going to drive to Auburn to watch you run."

My father had never attended one of my cross-country races: he was either working, or just getting off work, or out on a job with Uncle Dick. This time, his only excuse was deer season.

"What if you don't get your deer by then? This may be your last chance."

Dad planned to sell the cabin so we could renovate the house for Gramps. He wanted to add a walk-in bathtub, ramps leading to the front and back doors, and a sliding chair on the basement staircase, so Gramps could again operate his model railroad. Dad and Dick could install it all, but they had to buy the materials.

"There's been years I didn't get a deer," Dad said. "There'll be other years to go huntin.' Maybe not up there, but around here. But this is the only year you're going to win the state cross-country championship, right?"

"If I am gonna win, it'll be this year."

Jeez, that was a lot of pressure. If I didn't win, I hoped he at least got his deer. And if he didn't get his deer, I hoped I won.

My father returned from the cabin on Thursday afternoon, a day earlier than expected. I had just gotten home from practice when his car rolled into the driveway, without a deer across the trunk.

"I thought you weren't coming home until tomorrow," I said.

Dad pantomimed lifting a bottle to his lips.

"Too much drinking going on up there. Your uncle and I went through a case of Keystone. I decided to leave while I was still sober, to make sure I got back here in time."

Dad went inside to talk to Gramps, who was enthroned as usual in front of the television. I went to my room, to puzzle out algebraic equations for math class. From my end of the hallway, I couldn't hear everything Dad and Gramps were saying, but I did catch the few times Gramps raised his voice: "*My* name is on the deed"; "You're damn right we need the money down here"; "We're not going to hang onto something we use only one or two weeks a year now"; "Your brother has never been able to get along with anyone: not his foreman, not his wife, not you." That was all I heard. I didn't ask for any details. I had a race to think about.

All that season, I had lost to only one runner: Craig, from Frontenac Catholic Central. He would be at the state meet, of course. His school was the defending champion, and he had won his own sectional race, Coach told me. On the pre-dawn bus ride to Auburn, Coach and I talked about how to beat him. The bus was nearly empty because only the varsity seven went to state. On most trips, we also traveled with the JV and the girls' team, but the girls hadn't qualified. So Coach and I sat on adjoining benches. He rested his chin on the seat back and stared at me.

"When you ran against him at the Invitational, you went out too fast, because you didn't think anyone could catch you," Coach said. "Well, he caught you. You're going to have to run more conservatively this time. Just go with him from the start and make your move in the last half mile."

"How fast did he run at sectionals?"

"Fifteen, twenty-nine."

That made me nervous. I had only run fifteen, forty-three. Coach pointed out that Craig had run his race on a golf course, and that it hadn't rained in Frontenac that morning. Given the course, and the weather, my time was as good or better.

When we got off the bus and began our warm-up jog around the Arb, I looked everywhere for a bus with FRONTENAC CATHOLIC CENTRAL lettered on the side. I wondered whether Craig was searching for the Wenniway Central bus, or whether, having vanquished me at the Invitational, he wasn't thinking about me at all. If not, I could use that to my advantage, hang back just a little bit, then surprise him with my kick. When two runners are equally matched, the one who is better prepared, strategically and psychologically, usually wins.

I never located the bus. I didn't see Craig until we lined up at the starting stripe. It was cold again: thirty-five degrees. As I hugged myself and jogged in place, I looked among the spectators' faces, hoping to spot my parents. (I also examined the legs of my competitors: nobody was wearing pantyhose.)

"Runners set," the starter cried.

We leaned into our crouches—knees bent, hands balled, a hundred or so life-sized models for running trophies. When the gun went off, I didn't spring. I ran just fast enough to avoid getting boxed in by legs or elbows as the stampeding field collapsed from a rank to a file. I looked for Craig's black jersey: he was already pulling away from the rest of the runners. I rushed forward and fell in right behind Craig, following Coach's instructions not to set the pace. I was jogging casually, painlessly. That was how the first mile of the state meet was supposed to feel: it was the run-up to the race's real challenge, the Mother of All Hills—another reason Coach's strategy was so smart. The Arb needed to be taken slowly. We passed the first mile in five twenty. I was not alone with Craig. We were part of a four-man lead pack, alongside a runner in a red singlet and another in a blue singlet. I couldn't identify their schools. Since I didn't recognize them, I assumed they weren't from my part of the state.

The Mother of All Hills was longer and steeper than Mount Trashmore. As we began the ascent, my only goal was to hang with the lead pack until we reached the top. Then I would make a move on the ridge. That might drop the blue jersey or the red jersey. Craig would be with me to the finish. As they say in the army, "Everyone has a plan, until the shooting starts." Halfway up the hill, the red singlet pushed between me and Craig, digging hard for the summit. He was going *now*. I wondered if he was from one of those schools by the Big Lake, where the runners trained on sand dunes. I had to go with him. I couldn't wait and chase him down on tired legs. The blue singlet could not keep up, so at the top of the Mother, at the mid-point of the race, three of us were contending for the state championship. I abandoned my strategy of trying to break the race open there on the ridge. Coach had trained us to attack hills with short, quick bursts, so we didn't wear our-selves out by taking long strides. I had never attacked a hill *that* hard, though. Now I just wanted to keep up with these guys, and hope I had the fastest sprint left in my legs. I wanted to be the last survivor. I glanced at my watch. Nine minutes since the gun. Six and a half to go. That doesn't sound like a long time, but imagine you're holding your breath in a swimming pool and someone lowers a laminated sign that reads SIX MORE MINUTES. Or imagine the front wheel of a motorcycle is crushing your chest, and a friend says, "I'll have this thing off you in six minutes." I hoped I could endure this pain as long as those two other guys, if they were suffering as badly as I was. You never know what's happening inside another runner's head. I was afraid that if I turned to examine their faces for distress, they would see the distress on my own. At that moment, trapped within this effort, a part of me wished I were anyone but myself, and anywhere else but the Arb. Another part felt a sense of superiority to the common spectators, and to those who hadn't even made it to the sidelines but were still at home listening to music in their pajamas (as I imagined Sara was), because I had willed myself into a state of exhaustion that none of them could imagine. At the two-mile mark, just before the yellow flag signaling us to turn right, down a hill, I heard my father's voice, distinct among the shouts of encouragement from the parents and teammates and coaches.

"C'mon, Kevin!" he cried. "Let's go, buddy. Just a mile to go. You're hanging tough."

I had expected to see my father at the finish line. Instead, he was stationed at the point in the race where I needed his encouragement the most. Had Coach told him to stand at mile two? A surge of gratitude lightened my fatigue. Just a mile. I could run another mile. But I had to run it faster than Craig. We raced down the access road, our steps swishing in the gravel, our spikes flinging up dirt and pebbles. At the foot of the slope was a red flag, indicating a left turn into the meadow, where one of us would cross the finish line first. Rounding the pole, I accelerated, hoping to catch my rivals by surprise. For a moment, I took the lead; then I saw red out of the corner of my eye. Ahead of us lay three hundred yards of grass, the last three hundred yards of my high school cross-country career, the three hundred yards separating me from a state championship. I felt queasy, but I had to run through my qualms even if it meant I upchucked in the chute. I sprinted. I ran so hard that black curtains descended over my peripheral vision. I was running myself half-blind. I couldn't see the red jersey. I could only see ahead to the chute, and victory. At two hundred yards, there was no one ahead of me. At one hundred yards. At fifty. And then I was diving into the chute, tumbling into the grass, settling on my side. Reclining on the ground, I watched the red singlet jog to a halt ahead of me. I finally felt the pain of my effort, the nausea and the knives between my ribs. I had never run so hard, not even in the Dog Days 10K, and I had never hurt more. Unfamiliar faces hovered over me—old faces, beneath bald heads. Race marshals.

"Can you stand up, son?"

Old hands—speckled, veiny hands—guided me beneath the ropes, settling me in the grass beside the chute. More runners finished. Craig, Dave, then Tim. Coach was by my side now. My breathing was slowing. The sickness was subsiding. Still, I wasn't ready to stand up.

"You ran a great race, Ward," Coach said.

But had I won?

"That was the greatest race a Wenniway Central Warrior has ever run."

I pressed my hands into the crisp grass, pushing myself upright. I was cold. I wanted to find my sweats, and my parents.

"Who won?" I asked Coach.

"It came down to the lean."

So, he had won. All that pain, for second place.

"You've got nothing to be ashamed of. You couldn't have run any harder. He just leaned a little earlier than you did."

I might have leaned earlier if I'd known he was there. He must have come up behind me, in my temporary blind spot. Leaning: that was one aspect of racing we hadn't practiced. We had run up hills, we had run ten miles, we had raced intervals through the woods, but we hadn't leaned. Only sprinters were supposed to win races with their chests. And now I had been out-leaned for a state title. The guy in the red singlet would forever be listed as a champion, while the name Kevin Ward would be...forgotten.

I did receive a second-place trophy—silver-plated. The winner's trophy was gold. At the awards ceremony, my mother snapped a photo with her pocket Kodak of the president of the state cross-country association handing me my consolation prize. I smiled, not for the trophy, but for the family photo album. I didn't want to be remembered as a sore loser. Wenniway Central got a trophy, too, for finishing third in the team competition: Dave came in eleventh, Tim twelfth.

After the flags had been pulled out of the grass, my parents offered to take me to breakfast in Auburn. I'd gone to breakfast in Auburn after last year's state meet. At Waldo's, where Sara and Mr. Coonley sold me on running for the U. I didn't want to go to breakfast in Auburn again. I didn't want to be in Auburn, at that moment, or maybe any other moment. I told my parents I had no appetite, which was true. I still felt sick from the race. I just wanted to ride back to Wenniway on the team bus.

"Can you make pot roast for supper, though?" I asked. "I'll probably feel better by then."

"You've never asked for pot roast," Mom said. "If you want pot roast, I'll make pot roast."

"Well, it's weird. Last week, Coach sent us on a ten-mile run, and toward the end, I really wanted pot roast,

Fritos, and a chocolate shake from Burger King. I'm not gonna have to race again until next year, so I guess I can eat all that stuff."

(Someone could make a lot of money off runners by opening a restaurant called the Long Run Café, serving the junk food we crave to replace the fat, salt and sugar we lose over ten or twelve or fifteen miles.)

The next morning, the *Star* ran a photo of the finish, on page five of the sports section. I was captured in mid-fall—a fall I didn't even remember. My palms were splayed to cushion myself, my eyes squeezed shut, and my chin lifted. Beside me, the red singlet (as I knew him, for the photo was in black and white) looked like an astronaut just off the launch paid, with gravity times three dragging down his features. A grimace exposed his teeth and gums. He'd been hurting just as much as I was. I wouldn't have minded such an unflattering photo if it had shown me winning.

When I got home from school that Monday—early, because there was no cross-country practice—Dad was sitting on the front porch, smoking a cigarette and reading the classifieds from the Sunday *Star*. The paper was open to the Help Wanted ads, circled and underlined in red ink.

"I thought you had a job with Uncle Dick," I said.

Dad folded the newspaper. He took another drag on his cigarette. Mom did not allow him to smoke inside the house. It was unusual to see him smoking anywhere, since he'd vowed to quit. Usually, he only smoked at Pete's, but of course, Pete's was now closed.

"I'm going to give you some business advice," Dad said. "Never take a job with a family member. You may end up losing both."

Then, Dad told me the whole story of why he was looking for work. On the trip Up North, he had explained to Uncle Dick that he planned to sell the cabin, to pay for making

175

Gramps' house wheelchair friendly. Gramps, he said, had approved the sale. It didn't seem like a big deal: now that their kids were grown, or almost, they only used the cabin a few weekends each summer, and one week during deer season. It turned out to be a big deal to Uncle Dick, though.

Dad waited until late in the week to bring up the subject, after they were both sick of hunting and drinking. As he described the scene, they were sitting on the porch, wearing their camouflage jumpsuits against the chill, staring at the lake, buzzed on Keystone. Dad had hoped the beer would relax them both, but drinking didn't relax my uncle. It made him hostile. Nothing relaxed Uncle Dick.

"He said, 'G-D it, Gary, that house belongs to the *entire* family,'" Dad said, paraphrasing Uncle Dick's language out of respect for the Lord's name. "Then he told me I couldn't deal with Dad behind his back. He said, 'You got a grandkid. I'm gonna have grandkids. They should get the same summers that we had, and our kids had.' And he said I wouldn't need the money if I hadn't quit Empire. The last thing he told me was, 'I took you on to help you out, but I guess now you're not going to need the money—or the work.'"

After the argument, Dad packed up the car and drove back to Wenniway. That's why he came home on Thursday, instead of Friday as he'd originally planned. And that had been the subject of his heated conversation with Gramps in the living room. A year before, Dad had been on the outs with Gramps, because Dad had blamed the union for Empire's decision to abandon Wenniway. Now, Uncle Dick was on the outs with Gramps, because he had fired my father from his home renovation crew. Such were the shifting alliances of a family, or at least the shifting favor of my grandfather. Gramps had recovered enough from the stroke to regain his irascibility.

"I think he was angrier that I hadn't talked to him about it than he was that we were planning to do it," Dad said.

"But I *was* talking to him about it. If he had said, 'Hey, let's keep the cabin and I'll chip in on expanses for the house,' maybe I would have changed my mind. But now that he fired me, we're definitely going to have to sell it."

Dad picked up the folded newspaper and waved it at me.

"There's not a lot in here for a guy like me. Warehouse. Deliveries. I'm gonna have to ask around. Everyone knows the best jobs aren't advertised in the paper. And you know I'm not the only laid-off autoworker looking for work around here. A year ago, I was thinking about retirement. Now I gotta think about starting over."

Dad set the newspaper on the steps.

"I shouldn't have gone to work with your uncle in the first place," he said. "It's not just the family thing. He's just never worked well with other people. He never really got along with your aunt. I'm kind of amazed they made it twenty years. The last half, they would come to family dinners and just stand on opposite sides of the room, wouldn't even look at each other."

I remembered those dinners, and I remembered my cousin Jimmy saying he wished his parents would just go ahead and get divorced.

"Dick wants everyone to think he quit Empire because he's this independent free spirit who couldn't stand being shackled to an assembly line, but that's not exactly why he left," Dad went on. "He got into it with a foreman and threw a punch at him. You can call a foreman every dirty so-and-so name in the book, and your union steward will stand up for you, but once you throw a punch, that's it. Dick got fired. That's when he joined the Builders' Union. I guess he couldn't get along with the Builders' Union either, so he went to work for himself. He's where he should be in life now: living alone and working alone."

Dad ground out his cigarette on the concrete and went inside the house. I picked up the newspaper and looked through the want ads myself. If Dad wasn't working any-more, someone in this house had to. United Parcel Service was hiring package handlers for the Christmas rush. Indoor track didn't start until after the New Year, so I'd have time to work there after school. I borrowed the car keys from Mom, drove to the big UPS warehouse, somewhere be-tween the city limits and the countryside, and filled out an application. If UPS needed bodies so badly it was advertis-ing in the *Star*, maybe they'd even hire a little guy like me.

Coach taught my sixth period Government and Civ-ics class. One afternoon, the week after the state meet, he asked me to stay after school. It was always strange seeing Coach in any outfit other than a warmup suit. He hadn't really figured out how to dress as anything but a jock. That day, he wore Dockers a size too wide for his winnowed waist, a burgundy tartan shirt, and a black ribbed sweat-er vest. He always wore running shoes. "You never knew when you might have to make a get-away," he said. But really, Coach was a running bum who happened to hold a full-time job.

"Have you thought about where you want to take your running next?" Coach asked point blank, after I sat down next to his desk. "'Cause you're the best runner I've ever met—and that includes guys I went to college with. You could run Division I—*high* Division I."

For the first time, I told Coach about the letter I'd sent to Coach Harry Deane at the U, and the time goals he'd mailed me in response. I had never discussed my ambi-tions with Coach before. I wasn't sure they were possible. If they weren't, I didn't want to hear him tell me so. That would have convinced me they *were* impossible. But now that I'd nearly won the state cross-country championship, and Coach was telling me I could run a high D-I, maybe a 4:06 mile *was* possible.

"That's faster than I ever ran in college, but I went to Northern," Coach said. "My PR was 4:12. You could run at Northern for sure. My old coach is still there. I can call him tomorrow. It's not high D-I, though."

"I really want to go to the U," I told Coach. "Not just cause it's high D-I. It's only a hundred miles away. I need to stay close to my family. My dad's been having a tough time since Empire shut down. My grandfather had a stroke and we moved into his house to help him get around. The U's the only state school that can offer me a full scholarship. I'm gonna need that now that my dad's not working."

"The U's not the only school that could offer you a full scholarship," Coach said. "There're schools in Colorado, California, Wisconsin."

I tried to imagine wearing the uniform of a state I'd never visited. Part of the attraction of running for the U was showing the rest of the conference—the rest of the country, if I could get to NCAAs—how tough our state was. Our factories were closing, our unemployment rate was 15 percent, the magazines were calling us the buckle of the Rust Belt, but we endured. There was no better way to demonstrate that than winning endurance races. Plus, my dad had turned down a lot of money to not move to Tennessee because he'd wanted to stay close to me, my mom, Gramps, my sister and my nephew. Why would I take a lot of money to leave them? When I told Coach all this, he said, "I admire your devotion to your family. I really do. But I want to see you take your running as far as it can go. You think about Wiz Williams"—Dean "The Wiz" Williams was a basketball star who'd won a state championship for Central, and now played in the NBA. "The Wiz couldn't play for the Dallas Mavericks here in Wenniway. He couldn't play for any NBA team in Wenniway. Maybe he could have played for Frontenac, but you don't always get to choose in pro sports. You have to go where you're drafted. If you want to be the best you can be, you don't always get to choose. He's making six figures now, and he's taking care of his family. He bought his mom a house, and he's putting his sister through nursing school."

"That's pro basketball," I said. "There's only so many places you can play pro basketball, but you can run anywhere there's a road. Look at Bill Rodgers."

Coach sighed. He propped up the third-place plaque from the state cross-country meet, which he was displaying on his desk until it could be mounted in the school's trophy case.

"There's only one Bill Rodgers," he said. "And he didn't win all those marathons by himself. He trained with a lot of good runners in Boston. That's a big city. I'd hate to see you end up like those Wheel City guys, throwing everything away so maybe—maybe!—you can run in the Olympic Marathon Trials. So we'll work on getting you to the U. I want you to take it easy between now and New Year's. One run a day. You probably won't, but I have to say it anyway. Then, when indoor track starts, we'll go after that mile time."

NINETEEN

Hanging from the weave of the cyclone fence surrounding Empire Body was a sign with this slogan: CLARE CONSTRUCTION: DEMOLITION MEANS PROGRESS. I saw it every afternoon as I sped down the backstretch of the stadium track, running 400s, 800s, mile repeats, ladders of 200-400-800-1600-800-400-200. And every afternoon, I saw a little less of Empire Body, as backhoes nibbled away at its corrugated skin, and trains hauled equipment to still-functioning plants elsewhere in the Empire universe.

"That sign is…Orwellian," Tim commented one day, as we were stretching on the track before practice.

"What are you talking about?" Dave asked him.

"We're reading this book in English class, *Nineteen Eighty-Four*, by George Orwell. It's about this dictator called Big Brother who tells people that everything is the opposite of what it actually is, so they'll feel good about it and do what he says. Like, he'll say, 'War Is Peace,' so people will want to go to war. Or he'll say 'Freedom Is Slavery,' so they won't want to be free. That's what that sign is doing: trying to make you think Wenniway is progressing because they're tearing down the auto plants."

After practice, I crossed the street and peered through the fence, at what was now a demolition site. An outer wall had been peeled away, exposing the employee locker room, where my dad had stored his lunchbox, and, in the fall and winter, his mackinaw. Some of the locker doors had fallen open, others had fallen off, others still bore the personal imprints of men who would never open them again: stickers for STP Motor Oil, the Frontenac Foxes, a candidate for Local 151 president, WWAY radio. Vandals had broken in and spray-painted EMPIRE SUCKS across the bank of lockers. Tearing down the plant didn't look like progress to me, unless Empire intended to build a new one here, but maybe the company and the city had a plan they hadn't told anyone about yet.

After his falling out with Uncle Dick, my dad put in applications at a few machine shops and auto parts suppliers, some as far away as Grand Banks, sixty miles from Wenniway. For the time being, though, he was working behind the meat counter at Big Country Supermarket. One of his old high school classmates and Elks Lodge brothers, Ray Rink, was the meat manager. Dad wasn't thrilled about wearing a paper hat, an apron, and a name tag, or being recognized by people from church buying their Sunday pot roasts. Nor was he thrilled about working thirty hours a week for five dollars an hour—less than a quarter of what he'd earned at Empire—but it was just enough time to qualify him for the store's health insurance plan. That alone made tolerable the indignities of his new job as "Sam the Butcher," as he called himself, after Alice's boyfriend on *The Brady Bunch*. No longer was the household dependent on my mother for health insurance. Her job at the hospital paid more than his job at the supermarket, but with his Empire pension, he was bringing more money into the household, so he could feel like the provider. If my mother got too sick to work, her doctor bills would be taken care of. With his new free time, Dad was also restoring a 1951 Marquette for a car collector he knew at the Elks. That would bring in some cash, too. I was working part time at UPS. They *had* hired a little guy to buck packages during the Christmas rush. I guess they'd been impressed by my hustle, because they offered me four three-hour shifts a week, from five to eight in the evening. My dad, of all people, asked whether I really wanted the job. Dad, who loved to brag that he started working at age twelve—as a paperboy, a golf caddy, delivering groceries on his bike—and hired into the shop when he was eighteen.

"You sure it's not going to interfere with your running?" he asked anxiously. "Or your homework? You gotta do both if you want to get a scholarship."

"It'll help my running," I said. "I gotta get flats and spikes for outdoor track. That's expensive. The guys at The Athlete's Foot told me they jack up the prices on purpose so people will think they're getting a luxury item."

I didn't tell Dad that I couldn't ask him for the money. I knew he didn't want to hear that.

"I thought running was supposed to be the cheap sport. I remember the guy from Ethiopia who ran the marathon barefoot. Your mom and I watched him on TV."

"It was cheap," I said, "until it got popular."

In the spring of senior year, my schedule looked like this: 6 a.m. to 6:30 a.m.- morning run; 7:50 a.m. to 1:50 p.m.- school; 2 p.m. to 3:30 p.m.- track practice; 5 p.m. to 8 p.m.- work; 8:30 p.m. to 10:30 p.m.- homework. Honestly, though, after running intervals and lifting boxes onto trucks, I was usually too tired to do homework. During first period, I begged Dave to let me copy the answers to our algebra assignments. I had to keep my grade point average above 3.0 to get a scholarship. The U wasn't going to let me in with grades lower than that, no matter how fast I ran. Dave always let me, and he always joked, "Hey, Ward, since I'm giving you the answers, you have to give me the secret to running as fast as you do." Dave had stopped calling me Buzz and started calling me Ward again, since I'd grown my hair back to its normal length after Sara dumped me. I always told him, "If you ran that fast, you'd be too tired to do math homework."

If my life were a *Rocky* movie, that spring track season would have been the training montage. Coach came up with a "4:06 Mile Plan." He wanted it as badly as I did. I ran all the workouts the other milers ran, and then I ran more. Coach asked me to cut down my morning runs to half an hour, so I would be fresh for intense running in the afternoons. We were training for speed, not distance. The purpose of intervals, as we called sprints on the track, was to run faster than race pace, so that racing felt easy. We ran a lot of quarter miles. We ran them ten at a time, with a minute's rest in between. And we ran them as fast as Coach ordered us.

"Every one of these in 60 seconds, Ward," Coach ordered me, "or you're going to keep running them until you run ten that fast."

I ran every quarter mile in a minute, ending each lap in pinched pain. If I could run another three laps that fast, I'd be a four-minute miler. That seemed impossible. Even the next quarter seemed impossible. We ran 200-meter sprints, with 30 seconds in between, to get used to kicking. And I ran a single 1000-meter workout, at my 4:06 pace, to teach me not to go out too fast. Afterwards, Coach had me run 150s, alternating sprinting and cruising, so I would learn how to change speeds during a race. Twice, Coach drove me out to Mount Trashmore on a Saturday. There are no hills on a track, but "we need to strengthen your legs." He also asked me to lift weights, in the dank, cinder-block-walled training room that belonged to the football team in the fall and the basketball team in the winter.

"I'm lifting plenty of weight at UPS," I protested.

I had always hated weightlifting. It was oppressive. Running was liberating. Now I hated weightlifting even more because it reminded me of my job.

"We've got to work certain arm muscles. You'll need that power when you're sprinting in the stretch."

So, I bench pressed after practice. Coach spotted me, after pulling off plates left behind by real athletes, who could bench 250 or 300 pounds.

In our first meet of the season, against South, I won in 4:21, nearly a hundred yards ahead of the second-place finisher. Fifteen seconds short of what I needed. The closer I got to my goal, the harder won was each tick of the clock. I ran 4:17 against East Wenniway. Then, at an invitational in Grand Banks, I finally had some competition, racing another runner for three laps, until I dropped him on the backstretch and finished in 4:12—the fastest time in the state that season. It was even listed, in agate type, in the sports section of the Frontenac newspaper. I bought a copy from a box outside the old main gate at Empire Body. The box was still stocked every morning, even though the plant was disappearing, and autoworkers no longer streamed through the gate.

Our final dual meet of the season was against Oak Rapids, one of the country schools in our conference. I could make a run at 4:06, because I was going to win, even if I bonked on the last lap. That morning, after awakening to the chirping alarm on my digital watch, I hit start on the stopwatch and let it run for four minutes and six seconds, imagining myself racing as the digits turned over, and hitting the finish line the moment my thumb pressed stop. On my walk to school, I imagined the race again, and throughout all the classes I had to endure before the race, I wrote "Kevin Ward: 4:06" in my notebooks. I might have tattooed it on myself if I'd had a needle and ink.

"Go for it," Coach said, when I told him my plan. "You can run for time today. You're gonna have to run for points at sectional and state."

I knew I could run fast enough for 1,000 meters. I just needed to run that fast for another 600. I lined up by the rail, and never saw another runner after the gun.

"Sixty-two!" Coach shouted at the first lap. I was amazed to have learned my body so well that I could race a lap to the precise second. I did it again on the second lap, passing the half in 2:03, and on the third lap, which went in 3:05. I had carried my speed half a lap beyond my training. If I sprinted in the last 200, I'd have it!

How many terms are there for what happened to me on that final lap? I rigged up. I bonked. The bear jumped on my back. Suddenly, I felt as weak and helpless as on that day I'd tried to beat Joaquin in cross country. My heavy legs stopped running the race my mind had imagined. Not even the flailing of my weight-room toned arms could propel me faster. With half a lap left, I realized I wasn't going to make it. Instead of attempting a futile sprint to the finish, I jogged. No use burning myself out before the championship races to come. I won, but in 4:15—a step back from my state-best time.

When my dad asked me about the race at supper that night, I told him only, "I won." That wasn't news; it wasn't the result we were both thinking about, either. I felt I'd let him down by not running fast enough to win a full scholarship to the U. He felt he'd let me down by putting me in a position where I had to run that fast. I didn't tell him my winning time. It didn't feel like a victory. Now I only had two races left to do it: sectionals, and state. The Wenniway Central Warriors Boys Track Team had won every meet we'd entered that season. We didn't win just because of my points in the 1600 and the 3200. James Harris was the number one sprinter in the state, undefeated in the 100 meters. Donnell Taylor was one of the longest jumpers. We won our sectional meet (where I once again ran 4:12) to qualify for state, which would be run that year in the stadium of Frontenac State University. The meet was on a Saturday morning. That Thursday, after our final workout of the season, Coach gathered the entire team on the football field, and told us why we were going to win the state championship.

"You guys are the greatest track team I've ever coached," he shouted. Whenever he addressed the team, Coach shouted over our heads. He didn't like to make eye contact, because he wanted us to feel like he was talking to all of us, not singling out an individual. "You may be one of the greatest high school track teams in the history of this state. There may never be another team like you guys, and I'm gonna tell you why. Do you remember when some of you guys were in second or third grade, and your moms and dads said, 'Hey, you're not gonna be able to walk to school anymore? You're gonna have to get on a bus and go to school in a neighborhood where the kids don't look like you?'"

The black guys nodded. They had been bused to *our* elementary school. That fall, me and all the other eight-year-old punks couldn't stop talking about how "the nigger bus" was about to invade our neighborhood. On the first day of school, four of us lined up on a sidewalk, a block away from the school—away from the eyes of our principal, we thought—to await "the bus full of monkeys." When the bus rolled up the street, and we saw the black faces in the windows, we lifted our middle fingers, in a coordinated salute, then ran between two houses and jumped a fence into the cow pasture of the city's last working dairy farm. We did this every morning the first week of school. On Friday, the bus stopped. A short, round woman, her red face over-ripe with anger, emerged from the folding doors, shouting, "If you kids do that one more time, I'm gonna take down your names and call your parents!" That was the fastest I ran until I joined the junior high school track team.

We were afraid, of course. The stories of racial strife at Wenniway Central had filtered down to the elementary school level, through the recounting of older brothers and sisters: black students took over the principal's office, and rifled through the filing cabinets, demanding that they all receive passing grades. Black girls roamed the hallways with scissors in their purses, slicing off white girls' ponytails, collecting them like scalps. There were "black" bathrooms and "white" bathrooms, not marked, as in the Jim Crow South, but understood among the students. If you stepped into the wrong one, you risked a beating. There was even a local joke about the high school: "What's black and white and black and white and black and white? The lunch line at Central." (Integration ended at the lunch line. Black kids sat with black kids and white kids sat with white kids at segregated tables. It was still that way, mostly.)

My kindergarten had been all white, but there were a dozen black kids in my second-grade class. In our horseshoe-shaped desk arrangement, which allowed Mrs. Cartwright to instantly get into any student's face, I was seated directly across from Demetrius Mitchell. Surreptitiously, I drew cartoons of him with horns and fangs, indicating his skin color with diagonal pencil strokes, like Franklin in *Peanuts*. When Mrs. Cartwright discovered my drawings during one of her "desk inspections," she tore them up and forced me to write an apology to Demetrius. Demetrius crumpled it up without reading it. But to continue Coach's speech:

"The point is, your parents put you on that bus. That didn't happen everywhere. On Saturday, we're going to Frontenac. In Frontenac, when they heard their kids were gonna have to ride buses to go to school with kids who looked different, you know what they did? Some vigilantes burned the buses. Then they went to court to stop busing. And when that didn't work, all the white families moved to the suburbs. That's why Frontenac is all black, and the suburbs are all white. Here in Wenniway, we didn't do that. We didn't burn buses, or riot, like they did in Frontenac, or Boston. We came together. Wenniway Central is a better school because of that."

This was true. By the third grade, I had gotten over my little segregationist attitudes, and started to take the black kids for granted. I didn't have any black friends because our neighborhood was all white, but I played kickball and touch football with them during recess. (They were territorial about the basketball court, since they considered basketball a black game. They only allowed one white kid to play: tall, solid Jeff Hamaker, currently the starting center on the Wenniway Central basketball team.) By the fifth grade, I was so color blind I remember being shocked when Gramps referred to The Wiz as "that colored kid." I mean, he was a pro basketball player, so of course he was black, but to the schoolchildren of Wenniway, The Wiz was such a singular idol that he transcended any categorization.

As Coach pointed out, by the time we reached Central, there were no longer black bathrooms or white bathrooms, or office takeovers, or black girls scissoring off white girls' ponytails. (That wasn't a popular hairstyle anymore; now girls teased, sprayed and sculpted their hair.) Instead of being thrown together during puberty, we'd had years to get used to each other. We were no longer trying to beat each other up, but even on the integrated track team we didn't mingle much. That was less a result of racial prejudice than of the physiological fact that black kids were sprinters, hurdlers and jumpers, while us white kids were distance runners, and required different training. They ran on the track; we formed packs for long runs through the streets of Wenniway. (We only came together in the 800, which is either the longest sprint or the shortest endurance race, depending on whether you're moving up or down in distance. Coach didn't think I was fast enough for the race, and he knew I was guaranteed points in the 1600 and the 3200, but some of the other milers ran it. So did the quarter-milers.)

"We're not just a better school, we're a better *team*," Coach continued. "Track and field rewards integration more than any other sport. You know, Frontenac Catholic Central always beats us in cross country because they're a big school with a lot of great distance runners. But they don't have sprinters. Martin Luther King High School in Frontenac has got some great sprinters, but they don't have milers. On *this* team, we've got one of the best milers in the state *and* one of the best sprinters. So guys, that means we have a chance to make a statement about what it means to be a community where all different kinds of people live and play and go to school together. I'm not trying to put pressure on you guys or make this into something bigger than it is. You've all got to run your own races on Saturday. I'm just asking each of you to do your best, but I know that if you do, we're gonna show a lot of folks from the Frontenac area what they're missing out on. Now let me hear some school spirit."

Coach raised his fist in the air.

"WENNIWAY!" he shouted.

"ALL THE WAY!" we shouted back.

"WENNIWAY!"

"ALL THE WAY!"

And then we dispersed to our separate neighborhoods—the black sprinters to the West Side, the white distance runners to the East Side, the Mexicans to Mexicantown—to reunite again on Saturday morning.

During the hour-and-a-half bus ride to Frontenac, Coach shoved Tim off my seat and sat down to talk strategy. He really wanted to tell me that there was something more important than earning a full ride to the U: winning a state championship.

"I know you've been shooting for 4:06 all season, but today's not going to be the day," he said. "You've still got six seconds to make up. This isn't going to be a time trial like you did against Oak Rapids. This is a championship race. They hardly ever break world records at the Olympics. The world records are set in races with rabbits. No rabbits today. Everyone's trying to win. I don't want you going out at a 4:06 pace and dying on the last lap. You're the best 1600 guy in the state. If you run a smart race, you'll win. Even if you don't run 4:06, I'm sure a lot of colleges are going to have a lot of opportunities for a guy like you. Even the U will offer you something—maybe not a full ride, but something."

So now I had a decision to make: take one last shot at a 4:06 mile, and a full scholarship at the U, or guarantee myself a state championship. Of course, if I managed to run a 4:06, I'd get both. But if I went out hard, and bonked, I'd get passed on the last lap, and lose both. I wasn't running against a little country school today. I was running against the fastest milers in the state. The 1600 wasn't until the midpoint of the events, so I sat in the bleachers with the rest of the distance runners to cheer on our sprinters, hurdlers, throwers and jumpers. James won the 200 meters, scoring us ten points. I was sure he'd win the 100, for another ten points. Donnell took second in the long jump, after a kid from Frontenac, for eight points. We got third in the 4x400 and 110-meter hurdles, for six points apiece.

I sidled over to Coach. He was leaning against the railing, wearing that intense but frustrated look all coaches wear, the look of wanting to control everything on the field, but not being able to participate in anything. A coach knows exactly how everything should go. The players can only mess it up. I peeked at his clipboard. He was scoring the meet. We had an 11-point lead over the second-place team, Frontenac Martin Luther King. At that moment, I heard the meet announcer over the loudspeaker: "First call for the Boys' 1600. First call for the Boys' 1600." As I pulled off my sweatshirt, I thought *I don't actually have to win this race. We've got a lead so big no one can catch us. I can go for a PR and even if I fade to four or fifth, I'll still pick up a few points. Then I can come back and win the 3200.* As I jogged in lane eight, then cut loose with a hundred-meter stride to prepare my legs for the sprint off the line, I looked up into the stands, to see whether my parents had arrived. They had. My dad usually worked Saturday mornings, since that was the busiest shopping day of the week, but he'd begged Ray for time off so he could watch me run in the state meet. That must have been humiliating for a tradesman with twenty-five years' seniority. This race, in fact, was *why* my dad was working at the grocery store. If he had transferred to Tennessee, he might be in his mobile home this morning, sleeping off a Friday overtime shift. Dad had attended half a dozen track meets this season—every afternoon he didn't have to work at the supermarket, he'd been in the bleachers, even at rival schools' tracks. This moment was why he'd turned down the transfer. He wanted to see me run. I wanted to win a state championship for my dad, but I also wanted to spare him from feeling he was unable to pay for his son's education. Against Oak Rapids, I'd held a 4:06 pace for three laps. Maybe that was preparation I'd needed to hold it for four. If Coach got mad at me—well, he wasn't going to be my coach again after today. This was the final race of my high school career.

As the dozen finalists gathered at the distance stripe— the curved starting line that ensures runners in the outer lanes will cover no more ground than runners on the rail—I saw two familiar uniforms. Craig's black Frontenac Catholic Central singlet, and the red singlet of the guy who'd out-leaned me at the state cross-country championship. I now knew his name: Eric Novak, from Palmyra, a Frontenac suburb. I had to beat the only two guys who'd beaten me all year. As we leaned forward in anticipation of the gun, everyone in the stadium stopped to watch us, except the discus throwers in the infield. The 1600 is second only in glamour to the 100—the meet's final event.

When the gun popped, I went to the lead, alone. I was the rabbit. I passed the quarter in 62 seconds, exactly as I had against Oak Rapids. Out of the corner of my eye, I saw Coach flailing his arms in the stands. He was mouthing something I couldn't hear, probably, "Too fast, Ward!" Maybe with a swear word thrown in. All the great ones ran from the front. Jim Ryun ran from the front when he broke the four-minute mile in high school. Coach wasn't one of the great ones. I had already equaled his best college time, and I was only in high school. Who was he to tell me I was running too fast? On the second lap, I held my pace, going through the half in 2:04. This was the only way I could win, I told myself. Both of those guys outsprinted me in cross-country races. Craig ran the 4x800 relay, which meant he had some speed. He was a pure middle-distance runner. I was a long-distance runner. I could not allow this race to come down to a sprint in the homestretch. That was a race I would lose. I had to burn the speed out of my rivals. That had been the point of all those morning runs, all those Saturday ten-milers: if I couldn't be the fastest runner, I had to be the runner who could hold a hard pace longer than anyone else.

Coming out of the turn on the third lap, I saw the race marshal gripping the lanyard on the little brass bell cradled atop a metal pole pounded into the infield grass. As he yanked the lanyard, I glanced at my watch: 3:07. I had never run a 59-second lap in practice, and now I was going to have to do it when my legs were exhausted. I didn't know how far Craig and Eric were behind me, but I knew they'd be sprinting. I hoped I'd built a big enough margin to hold them off.

The final lap of the state championship 1600 was the longest minute of my life. I still remember how intensely it registered with all five of my senses: the sight of my teammates jumping up and down in the bleachers—a green wave of singlets; the sound of my spikes slapping against the track; the rubbery odor of the track's sunbaked surface; the taste of perspiration on my lips; the crimping, crushing feeling of my constricted lungs. Desperately, I gasped to inhale enough air to fuel a run that was in oxygen debt and approaching oxygen bankruptcy. Running is supposed to be a non-exploitive, non-zero-sum sport, in the sense that a runner's goal is not to interfere with or inflict pain on his opponents, as in boxing, or football, or basketball. In serious racing, though, there's always a desire to make the other guy hurt, to set a pace so intense and uncomfortable that only the runner with the most fortitude and desire can survive it. Pre used to say, "Somebody may beat me, but they are going to have to bleed to do it. I'm going to work so that it's a pure guts race at the end, and if it is, I am the only one who can win it."

Going into the final turn, I could feel myself rigging—that's short for rigor mortis, the feeling when you can no longer flush the lactic acid out of your legs. My strides were longer, less coordinated, my arms reached higher. It was happening later in the race than it had happened against Oak Rapids, so I had built my stamina, but it was still happening. In the final hundred yards, I heard footsteps. I heard breathing. I didn't know whose. I pumped my arms, strengthened by those afternoons in the weight room, hoping they could provide the power I was no longer getting from my legs. I don't remember crossing the finish line. There was no tape. All of a sudden, a race marshal was running alongside me, and no one was running ahead of me. I had won. I was the state 1600-meter champion. I didn't raise my arms in victory. Craig clapped me on the shoulder. As we shook sweaty hands, I thought, *This time I broke you.* And then I thought, *But how fast?* I knew it wasn't 4:06. I had felt myself slowing down on the final lap. Maybe it was just fast enough for Coach Harry Deane to make an exception for his state's high school champion.

"And the winner of the Boys' 1600 is Kevin Ward of Wenniway Central," I heard over the loudspeaker, "in a time of four minutes and eleven seconds."

Four minutes and eleven seconds. Not fast enough for a full scholarship at the U. Only a tick faster than my state-best time that year. For all my efforts, I had made only a single second of progress, the smallest amount measurable. I looked into the bleachers to see my parents jumping up and down, hugging each other. My teammates poured out of the bleachers and surrounded me, pounding my back, shaking my hands, just as we had done for James when he'd won the 200. I was a state champion. I had finally won a race that mattered, not just for myself, but for my school, and my hometown. Only Coach looked disappointed.

"You went for it, didn't you?" he said.

I nodded my head.

"You're lucky you're so good. I would have killed you if you'd lost. Now go up in the bleachers and cool off. You've got an even longer one to run in an hour."

That was the 3200, which I also won, in 8:41. I was a double state champion. So was James, who won the 100 meters at the end of the meet. We finished with 107 points, more than twice as many as the second-place school, Martin Luther King.

After the meet was over, and we had collected our trophy—a brass plaque embedded in a wooden cutout of the state—I listened to Coach talk to the sportswriters. He didn't talk about his coaching, he talked about the runners Wenniway had provided him. He enjoyed boasting about our integrated school, especially in Frontenac.

"I want you to take a look at the kids I got on my team," he said, as the men in sport shirts and khakis scribbled in little notebooks. "I got kids from all backgrounds: black, white, Mexican. Wenniway is a very diverse community. You have to have balance to win a championship in track and field. You can't be a team that's only good at distance, or sprinting, or jumping, or throwing, or whatever. At Wenniway Central, we've got kids who can do everything."

On the bus ride back to Wenniway, the guys chanted, "Wenniway, All the Way!" and "Who Dat Say Dey Gonna Beat Dem Warriors? Who Dat? Who Dat?" We threw sweatshirts and spikes at each other. We leaped over seat backs onto the soft landings of benches. Dave gave me three noogies. It didn't matter that I was state champion. We were *all* state champions. We were all getting championship pins to stick on our varsity letters, so we were all equally entitled to give each other shit. Coach didn't try to stop us, but the bus driver finally did. She'd driven the basketball team home after The Wiz had led to them to a state championship. She hadn't allowed basketball players to jump over the seats, so she sure wasn't going to allow a bunch of runners.

My parents left Frontenac after I won the 3200. Dad was waiting for me in the school parking lot when the bus dropped us off. As I got into the car, he put his hand on my shoulder, something he had never done before. Maybe it was easier for him than talking. He worked with things, not words, or people. After we sat there for a while, he took the hand away and said "Thanks," while looking out the windshield.

"For what?"

"For making me feel like I made the right decision to stay here. If I'd gone down to Tennessee, I'm not sure I could have gotten back up here to see you win those races. I definitely would have missed the rest of the season. I wouldn't have seen you grow into a state champ. I'm proud of you, but being a parent isn't just about being proud of the finished product, it's about seeing the whole journey."

I sank back into my seat, not just because I was tired, but because I felt self-conscious when my dad tried to say, "I love you" without actually saying it. When we pulled into our driveway, I saw a hand-painted banner stretched above the front door: CONGRATULATIONS, KEVIN! STATE CHAMP.

"Your mother's been busy," Dad said.

Mom ran down the driveway and practically dragged me out of the car, hugging me from behind as I tried to walk up the driveway.

"Did you just do that since I got home?" I asked, pointing at the banner.

"No! I worked on it all week because I knew you were going to win! You do so much running, I didn't see how anyone could beat you. You were so fast! I couldn't even run five steps as fast as you ran that mile. And I'm taking *all* the credit because I made you watch the Olympic marathon. I *knew* running would be your sport, because you're a little guy, like me and your dad. I can take credit for that, too."

After that long, exhausting, sweaty day, I just wanted to take a shower and go to bed. Shouldn't a state champion be allowed to take a shower and go to bed? Not in the Ward family. My achievement did not just belong to me, it belonged to all the Wards. My mother had already made a reservation for eight at Maggliano's, a pizza parlor with the softest crust and the ooziest cheese in Wenniway.

Even Gramps went to Maggliano's, shuffling through the carpeted dining room behind a walker cushioned with tennis balls. My sister Karen was there, too, pregnant again, which meant I was about to become a two-time uncle as well as a two-time state champion. So was my Aunt Sharon, although not Uncle Dick, who still wasn't talking to my dad. When the pies arrived, Mom stuck two candles into the cheese (it was that thick), one for each race I'd won.

"Our son just won the state track and field championship," Mom boasted to the waitress.

"Oh," said the waitress, who also looked to be in high school. She tried to look interested, for the sake of customer service, or her tip. "Do you run marathons?"

"Just the mile and the two-mile," I said, using the English distances. She was unimpressed that anyone would win a prize for only running a mile.

"Eat a lot," my dad said. "You're done running for a while, so you can pig out."

Was Dad was urging me to scarf down pizza to make sure he got his money's worth? We hadn't eaten out since Empire shut down. We'd never much of a restaurant family—we ate hamburgers and sundaes once a month after church at Big Top Family Dining. Ever since Dad stopped working in the shop, we'd eaten nothing but home cooking and leftovers. Dad got a ten percent employee discount at the supermarket. Four pizzas at Maggliano's cost thirty dollars, more than Dad took home from an entire shift behind the meat counter. But he paid in cash and left a big tip for the waitress.

"What are you gonna do next?" Dad asked me as we were waiting for the busboy to box up the uneaten slices. The Wards didn't waste, especially now. "Are you gonna do the mile in four?"

"I hope so. Coach says you don't hit your peak until you're twenty-five, so I've got eight years to get the last eleven seconds."

When I recited my time, though, I suddenly didn't feel like a winner. Dad could barely pay for these pizzas, and I hadn't run fast enough to spare him from paying for my college.

"I produced another Jim Ryun," Dad said wonderingly. "I don't know where the talent came from. I just did what the man does, and you came out that way."

"Jeez, you did more than that," I said, realizing as soon as I said "jeez" that I was about to get the dagger stare my mother was now directing at me. "You got up early every day to go to work, so I got up early every day to run."

"I used to run at Central," Gramps interrupted.

198

We all stared at him. The only time Gramps ever talked about the past was to brag about his exploits during the Wildcat Strike. Throughout all my years of running, he'd never mentioned that he'd run track, too. Maybe now he wanted to claim a share of the credit for my championship.

"In the '30s. When it was still just Wenniway High School. On the cinder track. In those thin leather shoes that practically fell apart if you tied the laces too tight. Quarter mile. Not as far or as fast as Kevin. I think I broke a minute one time."

Gramps gripped the handle of his walker with one hand and raised himself out of his chair.

"I hope I'm here to see that four-minute mile," he said. "Do as much as you can with it while you've got it."

Monday morning, our principal read the results of the state meet over the intercom. When he said, "Kevin Ward won the 1600 and the 3200," That was the extent of my celebrity at Wenniway Central.

The track team wasn't the football team. The cheerleaders decorated the football players' lockers before every game, with tissue paper flowers and hand-painted motivational posters, even though the team had gone two and nine last season. Or the basketball team, which was introduced at a pep rally before every season opener. WWAY broadcast the basketball games. As an individual sport, track was presumed to be important to the participants only, and not a source of school pride. Like the swimmers and golfers, we were indulging in hobbies which could be pursued into old age, not gladiatorial contests in which we imperiled our arms, legs, elbows, knees and brains for the glory of Central High. To the average high school student, the fastest 1600 time in the state was as impressive as the highest Defender score at the local arcade. Running didn't get you girls—unless they were girls who also ran and had no better way of meeting guys. Even though I'd found Sara, I'd lost her to a "musician" who owned an electric guitar and an amplifier.

TWENTY

The letter arrived in a heavy-grained envelope, with the U's address and logo in the upper left-hand corner. Coach Deane had hand-written his name above the return address. I took it up to my room and sliced it open neatly with a pair of scissors.

"Dear Kevin," the typewritten letter began.

First of all, let me congratulate you on winning the state championship in both the 1600 and the 3200. I've talked to your coach, and he said you ran a smart, gutsy race, especially in the second event.

Since you wrote me last year about your interest in running for the U, I've been following your progress, and I believe you would be an asset to both our track and cross-country programs. Based on your achievements, I am prepared to offer you a partial scholarship, provided you can demonstrate you meet our academic standards for intercollegiate athletes.

If you are still interested in running for the U, I would like to invite you to visit our campus on the 24th of this month, along with some other freshman prospects. You will get a chance to tour our facilities and learn more about our program from current members of the team.

Sincerely Yours,
Harry Deane
Coach, Men's Cross Country and Track

A partial scholarship? How much was that? A quarter? A half? Three quarters? Any one of those fractions could be a part. I took the letter into the kitchen, grateful that only Gramps was home, and asleep in his chair. Lifting the telephone from its wall cradle, I dialed the number. A secretary answered.

"Athletic department."

"May I speak to Coach Deane?"

"May I ask who's calling?"

"Kevin Ward. He sent me a letter about a track scholarship."

"I'll see if he's available."

I heard a click. Moments later, a man's voice was on the line.

"Kevin?"

It was a high-pitched, astringent voice, but it matched my physical impression of Coach Deane from the meet in Auburn. He'd been a tall, slight, balding man in a crimson-and-gold windbreaker, probably a distance runner in his own day. "You must have gotten my letter," he said. "I hope you'll be able to come out and see us on the 24th."

"Yes, sir," I said.

Coach Deane spoke rapidly, with an East Coast accent, almost like a character on *Welcome Back, Kotter* or *Barney Miller*. The U was world-famous. Students and athletes flocked from all corners of the country to study in its classrooms and play for its teams.

"Terrific. We'll be really excited to have the state mile champion here." He still called it the mile, the distance run during his pre-metric career—the 1950s, I guessed. "We'd like to have you stay over one night, so you can run with some of the guys and see the campus. Bring an overnight bag and your running gear. Get here in the morning and stop by the athletic department. We'll have a talk about what the U can do for you."

I told Coach Deane I would do that. There was nothing else to say over the phone. The coach, I could tell already, was a man accustomed to giving orders to his runners, not engaging in conversations with us. Sports were serious business at the U, even track; apparently.

James also got a scholarship offer. Not from the U, but Ohio State, an even bigger school. Ohio State was Jesse Owens's alma mater. Coach told me about it, then I saw it in the *Star*'s "People Going Places" column.

"He took it," Coach said. "He's going to college out of state in the fall. Talk to him about it."

I found James in the lunchroom, sitting with a couple of other sprinters. I walked over to their table. I felt I could cross that color line. We were teammates. More than that, I wasn't just some random miler who thought he was cool with the black guys because he ran track. James and I were state champions.

"James?" I said.

He looked startled at the sound of his name. Recognizing me, he turned in his chair, and shook my hand.

"Kev!"

The other sprinters smiled, too. Derrick Williams reached across the table to offer his hand.

"Man won us the championship," Derrick said.

"Congratulations," I told James. "I hear you're going to Ohio State."

"Full ride," he said.

"Wow. The U only offered me a partial scholarship."

"That's all they offered me, too. I wanted to run there, but Ohio State gave me a better deal."

"That's a long way to go."

"Five hours. I can come back to see Mom on weekends."

"I'm going down to Auburn next week to talk to the coach and see the campus."

"We'll be in the same conference. I'll see you at the dual meet. You're gonna make the U tough to beat."

"You're gonna make Ohio State tough to beat."

I walked away, back to the white side of the lunchroom. James had been cordial, but he hadn't invited me to sit down. He'd been right to take Ohio State's full scholarship, when the U had only offered him a partial. I didn't know whether I would have done the same. Five hours was a long way from home.

Dad was having trouble with his tenants. They hadn't paid rent in three months. He went over to the house to talk to them, bringing me along in case there was trouble. I thought a gun would have been more effective, but Dad only owned a hunting rifle.

It was strange to see our old home so empty. The new family owned a sagging, wood-paneled station wagon that had stained the driveway with dripping oil. The only furniture in the living room was a sofa, whose stuffing burst free at the unraveled seams. The television sat on the floor. This was all I could see from the front door. I looked through the window, which was not covered with curtains or blinds. On a wooden dining table, I could see an open box of Fruit Loops. When Dad knocked, the father opened the door. He stepped out onto the porch in his bare feet. Maybe his family didn't know he he'd missed the rent.

The man apologized to my father, without making eye contact. He hadn't been working. He'd been laid off from his job, at one of the mini-marts near the shop. Business was slow. He had applied for unemployment, but his claim was still waiting approval.

Dad said he understood. Times were tough in Wenniway. Perhaps they could work out a payment plan—a little now, and the rest when he started working again? The man pulled a cloth wallet from his back pocket, and tore open the vinyl clasp. There were five twenty-dollar bills inside. He handed four to Dad. The last, I supposed, was his family's grocery money for the week.

"That's a start," Dad said. "Let's talk again next month."

The next month, though, the man paid nothing. Nor the month after. So, Dad went to court to file eviction papers.

"I don't want to be a hard guy," he told Gramps, "but no one gets to live for free."

As a veteran of the Wildcat Strike, Gramps had often expressed his mistrust of the courts, and the sheriff's department, who had tried to evict the strikers from the plants they'd occupied. Now he just shrugged. The rent on our old house was supposed to pay for his medical care.

"You paid for that house," he said. "You have a right to decide who gets to live there."

Shortly after Dad filed the papers, we received a phone call from Mr. Ockenfels. He must have found Gramps' name in the book. Even though Dad held the receiver close to his ear, I could hear Mr. Ockenfels screaming that he'd better get the hell over there and see just what his trashy tenants had done.

When we got there, the station wagon was gone. Only a black spot remained in the driveway. The house was trashed. In the living room, still furnished with that sagging couch, plastic wiring sleeves dangled from the light fixture. Upstairs, the floors were powdered with flakes of drywall, which had sifted out of the hacked-open walls. In the bathroom, The tenants had yanked the brass knobs off the tub and toilet and cut the piping from under the sink. The stove and the refrigerator were missing from the kitchen. Dad clicked on his flashlight and led me to the basement. The boiler was gone, along with the copper pipe that had run beneath the ceiling.

"They scrapped the whole place," Dad mumbled, shining a disc of light over the cinderblock walls. "Every piece of metal in here. I'm sure they took it to a scrapyard and got ten cents a pound or whatever. I thought having tenants in here would keep the scrappers out, but they turned into scrappers. I guess once I tried to evict them, they just decided to take what they could get."

We walked back up the narrow stairs to my old bedroom, under the roof, where I had taped my Steve Scott poster on the sloping wall. The room was empty, except for a soiled, king-sized mattress, broad enough to sleep three children.

"This was your childhood home, and now it's...nothing," Dad said apologetically. "There's no way I can repair all this for what this place is worth, not in this market. If I'd taken twenty or twenty-five thousand for it after we moved, I would have gotten something out of it. Now I've got nothing. It's not even going to be worth paying taxes on. I may as well let the city foreclose and tear it down. Sorry, Kev, we could have used the money. I guess I wasn't cut out to be a landlord."

Dad didn't even bother to lock the door when we left the house. There was nothing inside worth stealing now. Mr. Ockenfels was standing on his porch, griping the balustrade even more tightly than usual.

"You got what you deserved," he taunted my father. "Last night, I heard an old truck with squeaky shocks pull up here. I didn't call the police because I was just glad they were moving out. It wasn't my business what they took. It's not my property."

"Well, Frank, it can be your property. I'll sell it to you for a thousand dollars. Then you'll have twice as much yard to keep the kids off."

"A thousand? It would cost me more than that to tear it down. I'll take it from you if you pay the demolition fees."

"A thousand's my offer. Call me if you change your mind. You've got our number."

Dad got behind the wheel of the car, and we drove away.

Dad called the police to report the family for theft and malicious destruction of property. We didn't know where they'd gone, though. They might have left Wenniway. The cops promised to visit the local scrapyards, to find out whether anyone fitting their description had recently sold a truckload of copper piping and appliances. Even if they found the family, though, there wouldn't be much point in pressing charges. We would never get any money out of them. All we could do was imprison their main breadwinner.

Mom took it hard. I don't know if she took it harder than Dad, but after Dad described the damage, she showed it more.

"That was our home," she said tensely. Then she burst into tears. I think Mom was so small and thin because she was so high-strung. Lately, as a result of our money troubles since Dad had quit his job, worry had whittled her down to a girl's figure, bustless and hipless. "That was where we raised our family. That was the only thing we owned! If you hadn't..."

"It had nothing to do with what I did or didn't do," Dad retorted. "We moved out of there to take care of my dad. I'm never going to regret doing that. He'd be in a nursing home if I'd gone to Tennessee. We just couldn't sell the house after Empire closed. You can't sell anything around here now."

Then Dad hugged her. Mom clutched her arms to her chest, but she let him hug her. She always did.

"My dad is going to leave us this place," Dad reassured Mom. "He appreciates what we did. We'll always have a place to live."

I went to my room, so they could work this out in private. I was sure there would be more fallout tomorrow, but

I wouldn't be there to hear it. The next day was the 24th—
the day of my visit to the U.

Twenty-One

I drove down to Auburn in Dad's car. Riding shotgun was a duffel bag packed with training flats, two t-shirts, two pairs of nylon shorts, two pairs of socks, a clean pair of blue jeans, a button-down plaid shirt and a change of underwear. I wore my Wenniway Central jacket, with the state championship pin affixed to my varsity letter, even though the temperature was in the 70s. Coach had handed out the pins at the team banquet—actually just a pizza party in the basement of Maggliano's. Every runner, jumper, and thrower got one, because we all ran, jumped, and threw together. Before he presented my pin, Coach gave a speech: "In the ten years I've been here at Central, Kevin is the hardest-working runner I've ever coached. He really deserved those state championships after coming so close in the state cross-country meet last fall. I want all you guys to talk to Kevin about his training, because if you work as hard as he did, we'll be state champs every year." And then the guys gave me a standing ovation. That was more thrilling than winning the races. After I won those races, I was too exhausted, and too disappointed in my 1600 time, to appreciate anyone's accolades. The ovation was the culmination of my high school career—of my entire life, up to this point. Now, on the drive to Auburn, I was leaving a world I had conquered for a new world in which I might start out as the youngest, and slowest, runner on the team.

"Whatever they offer you, get it in writing," Dad told me, before I embarked at eight o'clock. "Bring it back here so we can show it to your grandfather. He used to negotiate union contracts."

Two hours later, I parked the car outside the athletic department office. It was a gleaming glass cube, eight stories of morning-bronzed windows. Standing on the plaza, before the chrome-handled doors, I could spin around and gather in all the grandeur of U sports, in a single three-hundred-and-sixty-degree circuit. The natatorium, as it was called, emblazoned with a Roman-coin bas relief of Casey Clark, the 1936 Olympic breaststroke champion, who had coached here for three decades; the Fieldhouse, a brick representation of the Midwestern barns in which basketball was played after migrating here from Massachusetts; the domed igloo, a flying saucer landed in Auburn by aliens who'd brought the planet ice and hockey; and, of course, the Coliseum, the emperor of American college football stadiums, with 108,000 seats—enough to hold the entire population of Wenniway—embedded in the Earth. To my right, to my left, in front of me, behind me, backpack-toting students pedaled past on bicycles, every face intent on a destination. In imitation of their ambition, I hurried through the glass doors.

At Central, Coach Funkhouser did business from behind his classroom desk. At the U, Coach Deane had his own office, on the third floor. The walls were adorned with conference championship plaques and photos of NCAA champions. The shelves bore trophies, and bronzed spikes. My eyes fixed on Matt Steensma, who still held the course record for the state high school cross-country meet in the Arb. After the U, Matt qualified for the Olympics, in the 10,000 meters, but couldn't run, because of the boycott. As Coach Deane invited me to sit in front of his desk, I had the disembodied feeling that I was not there as Kevin Ward, but as a 4:11 miler—a number, not a name. It was clear from these surroundings, and from Coach Deane's demeanor, ("Would you like something to drink?" "Sharon, can you get Kevin some water!") that this meeting was business.

"The first thing I want to know about you, Kevin," Coach Deane said, smiling, "is what you want to accomplish at the U. I've already seen what you can do for us, now I want to know what we can do for you."

I looked at some of the other photos on the wall. I recognized the names and faces from *Track and Field News*. NCAA champions. Four-minute milers. Olympians, although none of them medalists. I tried not to think that far ahead. I tried to think only of what I could do here, in the next four years.

"I'd like to run a four-minute mile," I said. "I know that would make my dad happy."

Coach Deane smiled again.

"We always like to make the parents happy," he said. "We've got a couple seniors who started out where you are now and broke four minutes last year. They can help you get there."

"And I'd like to keep running for a few years after college. Get a shoe contract, see if I can qualify for the Olympic trials."

"I can't promise you that," Coach Deane said, looking more serious now. "I can promise that if you come here and work hard, you'll find out whether you're capable of that. I want to make sure you reach your full potential. In fact, I won't settle for anything less from you."

"You only get one chance to find that out," I said. "You can't wait until you retire."

"Exactly. And you'll see on these walls plenty of young men who've done exactly what you want to do. It can happen at the U."

Coach Deane withdrew a sheet of paper from a drawer and slid it across his desk.

"This is a formal scholarship offer," he said. "We can pay half your tuition and room and board. We're not the football program, with dozens of full scholarships to hand out. For an in-stater like you, that'll cover about six thousand dollars a year. You can take that home and talk to your parents about it, but right now, I want you to meet a couple of your prospective teammates. They'll help you get checked into your room and take you out for a run in the Arb. I know you're familiar with the Arb."

Coach Deane smiled again.

"They'll meet you in front of Richard Hall." He pronounced it "ree-SHARD." As I would learn from a plaque outside the building, Richard was the French priest who founded the U. It was one of those things you had to know to fit in there. Ree-shard Hall was a fifteen-story dormitory, taller than any building in Wenniway, so tall it had a real aircraft warning beacon on its roof.

Darren and Jay met me in front of the building. Both were six feet tall and lanky, built more like classic middle-distance runners than I was. (Was I an overachiever, to have run my times at five foot seven? Would I be better suited for long distance? In college, the cross-country races were eight thousand meters, and the track races went on as long as ten thousand.)

"Where's W?" Jay asked, nodding at the letter on my jacket.

"Wenniway," I said, straightening myself as much as I could, to minimize the height difference.

"You'll love Auburn, then," Jay said. "It's definitely a step up from Wenniway."

"Where are *you* from?" I asked, trying not to sound as irritated as I felt.

"Palmyra. It's a step up from there, too. And then it's a step out. You can go anywhere with a degree from the U."

"I'm from Colorado," Darren said. He had picked up on my bristling tone and was trying to defuse this intrastate conflict. "I don't know all the different towns in this state, but I love it. All you ever hear about is the auto plants, but it's so beautiful."

Coach Deane had given me a room key, so I took the elevator to 119, where I changed into my running clothes. On the bottom bunk was a duffel bag stenciled GLEN-BROOK NORTH, a high school I'd never heard of. It must have belonged to an out-of-stater. The U didn't just recruit the fastest runners in our state, it recruited the fastest runners in the country. Athletically, it competed with Ohio State, and Texas, and Alabama. Academically, only the Ivy League schools were better. That's what Mr. Coonley had told me, anyway.

As we jogged across the Quad, towards the Arb, I noticed two types of students: one wore lace-up leather moccasins, chino shorts, and polo shirts. The other wore Chuck Taylor sneakers, stovepipe jeans and t-shirts with a rock band's name and logo, underneath a plaid button-down shirt. Everyone was using brand names or band names to advertise their personalities. I imagined Sara would adopt the latter uniform. Would I see Sara at the U? I'd passed her a few times in the hallways at Central. We exchanged glances, but no words. Once, she opened her mouth as she looked at me, as though she wanted to say something—to apologize, perhaps. I kept walking. A runner has to stay on the move. On a campus this big, Sara would be easier to avoid. I wondered, though, whether all the girls here were like Sara. Did they all buy Echo and the Bunnymen albums at the Black Platter? Did they all aspire to go to grad school, then move to a big city? Would there be any point in dating a girl like that? I could never bring her home to Wenniway.

"We're gonna run through the Arb," Darren said. "Do you know about the Arb?"

"He knows about the Arb," Jay nodded at me. "Everyone in this state knows about the Arb. He almost won the state cross-country championship there. That's when Coach started keeping an eye on him."

We ran between the library and the art museum, a pair of nearly identical Greek edifices, with long, flat roofs and fluted stone columns. Before it could educate, the U evidently meant to intimidate. We passed through a black wrought iron gate. Above the entrance was the number 1819, the year of the U's founding. The school was older than the state itself. After leaving campus, we ran past a shabby block of diners and used record shops. We passed Waldo's. We passed the Black Platter, where Sara purchased the punk rock and New Wave imports she couldn't find in Wenniway. Now she wouldn't have to travel a hundred miles for "culture."

At the entrance to the Arb, we made a hard left on the oiled service road that ran steeply downhill. When we emerged from the trees, onto the spreading grass, I saw the Meadow for the first time since I was out-leaned there at the state cross-country meet.

"We run our cross-country meets here," Jay informed me. "Most of this part of the country is flat, so we kill the other teams on the hills."

"Colorado's not flat," said Darren. "Maybe that's why they recruited me. So they wouldn't have to train me to run hills."

I wanted to tell them about Coach Funkhouser driving me to Mount Trashmore, but I knew, from being the boss of my high school team, that no one wanted to hear a freshman's stories. No one wanted to hear about Wenniway, either. I regretted wearing my letterman's jacket. I resolved to leave it at home in the fall.

Our run ended at the track, which had its own grandstand seating five thousand spectators. That was nearly as many as Hayward Field, at the University of Oregon, where track was bigger than football, where fans still wore

STOP PRE t-shirts, in honor of the unstoppable Steve Prefontaine. Stepping onto the spongy surface, painted crimson, with gold lane stripes, I felt ready to run in the Olympics, or at least the NCAA Championships, which had been held here four times. Inside lane one, a metal rail encircled the infield. The track had a water pit, for the steeplechase, and a caged ring for the discus, the shot put, and the hammer throw. A crimson and gold riding mower was barbering the grass to a fairway trim.

"You want to finish this with a sixty?" Jay asked Darren.

"Sure."

"Can you do a sixty?" Jay asked me.

I nodded. It was a challenge, not a question. They were busting my balls, making me prove I belonged on a Division I track team.

"Go!" Jay shouted, trying to catch me off guard. We tore down the backstretch, feet pinwheeling, arms pumping. Half-way through, Jay peeked at his watch. He didn't slow down, so I assumed we were on pace. I knew then that I was going to make it, and I did.

"Good run," Jay said, after we braked to a finish-line halt, our rubber soles slapping the rubberized track, ending the 400 three abreast. "There's a mixer at the Union tonight. Six o'clock. The women's team is gonna be there, too."

I walked over to the Union with my roommate for the night, the owner of the Glenbrook North duffel bag. His name was Jim. He was from Illinois, where, like me, he'd been runner up at the state cross-country meet.

"Detweiller Park in Peoria!" I said excitedly.

"You know about Detweiller Park?" He seemed put off. Not every track star was a track nerd. Craig Virgin had set the course record in the Illinois State Cross-Country meet. Then he'd won the NCAA cross-country championship for the University of Illinois, and the *world* cross-country championship for the USA. I'd read all about him in *Runner's World*. A small-town kid from the Midwest, running in the same conference as the U, Craig Virgin was one of my idols, because he'd proven that you could get there from here.

"We didn't break his record," Jim said. "No one's ever broken his record. It's a legend."

Glenbrook North, it turned out, was "near Chicago."

"I mean, not in Chicago," Jim said. "It's just a bunch of houses out there before the cornfields start. I got offers from U of I and Notre Dame, but I wanted to get as far away from there as possible."

The mixer was in the Union's food court. We all got a ticket for a slice of pizza and a can of pop. Everyone, it seemed, was from somewhere near somewhere else, and talked about home like it was nowhere at all. "Near Chicago." "Near New York." "Near Frontenac," of course. Like Jim, none of them seemed sentimental about their hometowns, or even considered them hometowns. They were launching pads where they had prepared for lives of achievement, and to which they would return only for obligatory holidays.

"Where are you from?" a women's team recruit asked me.

"Wenniway."

"That's a nice sounding name," she said.

I had never thought about how "Wenniway" landed on the ear, but I supposed it *was* a nice-sounding name. I recalled a third-grade pageant, attended by the mayor, in which our class sang about the state's sibilant Indian names: Wenniway. Sinnising. Kamanack.

"Where is Wenniway?" she asked.

"You're from out of state." I tried not to make it sound like an accusation. No one could help where they grew up.

"Yeah," she said.

"From where?"

"Short Hills. New Jersey."

"Near?"

"New York."

I tried to picture a map of the United States. If she said New Jersey was near New York, I would take her word for it.

"Wenniway is west of here," I explained. "Home of the Empire Marquette. Or it used to be, before they moved the plant to Tennessee."

"Oh yeah." I had kindled a glimmer of recognition in her eyes. "My parents had a Marquette. Now we've got a Datsun. Better mileage. Better for the environment."

I moved on, back toward the pizza counter. As an athlete, I was used to competition, and bragging about race times, but everyone seemed to be trying to one-up everyone else in more subtle ways. I overheard half a conversation about Spain: "I did language immersion summer study. I couldn't do a whole semester because we're running all school year...Oh, you went? For real? When?...Did you go to Barcelona...Oh yeah, the cathedral is amazing."

I felt like an extra in *Risky Business*, that other Tom Cruise movie where he plays a kid from "near Chicago" who wants to go to Princeton. When the recruiter turns him down, he puts on a pair of Ray-Ban sunglasses and tells a hooker, "Looks like University of Illinois!" (Was every Tom Cruise movie about a young hotshot trying to escape home for a big college?) Or maybe I was in a John Hughes movie. Those took place "near Chicago." Wenniway was someplace that wasn't near anyplace. Wenniway had an identity all its own, even if that identity had so recently been stripped away. It would always be the birthplace of the Marquette, even if that car was now manufactured "near Nashville."

Before Jim and I went back to the dorm, Jay put his arms on our shoulders.

"They say nine out of ten girls in this conference are good looking, and the tenth goes to the U," he said. He pointed at the girl from New Jersey. "You can see that's not true on this team."

I belonged on the U's cross-country team, even if I hadn't been offered a full scholarship. I'd hammered that 400 with Jay and Darren, matching them stride for stride. My 1600 time was faster than some of the freshmen and sophomores. As I drove home to Wenniway, though, I wondered whether I really belonged at the U. Sara did. The U was the steppingstone between Wenniway and her ambitions. She'd leave nothing behind but two parents, who themselves would leave as soon as they retired from teaching. The U could, I supposed, be my steppingstone back to Wenniway: if I ran fast enough in my four years there, I could train wherever I wanted. My running idols lived all over the map: in Eugene, Oregon; in Clinton, Iowa; in Boston, Massachusetts; in Gainesville, Florida. They had made their hometowns famous. Bill Rodgers was "Boston Billy." Could I do the same for Wenniway? Could I replace "Home of the Marquette" with "Home of an Olympian"?

My family sat around the dining room table, with the U's scholarship offer in front of us: Mom, Dad, even Gramps, who had wandered over from his TV chair for this meeting.

"The coach said the scholarship would cover six thousand a year," I said. "We'd have to come up with the other six."

Dad stared at the paper. He slumped and exhaled.

"We're just breaking even now," he said. "If this had come up even a few months ago, we could have sold the house for enough to cover that. Now I don't know what I can get for it."

"We could take out another mortgage on *this* place," Gramps suggested. It was an extraordinary proposal. No one in our family had ever carried a mortgage. Gramps, Dad, and Uncle Dick had all bought their houses in cash. Real estate was just that cheap in Wenniway, and Empire paychecks had been just that good.

"But, Dad, who's going to pay that back?" my dad asked. "You can make the payments now, but a mortgage is thirty years."

"There are student loans," my mother said, "but you end up paying those off forever. They can be worse than a mortgage."

My mother folded her arms across her thin chest and glared at my father. I knew what she was thinking: if you had just sucked it up for five years in Tennessee, Kevin would be on his way to the U, and we wouldn't be having this conversation. Before she could say that, I spoke up.

"I don't have to go to the U."

They all stared at me.

"I'm not going there if it's going to put us further in a hole. I can run at WCC. Joaquin runs there. He beat me in high school. They've got a track. If I get my times down, maybe I can earn a full scholarship and transfer."

I didn't say what else I was thinking: this didn't seem like the right time to leave home. Gramps was sick. These might be his final years. Dad's new job at the supermarket had left him struggling, both financially, and with his identity as head of the family. He needed an ally, especially since Mom seemed increasingly bitter about his decision not to take the transfer. Maybe in two years, Gramps would be better, or else his struggles would be over. Maybe Dad would have a better job. In the meantime, I could get more hours at UPS, and pay my own tuition at the community college. I could contribute to the family, instead of putting us deeper in debt.

"Kevin," my mother said, in an imploring voice, as tense as an electrical wire. "You have a talent. You've always wanted to be the best you can be at running. You can do that at the U. I know you think we're going to have to make sacrifices for you, but helping your children achieve their dreams is *not* a sacrifice."

Mom's eyes were misty. She looked only at me. Not at Dad. Not at Gramps.

"My running doesn't own me," I said to Mom. "I own my running. I can run wherever I want. I'm going to do it right now."

I stood up from the table. I had the day off from work. It was newly summer, so I'd planned a ten-mile run through the long, mellow evening. I put on my shorts, my Dog Days 10K shirt, and my Etonics, and opened the front door. As I ran, I heard that nasal announcer's voice in my head.

"Mile sixteen of the Olympic marathon here in Seoul, South Korea, and still one American among the leaders. Kevin Ward, a young man from a small town called Wenniway. You might not have heard of it, but you're hearing about it now."

I ran past the high school. Across the street, nothing remained of Empire Body, except a few gnarled metal struts, twisting out of hillocks of bare dirt. Behind the fence waved wildflowers that thrive in abandoned places: Queen Anne's lace, peppergrass, teasel. Looking beyond the empty site, toward the railroad tracks that once carried the cars away, I decided to speed up until I reached the gates.

"Ward is making a move here at mile sixteen. Can anyone else cover it? No one is going with him! It looks like Kevin Ward is breaking away!"

About the Author

Edward (Ted) McClelland is a native of Lansing, Michigan, also the birthplace of Burt Reynolds and the Oldsmobile. He ran track and cross country at J.W. Sexton High School, which was across the street from a Fisher Body plant.

After getting his start in journalism at the Lansing Community College *Lookout*, Ted went on to the *Chicago Reader*, where he met Barack Obama during his failed 2000 campaign for Congress. Ted's coverage of that race became the basis of *Young Mr. Obama: Chicago and the Making of a Black President*. His book *The Third Coast: Sailors, Strippers, Fishermen, Folksingers, Long-Haired Ojibway Painters and God-Save-the-Queen Monarchists of the Great Lakes*, a travelogue of a 10,000-mile journey around the Lakes, won the 2008 Great Lakes Book Award in General Nonfiction. *Nothin' But Blue Skies: The Heyday, Hard Times and Hopes of America's Industrial Heartland* (Bloomsbury Press, 2013) is a history of the Rust Belt, inspired by seeing the Fisher Body plant across the street from his old high school torn down.

Ted's book *How to Speak Midwestern* is a guide to the speech and sayings of Middle America, which *The New York Times* called "a dictionary wrapped in some serious dialectology inside a gift book trailing a serious whiff of Relevance." His most recent book, *Midnight in Vehicle City: General Motors, Flint, and the Strike That Created the Middle Class*, is about the 1936-37 Flint Sit Down Strike, which led to the establishment of the United Auto Workers as the nation's preeminent labor union.

Ted's writing has also appeared in *The New York Times, Los Angeles Times, Columbia Journalism Review, Salon, Slate*, and *Playboy*. *Running for Home* is his first novel.

BOOKS BY BOTTOM DOG PRESS

HARMONY SERIES

The Pears: Poems, by Larry Smith, 66 pgs, $15
Without a Plea, by Jeff Gundy, 96 pgs, $16
Taking a Walk in My Animal Hat, by Charlene Fix, 90 pgs, $16
Pieces: A Composite Novel, by Mary Ann McGuigan, 250 pgs, $18
Crows in the Jukebox: Poems, by Mike James, 106 pgs, $16
Cold Air Return: A Novel, by Patrick Lawrence O'Keeffe, 390 pgs, $20
Flesh and Stones: A Memoir, by Jan Shoemaker, 176 pgs, $18
Waiting to Begin: A Memoir, by Patricia O'Donnell, 166 pgs, $18
And Waking: Poems, by Kevin Casey, 80 pgs, $16
Both Shoes Off: Poems, by Jeanne Bryner, 112 pgs, $16
Abandoned Homeland: Poems, by Jeff Gundy, 96 pgs, $16
Stolen Child: A Novel, by Suzanne Kelly, 338 pgs, $18
The Canary: A Novel, by Michael Loyd Gray, 196 pgs, $18
On the Flyleaf: Poems, by Herbert Woodward Martin, 106 pgs, $16
The Harmonist at Nightfall: Poems of Indiana, by Shari Wagner, 114 pgs, $16
Painting Bridges: A Novel, by Patricia Averbach, 234 pgs, $18
Ariadne & Other Poems, by Ingrid Swanberg, 120 pgs, $16
The Search for the Reason Why: New and Selected Poems, by Tom Kryss, 192 pgs, $16
Kenneth Patchen: Rebel Poet in America, by Larry Smith,
Revised 2nd Edition, 326 pgs, Cloth $28
Selected Correspondence of Kenneth Patchen,
Edited with introduction by Allen Frost, Paper $18/ Cloth $28
Awash with Roses: Collected Love Poems of Kenneth Patchen,
Eds. Laura Smith and Larry Smith
with introduction by Larry Smith, 200 pgs, $16
Breathing the West: Great Basin Poems, by Liane Ellison Norman, 96 pgs, $16

APPALACHIAN WRITING SERIES ANTHOLOGIES

Unbroken Circle: Stories of Cultural Diversity in the South,
Eds. Julia Watts and Larry Smith, 194 pgs, $18
Appalachia Now: Short Stories of Contemporary Appalachia,
Eds. Charles Dodd White and Larry Smith, 178 pgs, $18
Degrees of Elevation: Short Stories of Contemporary Appalachia,
Eds. Charles Dodd White and Page Seay, 186 pgs, $18

BOTTOM DOG PRESS, INC.
P.O. BOX 425 /HURON, OHIO 44839
HTTP://SMITHDOCS.NET